D0776886

THE DIG

THE DIG

A NOVEL

Anne Burt

COUNTERPOINT

BERKELEY

First Counterpoint edition: 2023

Library of Congress Cataloging-in-Publication Data
Names: Burt, Anne, author.
Title: The dig : a novel / Anne Burt.
Description: First Counterpoint edition. | Berkeley, CA : Counterpoint Press, 2023.
Identifiers: LCCN 2022038675 | ISBN 9781640096042 (hardcover) | ISBN 9781640096059 (ebook) Subjects: LCGFT: Novels.
Classification: LCC PS3602.U76945 D54 2023 | DDC 813/.6—dc23/eng/20220817
LC record available at https://lccn.loc.gov/2022038675

Jacket design by Faceout Studio
Book design by Laura Berry

COUNTERPOINT
2560 Ninth Street, Suite 318
Berkeley, CA 94710
www.counterpointpress.com

Printed in the United States of America

1 3 5 7 9 10 8 6 4 2

For Tessa and Delayna

It is the dead, not the living, who make the longest demands.

—SOPHOCLES, *Antigone*
(tr. Fitts & Fitzgerald)

THE DIG

BEFORE

IT BEGINS HERE. IN THE CITY OF SARAJEVO, BOSNIA, ON a bitter November day in 1993. A city where minarets and steeples once shared the skyline; where men drinking cardamom-scented coffee from brass cups argued and sang into the night. In 1984, Olympic athletes skied down the slopes of Mount Igman to the cheers of the world. Only nine years later, the abandoned bobsled track overflows with stockpiles of Serbian artillery. The mosques are rubble. Petals of collapsed concrete, blown apart by shell after shell, pock the streets—gaping wounds that will be filled with scarlet resin when the bombings end. Sarajevo Roses, they will call them. To commemorate the dead.

A nondescript gray cinderblock apartment complex looms above the bombed-out buildings on the west side of the Miljacka River. Imagine yourself there, picking your way across the debris to building number 4, carefully, slowly, while sirens wail around you. When you're close enough to touch the walls, wipe a circle in the dust that covers the ground-floor window on the left.

Look inside.

At first, you won't see any signs of life. But don't turn away. Look closer. In the back corner of the darkened room, a three-year-old girl lies on the dirty floor under a cot. She stares at a diamond pattern of rusted bedsprings above her head. Tufts of ticking from rips in the mattress hover over her like the clouds above the hills that ring the city. The scent of cabbage and garlic rises from the pot that's been simmering on the hot plate for hours.

Her six-year-old brother huddles against her, pressing his sweaty hands over her ears to dull the sound of exploding concrete. *Close your eyes*, he says. But she's too frightened. Without shifting, she moves her head as much as she can until she sees the wedge of floor beneath the kitchen counter. Shards of glass and piles of concrete on green tile. Dust motes swirl in a gash of daylight streaming from a new hole in the front wall. The round yellow rug, covered in soot; her stick horse crosswise atop it, one glazed button eye peering out from a pile of shattered brick. And, from the corner of her field of vision, a pale hand, motionless amid the debris. A hand whose wrist sports the brown sleeve of her mother's dress—the dress the girl helped fold that very morning, warm and sun-sweet from the clothesline in the back.

A giant boot steps between the girl and the hand, then more boots. Two male voices whisper. It's not a language she's used to hearing in their home. Her brother covers her mouth now instead of her ears—keep quiet, keep still, his gestures tell her. He's always trying to shush her! She wrests herself away.

The whispering stops. Suddenly a man's head appears, blond hair and beard, smears of dirt across his face, startling blue eyes.

"Shit!" he says. The girl recognizes this word: she's heard men shouting it from the trucks that rumble back and forth on the street outside their apartment. It's a word about things you don't want.

Another man, who looks like the first one but with no beard, appears. His eyes are kinder.

The bearded one shakes his head. "Vlado never said there were kids."

Vlado. This is the name of the tall man who's been sleeping next to her mother on the cot every night since he brought them out of the camp. The rest of the bearded man's words sound like nonsense to her. But she knows Vlado. She yells: "Vlado! Poznajem ga!" despite her brother's agonized hisses of "Ne! Ne!"

The bearded man's thick hands slide under the cot toward her. His fingernails are split and caked with grime. Her brother pulls her back toward the wall, trying as hard as he can to make them both disappear. The girl feels the man's hands grab her ankles. She tightens her grip on her brother's narrow shoulders. She'll be ripped in two, she thinks. Then another blast screams from outside. The apartment tilts again. The girl shuts her eyes, and the world closes in.

She lets go.

———

Yes, that girl was me. But she doesn't exist anymore, other than in the nightmare that still shakes me from my sleep. Is it true? Or is it a twisted, truncated dream version of events I've been told about over and over again by my adopted family: the story of how Paul and Antonia came to America, rescued by two brave brothers from Thebes, Minnesota, working as contractors in Sarajevo when the siege began?

Christopher, the one with the beard, told us to forget everything that happened in Bosnia. That our arrival in Thebes was the beginning of our real lives.

Eddie, the one with the kind eyes, told us nothing.

Before we even learned to call him Dad, Edward King was gone.

PART I

Thursday, June 11, 2014

Afternoon

"TELL ME ABOUT YOURSELF. WHO *IS* ANTONIA KING?"

Per Olufsen leans back against the damask-covered seat in the lounge at the Minneapolis Four Seasons and crosses his legs. Raindrops pelt the window by our table, running in rivulets down the glass.

I sit up straighter and square my shoulders under my navy suit jacket— the same one I've worn to every interview and meeting since graduating from law school last month. Per is CEO of Sweden's Air Trek Industries, the fastest-growing luxury airline company in the world. He's dressed in a white linen shirt, open at the collar, no tie, and jeans. An outfit only a hipster billionaire would wear at the Four Seasons.

I sneak a glance at myself in the mirrored wall behind him. The young lawyer who meets my gaze looks the part, for sure: black hair tamed into a sleek low ponytail. Serious dark eyes. Pale olive skin, smooth from the moisturizing sunscreen my aunt has drilled me into wearing, even on a rainy day. Does the woman in the mirror seem a bit desperate for approval, though? Does a scared little girl, shaking under a dirty cot, peer out at me from behind her polished exterior?

I rearrange her expression, willing her to soften around the forehead, the mouth. Blink twice, banish the fear from her eyes.

Better.

Before he can notice my lightning-quick fix, I turn my attention back to the man across the table to begin the most significant conversation of my career. That is, the career I'll have if I can nail it today.

All the businesses in town went crazy when Air Trek announced weeks ago that its first midwestern hub would be the Twin Cities. My cousin Harrison, whose self-proclaimed purpose during my last seven years at Harvard has been to remind me that Minnesota remains the center of the universe, emailed me local news coverage of ordinarily staid and emotionless MBAs filling the downtown bars, cheering "In your face, Chicago!" Everyone began to plan for the thousands of humans with fat wallets the airline would bring through the Cities. Especially those stranded by blizzards. Hotels! Restaurants! Pricey down-filled products!

I was prepping my resume for my real dream—a future in Washington, DC, where I could bring power to people like the little girl I used to be—when Air Trek's announcement hit the news. Each of the Big Four law firms in Minneapolis–St. Paul threw in a bid to become Olufsen's local counsel of record, producing a cyclone of recruiters who descended on campus, trying to sweep any of us who were still available into their game. I showed up out of home-state curiosity, nothing more. Then I met Melanie.

Melanie Dwyer, of Grogan, Dwyer, and Lenz. The only woman who was a named partner in any of the firms, she dominated during their presentations with her velvety alto and encyclopedic knowledge of corporate governance.

"You were meant for this opportunity, Toni," she said when we met in the Law School faculty lounge, with its sweeping grandeur, its ornate framed portraits of old, old white men. Presidents, Supreme Court justices, alumni all. "Come to Minneapolis and win Air Trek with me. Let's make our mark together."

She said I could leverage my Minnesota roots to take me to the halls of power someday, and that success at Grogan, Dwyer would position me better as a leader for my state than an entry-level legislative assistant role on the Hill ever could. And if things worked out, she'd mentor me right to the top.

My problem wasn't envisioning a different path to a future in DC—it was returning to Minnesota at all.

I was furious at my brother for bailing on me, and I blamed my uncle for driving him away. I back talked, scowled, slammed my bedroom door from age fourteen till the day I left for college.

And yet, Christopher wanted me back. As counsel of record for King Family Construction.

My uncle called me in Cambridge at the start of my third year of law school to announce his intentions. I had a bigger reason to stay away from Thebes than I did to return: James Hollings still lived there.

"You belong back here with us," Christopher said. "You're family."

Part of me lit up with hope to hear him say that word. *Family.* I had to admit—hearing he wanted me to return, even with all my ambivalence, felt surprisingly . . . good.

But his demands for all of us—Paul and me, his own kids—to toe the family line, business included, had pushed my brother to leave. And as much as I disapproved of my older brother's decisions, our fights belonged to us. We brought them with us from our past. I might judge Paul, but no one else, certainly not my uncle, got a pass from me to do the same. My loyalty to my brother gave me yet another reason to feel squeamish about returning to the fold.

Christopher, as usual, pressed his case.

"What about your aunt? She would be thrilled to have you back," he said.

Would she? Thrilled required a capacity for excitement that Evelyn had long ago relinquished. She started dulling all emotions with vodka martinis around the same time that Paul left. And who could blame her? After Harrison and I discovered her upstairs stash of Smirnoff in a cabinet behind the toilet in the guest bathroom, vodka helped our days go down easier too.

"Corporate law isn't really my thing," I said.

"Fair enough, Antonia. But remember: every other potential employer you'll meet is only interested in that piece of paper from Harvard Law School. Don't rule out a future with us."

To placate my uncle, I took the Minnesota Bar Exam in February, even before graduating. It was practice for DC, I told myself, although I didn't tell Christopher.

Then Melanie Dwyer came to campus and convinced me that my admission to the Minnesota Bar had been no practice run. "Start your career at a leading firm and all the pols in the state will know your name," she said. "Build up a war chest. Do well with me, and you'll earn the support you'll need for a future in Washington."

Maybe this kind of corporate law could be my thing. Or at least, as Melanie promised, my first thing on the way to my next thing.

PER OLUFSEN INSISTED ON MEETING INDIVIDUALLY WITH every lawyer who might be assigned to his team before making his choice between law firms. If Grogan won, my place was guaranteed. If they lost, I'd get the boot. A challenge I couldn't resist.

To say I was nervous about meeting with Olufsen was an understatement. But I couldn't let Melanie, or anyone, know that.

"I'll impress him," I told her yesterday when she informed me of my upcoming interview. "I've got this."

I spent hours last night with my laptop, researching Per's business from my room at the Motel 6 on Freeway Boulevard, where I've been staying since I moved from Cambridge two weeks ago. When I'm in work mode, my surroundings never matter. Fast Wi-Fi, a microwave in my room to heat up my Stouffer's mac-and-cheese dinners, a bed that's not my car. The opposite of the poufy French country sofas and Wedgwood Florentine china settings Aunt Evelyn favored. I finally passed out on top of the scratchy bedspread around 3:00 a.m. after scrolling past the millionth tabloid profile of Per and his latest model-girlfriend.

Now I'm bleary with exhaustion. But I've memorized his background, Air Trek's top line financials from the past eight years, and all the international flight patterns out of the Twin Cities. I'm ready to ace this test.

"Well," I say, "I'm fascinated by the third-quarter turnaround Air Trek made in 2012 after the Düsseldorf factory opened. I've analyzed some of the numbers and—"

He waves his hand to stop me.

"No, no, I don't care. Tell me about you."

I force a laugh. "I'm so boring. Really. Um, I graduated in the top ten percent of my class?"

"Ms. King. May I call you Toni? Good. You see, I want to know the person behind the person on my team. I have your resume. I know your academic credentials. Instead, let's work to find common ground, you and I." He uncrosses his legs and leans forward. "People, Toni. People make Air Trek a success, not its 2012 third-quarter financials. So, tell me. What is it that you think could bring us together?"

Per's clear blue eyes are trained on me like I'm the only one in the lobby restaurant. With his deliberately mussed white-blond hair and his complete self-assurance, I can see how the most beautiful women in the world melt in his presence. I, however, feel my throat close.

He sips his cappuccino. That unrelenting gaze over the rim of his cup makes my right leg twitch.

I have to say something.

"Um, okay. Well, one thing we have in common: I'm from Europe too."

"Really! Where?"

I see him trying to read my face with curiosity: she's too dark to be from Northern Europe, not dark enough to be an African transplant, could be Middle Eastern . . .

"Sarajevo."

"Ah. Post-Milošević? You must have been very young during the war. Bosniak, I assume, if you ended up in the States?"

I'm surprised by his easy knowledge of my context. Then I remember that I'm talking with a real Swede, not a third-generation Thebes farm-family Swede. Most Americans I've spoken with aren't quite sure where Bosnia is—Asia maybe? Some know, vaguely, that Serbia and Bosnia were fighting. Or wait, wasn't it a genocide? What are you, they ask? I try to explain that ethnically I'm Bosniak, but my parents converted from Islam to Christianity before I was born to try to survive and . . . that's when I feel their interest drain away.

By the time I left Thebes, I was tired of having to explain myself, explain away my dark features in a family of sunshine blonds, tired of the whispers and side glances from townspeople who remember when Eddie King lived in the house on the hill outside of town and how taking on those Bosnian orphans did him in. Eddie, who still lurked, ghostlike, in the hidden corners of Thebes's collective memory, twenty years later.

"Antonia King" was a costume I'd worn for most of my life anyhow, so I just put on a slightly different costume when I left for college. Midwestern girl, typical American upbringing, blah, blah, no drama. It was a huge relief. At Harvard, I met real European royalty. And American versions of royalty. A girl from northwestern Minnesota brings her own kind of exoticism into that context, and it was more than enough for me to handle. I shook off my origins like a dog coming in from the rain.

But here's Per Olufsen, responding to my origins with neither boredom nor horror, but simply as fact.

I can work with facts.

"I was so little when we were brought over," I say, wrapping my hands around the warm mug in front of me. "My brother told me stories about our past in secret, at night, because we were expected to erase it all to become Americans. We'd be scolded by our uncle for asking questions about Sarajevo, or our birth parents. And nothing but English was permitted in our house. I lost what few words of Serbo-Croatian I had."

"Your uncle?"

"Adopted. He brought us to the States from Bosnia to live with him and my aunt and cousins. Christopher King. He runs a manufacturing company in a small town a few hours northwest of here."

"Why was an American from Minnesota in Sarajevo during the siege? Was he with the United Nations peacekeeping forces?"

My uncle is a lot of things. Intently persuasive. Almost impossible to defy. Even loving, in his gruff, demanding way. But peacekeeper? Not one bit.

"He and his older brother were working construction for Barrington Development, an American company contracted to build hotels in Sarajevo. People here thought the Balkans would be capitalist hubs after Yugoslavia dissolved."

"Sure, I know about Barrington," says Per. "Some of their buildings from that era are still unfinished. Lots of lawsuits back in the day. A case study in what not to do at Air Trek."

"I guess at the time they were a big deal. Anyhow, they had lots of money to hire lots of people. Christopher and Eddie were just back from the Gulf War. Eddie was injured, there was a recession, and the economy was bad in Thebes."

"They worked in Greece too?"

I laugh. "It's the Thebes you've never heard of. Thebes, Minnesota. Christopher and Eddie went to Bosnia to earn enough cash to start the family business. Then the siege happened. They found us totally by accident after a bombing several months in, while they were surveilling the area to make sure it was safe to go back to work."

"They saved your lives. Miraculous."

I go numb. What am I doing? Christopher saved my life and I'm repaying him by interviewing for a job in Minnesota that isn't with King Family Construction. Behind his back. After I told him that corporate law wasn't my thing. I swore Harrison to secrecy when I told him about the Grogan possibility. We both know that any plan Christopher doesn't make himself he considers to be the wrong plan.

Be the woman in the mirror, Toni, I remind myself. *Win this job and you can win his approval. He will come around. He has to.*

"So, the business is run by Christopher and Eddie?" Per asks.

Eddie. When I was four, I watched our new American father nod off in a corner of the living room, his bottle of blue pain pills overturned on the floor. Pus oozing from the stump that had been his lower leg before Iraq. Paul was at school. And me? Quaking under the sofa. Paralyzed by the memory of my mother's stilled hand, half a world away.

I could see the moss-green phone in the kitchen from my hiding place on the floor. The metal step stool below it. I knew there were three buttons I was supposed to push in an emergency. But I was frozen.

Paul found us this way when he came home. "What's wrong with you?" he screamed. I had no answer. He made it look so easy to grab the receiver and press the right numbers. "If he dies, it's all your fault!"

When the ambulance came, Paul was thumping on Eddie's chest while tears ran down his face. "Please wake up," he recited in a whisper. "Please, please." And by the time Christopher arrived, I was huddled next to Paul on top of the blue sofa, clinging to him as if for my life. Presenting a united front, once again. But my brother's accusation had lodged itself in my heart.

"Eddie died years ago," I say.

Facts, I remind myself. That's what I'm trading with Per. "Christopher turned their earnings into a manufacturing company. It's grown into the leading business of Thebes."

"The manufacturing industry. How compelling! I find fewer and fewer people I meet these days have any connection to how things are made. And ultimately, airplanes are things."

"I grew up seeing the before and after whenever King Family Construction took on a project."

"A Bosnian migrant *and* a child raised in the great tradition of American manufacturing. This is fascinating! So, what stays with you from your earliest years?"

Per's glowing attention is like Helios the sun god himself, bursting out of ancient Greek mythology to quell the Minneapolis rain. Impossible to resist. He wants to know about stories I've buried so deeply that I've only ever spoken with Paul about them. Per is my uncle's opposite. He says: tell me your stories and we shall be friends. Christopher says: ignore the past, what good will it do?

I'm enveloped by the warmth of Per's bright light. I want to feel how he makes me feel: Important. Suffused with meaning. Safe.

"My brother was the caretaker of all the stories from our former life," I say. "Our past is a fairy tale to me. Even my real name became imaginary. Nobody used it but Paul."

I was Mujo, and you were Andela, he would whisper to me, *before we were Paul and Toni. Our mother gave us those names and we can't forget them. Or her.*

Andela, after my mother's mother, I say to Per, who died when she was still a girl. Mujo, after her favorite folk song: a boy, shoeing his horse in the moonlight so he can ride off to fight the invading Turks, while his mother begs him to stay.

Once I start, I can't seem to stop. It's as if I'm floating above myself and this man sitting at the Four Seasons, watching myself talk. I tell Per how just before my brother dropped out of high school, he had his old name tattooed across his chest, along with the turbaned, bearded face of a nineteenth-century folk hero known as the Dragon of Bosnia. Paul remembers our birth father telling us the tale. The swirls of ink that permeated my brother's skin both repulsed and fascinated me. Was this Bosnian face over his heart a signal that our American life wasn't real? Was I less real to him than a story? The dark beard and dark eyes: could this be what our father looked like too?

I tell Per that our father was taken away when I was only months old.

"Taken?" he asks.

"Paul says it must have been to a prison camp. He did a bunch of online research at one point, but he never found anything specific."

Per shakes his head and sighs. "Tragic," he mutters.

Oh no. Is he tipping away from fascination and into sympathy for the poor little orphan girl sitting across from him? That won't do. I force myself back into my body, shake off the floating sensation. No matter how brilliant Per is at drawing out personal information, this is still an interview. My goal isn't to make him feel sorry for me. Sweat begins to creep along my neck and under my arms. Am I screwing this up? Is my past too much for anyone "normal"?

"And your mother?" Per leans even closer to me over the table. "What happened to her?"

No.

He can't have her, no matter how kind the sound of his voice.

My exhaustion, his golden gaze: all of it weakened me temporarily, allowed me to go soft. Time to snap back into place.

I lean forward to meet him.

"Per," I say, "this is all pretty personal stuff. I'd hate to have my potential new boss think I'm oversharing on such an important client interview. Can I ask you, if it isn't too bold, to keep this piece of my history between us? Please?"

I make sure my eyes radiate vulnerability. Innocence. Dark pools of . . . whatever he wants to see.

"Of course," he says, squeezing my hands. "Your secrets are safe with me."

————

The day after our meeting, I flip-flop between panic that I've thrown the deal with my revelations (Per thinks: *How could a weak little runt with a tragic past represent me and my multi-billion-dollar company?*) and panic that I've talked myself out of a job (Per says: "Melanie, get rid of the weak little runt with the tragic past and you'll have my business."). How did something I never wanted turn into something I want more than anything? But Per's magnitude, Melanie's panache—the sheer brain power involved in the operations has seduced me. And even though it's unexpected, won't my uncle be excited for me if I land such a prominent gig in his own state? With a salary worth writing home about. If I went straight to Washington, there's no question I'd be working for someone whose politics he despises. For pennies. All decisions he would disagree with, to say the least. Working at Grogan would be an olive branch, wouldn't it? If I win this job, will he finally say to me, "Antonia, you've made me so proud"?

WHEN GROGAN'S PARTNERS EMERGE FROM THE CONFERence room at 4:00 p.m. with thirty-year-old scotch and shot glasses for all to announce that we've won the biggest client the Twin Cities had seen in a generation, I almost pass out from relief amid the cheers and high fives. And when Melanie pulls me aside to say Per told her she'd assembled exactly the team he had hoped to find, right down to the marvelous young recruit straight out of Harvard Law School who sealed the deal for him, all is right with the world.

With Melanie's perfectly manicured hand on my shoulder, I sign my life away to Grogan, Dwyer, and Lenz, my heart pounding with excitement about my win and fear about sharing the news with my uncle.

MY FEAR IS WELL PLACED. THE DAY AFTER I TELL HIM, Christopher emails me a bill for my full three-year ride at law school. And announces that I'll never see another cent.

Saturday, June 20, 2014

Evening

IT'S 8:00 P.M. AND I'M IN A BATHROOM STALL ON THE fiftieth floor of the IDS Center building, wriggling into a pair of pantyhose. Grogan's pull-out-all-the-stops cocktail reception to celebrate the acquisition of Air Trek is about to begin.

The main bathroom door squeaks open. The scent of Melanie's Chanel No. 5 announces her entrance.

"Toni? Are you ready? Per just arrived!"

"Coming!" I shimmy my red Alaïa bandage dress down over the hose and reach behind my neck to tuck the tag into my bra strap. The dress goes back to Nordstrom next week, along with the Manolo Blahnik black pumps I slip onto my feet. I don't trust any item of clothing I own to give me the confidence I need to exude tonight, and thanks to my brand-new six-figure debt, I'm without a wardrobe budget for the foreseeable future.

I open the stall door to see Melanie in front of the bathroom mirror, searching her own face for anything that needs fixing. Nothing does. She's everything I want to be someday: brilliant, respected, gloriously single; her outfit—ivory silk blouse, black velvet palazzo pants, stilettos—perfectly balanced between professional and goddess. Even her skin looks expensive.

A career like Melanie's, filled with mundane rules and regulations, might look like a yawn from the outside. But I see something else when I watch her: Control. Certainty. A haven from the dreams that still shake me from my sleep. The one where I'm reaching for my mother to pick me up, but she floats away, carried into the night sky by giant wooden clothespins while dust glitters all around. The one where she feeds me sour cabbage from a green plastic spoon with a metal handle; I want her to stop, I hate it, but she shoves more into my mouth, and more, until I wake in a sweat, gagging on nothing, tears running down my cheeks.

No. Melanie's work is a pathway to mastery, filled with handholds and footholds I can use to climb even further away from the little girl I used to be, the one who still invades my nightmares, even two languages, twenty years, and ten thousand miles later. And away from Thebes, where every twist and turn of King family drama rises to epic reality-television levels of intrigue among the locals.

Half the town blamed me and Paul for what happened to Eddie after he brought us back from Bosnia. The stress of raising those foreign orphans alone was too much for that poor injured man, they whispered to each other when they saw us with Christopher and Evelyn at church. We heard. We knew. And sometimes—okay, most of the time—I blamed myself. Why didn't I get to the phone when Eddie collapsed instead of hiding under the sofa? Even now, although my rational mind understands that I was only four years old, I still wonder: If I hadn't been Andela, that terrified orphan from a world away, if I had been a proper little American girl, would I have made the call to 911 and saved Eddie's life?

Minneapolis is awfully close to Thebes. However, standing next to Melanie Dwyer in front of the perfectly lit mirror in the perfectly lit ladies' bathroom, I know I made the right decision. The Cities might be only a three-hour drive from my childhood home, but Melanie's hushed power makes it all feel worlds away.

She appraises me, her new protégée.

"Just one thing." She pulls a lipstick out of her clutch and passes it my way. Chanel again. Rouge Allure. The woman is brand loyal.

The red is the precise color of my dress and sets off my black hair and eyes. It's like adding a sword to a suit of armor.

Melanie puts an arm over my shoulders and leans into the mirror.

"We are a formidable team tonight," she says.

I want to believe that she's right. I want to feel rooms stir when the two of us walk in looking impeccable and fierce. Because Melanie promised this will lead to everything I've been working for.

Enormous arrangements of creamy calla lilies and purple-blue hydrangeas reign over the two bars in the main hall. Dom Pérignon is flowing, and a jazz trio swings out Basie tunes—all Olufsen's favorites, according to my pre-party research. First-year associates: we do whatever we can to stand out. Even event planning if that's what it takes.

Melanie is immediately swept away by the other partners at Grogan, leaving me to gaze around the hall, alight with chandeliers above and tea lights on every cocktail table. The wide bank of windows across from me showcases Minneapolis under a twilit sky, with St. Paul right across the Mississippi River.

Look where I am, I say in my head to my uncle. *Shouldn't you be proud of me?*

Shouldn't he brag to his cronies about the little girl he rescued twice—once from certain death on the other side of the world and a second time from the loss of his own brother on the other side of town? Isn't it a feather in his cap that the little girl made it from Sarajevo to Thebes and all the way to Harvard under his tutelage?

I get only his disappointment. His sense of my betrayal.

Then there's Paul.

My brother didn't have to say the word *sellout* aloud for me to hear it ricochet between us during our last call. When I told him about my new job, I could feel his judgment crawl through the phone and onto my skin.

"You have lots of options, Toni. What happened to politics? Are you just stuck on making money?"

"Would you rather I came back there to defend the right of King Family Construction to blow up any piece of land in northern Minnesota to build a Starbucks? Because that was my other option, Paul. And anyhow, with money comes influence. You can protest all you want, but do it without influence and you're nowhere."

When Paul dropped out after his junior year of high school, he hit the road, dumpster-diving his way across the Midwest, from one antiwar protest to the next, leaving me behind to shoulder the brunt of Christopher's disappointment. I became a stand-in for my brother's failure to live up to our uncle's dreams. And in retaliation, I became anti-Paul. I deleted his emails imploring me to learn more about Islam or the Bosnian genocide and the destruction of our people. Ripped up the letters he sent without reading them.

And when I got myself out three years later, the only student from Mt. Olympus High School ever to apply to Harvard, let alone receive admission, what did Paul do? He came back to Thebes. Not right away, but soon after I'd made the decision to stay in Cambridge for law school. And not to our uncle's house, but to live in the area of town where a small group of Somali refugees had recently settled.

Christopher was in negotiations with the county to declare eminent domain over the four-block Somali section that included Paul's building. My brother threw himself right in the middle.

Thousands of Somalis had been coming to the Twin Cities for a few years. Minnesota's immigration laws were friendly, and the social service network for refugees had been around for decades. Since, well, Bosnians. Maybe even before. But not in northwestern towns like Thebes—I never even met a Black person until I left for college.

Paul was repurposing his activism on home soil. While I agreed with him in theory, I couldn't in practice. Thebes was Thebes. Xenophobic. Racist. Small-minded and proud of it. My brother was expending all his energy for social change on four blocks in a tiny town where our uncle was royalty and called all the shots.

Why? I kept asking Paul. We were on speaking terms again by then; however, our life choices had taken us in such different directions that it was hard to find our way back. Our phone calls became terse as we rehashed the same exhausting fight over and over again.

Him: "You forget where you come from."

Me: "Oh, I know where I come from. The Kings gave us our actual American lives, by the way, not our fake oppressed lives that you're appropriating to make yourself seem like a man of the people. Take what you've been given, Paul, and do something with it!"

"That's exactly what I'm doing, Andela."

He knows that my given name is both nails on a chalkboard and my weakness when it comes to him. Yet, as annoying and self-righteous as he's become, I'll do anything for him, even if I can't bring myself to tell him so.

He's also the only one who knows about my nightmares. I've cultivated my stance for years—Antonia King, cool as a cucumber, smart as a whip, every cliché of unflappability ever written. My dreams, my night sweats, they don't match. Paul helps. When I see my brother's thick mess of brown hair, the shadows under his brown eyes that never quite fade, I can imagine our parents, once upon a time and long ago. I used to ask: Did I look more like our mother, or did he? (You did, said Paul.) Did our father tell us stories all the time or only before bed? (At bedtime, said Paul.) I remember nothing without my brother to remember it for me.

I'd be lying to myself if I didn't confess that his disapproval strikes a chord. Fancy corporate law, glittering evenings like this—what am I doing here? Maybe he's right. Maybe Christopher is too. I could have chosen Washington, or I could have chosen family. And I chose neither. Have I lost my way?

Who is Antonia King? Per's question echoes in my mind. Ask my uncle, and he'll say: family betrayer. Ask my brother, and he'll say: corporate tool.

After a quick glance around the room to make sure Melanie isn't watching, I pick up a crystal flute of Dom from the bar near the entrance and down it in a few fast gulps.

Two years, I remind myself. Maybe three. Then Washington. Working on behalf of the ideals I hold: Justice. Truth. I know what I want, I do.

The banquet hall glows with women in their cocktail finery: a parade of updos, of flawless makeup, of intricately draped and beaded dresses, all the result of hours of labor. The men wear the same kind of suits I see each day, with just a pocket square and a fancy tie marking the difference between work and play.

"Looking the part is how we have to play the game," Melanie said when she approved my outfit for tonight. "No missteps allowed."

Melanie. That's the image that wipes my mental slate clean. She is my goal, my mantra. *Be Melanie.* I close my eyes. The sounds of "Take the A Train" and the clinking of expensive crystal hum beneath the mounting party chatter.

Fuck Thebes. And fuck our past. Paul can have them both.

"Does the lady need a refill?"

Per Olufsen holds a new flute of bubbly before me and places his other hand on my back. I allow him to double-cheek kiss me and leave his hand where it rests.

"Toni, I need you. Melanie assures me that you'll help me keep track of all the Twin City doyennes and—oh, whatever the men are called—to whom I promise anything tonight."

"Absolutely." Relief. I'm better when I have a task. And a second glass of champagne.

Tonight is both a celebration of Air Trek Industries' future in

Minneapolis and a debutante ball for Per himself. Executives from every major business operating in the Cities are here, as well as trustees of every cultural institution. I stand by his side while the fancy people press up against each other in their eagerness to shake his hand. When I sense him losing interest in the parade of new subjects, I steer him to a quiet corner. Per and I sit close together at a tiny cocktail table, knees touching lightly but never more than what could be construed as accidental. I've calibrated the line between "tolerable" and "no" with precision. We'll remain on the correct side of proper. My experience with James Hollings taught me never to cross that line again. The only men allowed in my bed now are men I can send away when it's done. No baggage, no questions.

A young cater-waiter in an ill-fitting tux stops by with his silver tray: glistening orange caviar on toast. Roe imported from Per's native Scandinavia. At last, I can sample the menu that my new employer chose to convince the man across from me that Minneapolis is world-class, and Air Trek belongs. Silky, briny eggs that taste like oceans and luxury. I reach for another, but Per dismisses the waiter with a slight wave of his hand.

"Not hungry?" I ask.

He throws his sun-god smile. "I hate caviar. But don't tell anyone—it's too far off-brand."

"Attorney-client privilege extends to food."

"Ah, I knew I hired well. Next time, let's wear disguises and you can take me out for some true local fare."

"Two Juicy Lucys coming right up!"

He raises an eyebrow.

"Folks here take credit for inventing cheese stuffed inside of burgers instead of melted on top," I say. "Honestly, it's so good that way. I couldn't find a Boston burger that didn't taste dry as dirt."

He laughs—a real laugh this time, not a cocktail-party laugh.

I feel loose, sparkly. The star of this show approves of me. "If you want to sample real Minnesota food, come up north for potluck supper at my uncle's church. Hot dish for days. The people here might look fancy, but we all love our frozen tater tots."

"Up north. That's Thebes, right?"

"You remember."

"You're quite memorable. Your uncle is a churchgoer? May I ask, was that ever . . . a conflict? With your history?"

My usual cue to shift the subject. But Per asks so gently. No judgment, just curiosity. With a hint of concern that feels almost fatherly.

"Christopher was president of the board at Northern Baptist. Probably still is. So church was important to him and Evelyn. It was their way. The King family name means something in a town as small as Thebes. My brother and I were under their protection; nobody dared question our religious roots."

"Did you?" Again, that intense gaze, as if I'm the most interesting person on the planet.

I take another sip of champagne. A performance of my secular tastes, I suppose. Honed in teenaged opposition to my brother's path. Solidified as I traveled further down my own. "My first people were destroyed because of religion. My parents converted to hide, not to believe—and it didn't work. I prefer being nothing from nowhere. I'm sorry if that offends."

"You can't offend me."

He's safe. A force field, keeping the partygoers in the room—and the demons in my head—at bay.

"Paul and I were the only kids from another country in school and in church. Christopher's money and prominence kept people from saying stuff to our faces—but we knew the difference between the smiles for our cute blond cousins and what we got. My brother was always curious about Muslim culture because of our ancestors. Now he identifies with the community of Somali refugees in Thebes, even though they're from such a different place. Maybe he wants to re-create something we never had."

Per is nodding. "That would explain a lot."

I'm a little soft from the champagne and the attention, but I'm not sure what he thinks I'm explaining. Have I told him even more about my family than I intended?

Melanie materializes at our table. I sit up straight, blink myself back to attention.

"Is my new associate taking good care of you, Per?" She's checking me, reminding me about the new part.

"And how!" He's relaxed, his expression unchanged. *Your secrets are safe with me.* His pledge over coffee at the Four Seasons holds.

Melanie catches my eye, signals her approval. Good. She plans to make Grogan lots and lots of beautiful money with Per as our client, and she needs to see that I'm fully on board to help. Okay, my brother isn't totally off base. But what else can I do now? Christopher cut us both off when we defied his wishes. I will scrimp and save and return all my clothes and tithe my entire salary at Grogan to pay back my uncle, but I will not end up in poverty like Paul. I will earn my way to the places where all the real decisions are made about justice in the world. And I refuse to be ashamed.

———

At the end of the party, Melanie and I escort Per to the elevators with more double-cheek kisses and promises to start working on behalf of our new number-one account in the morning. Per leans over to Melanie and says, "You know what the first order of business is."

Melanie nods.

"And you'll tell her what we need?" he continues, angling his head my way.

"Trust me," says Melanie, "she's exactly what you've been looking for."

I'm still feeling the champagne, but not enough that I don't pick up on my cue.

"Per," I say in my Harvard Law School voice, "thank you for the opportunity. You won't regret it. I'll do whatever it takes." I will, even though I don't know what they're talking about.

He takes my hand in both of his, squeezes it in appreciation.

"You know, tomorrow is the summer solstice," he says. "I think this evening marks an auspicious beginning to the turn of the season."

A gentle chime. The elevator doors slide open.

"I'll see you down," says Melanie. "Toni, we'll talk in the morning."

I watch the doors close and wait for the indicator light to show that they've really left.

Done. Success. Relief.

I turn back to the remains of the party, teetering slightly in my "borrowed" heels. I'll have a whopping couple of blisters to bandage up when I go running tomorrow, but it will have been worth it.

Most everyone has left, gone out into the beautiful June night. Only the staff and a few stragglers remain. My final job is making sure the cleanup goes smoothly, but there's nothing to do other than wait around. I wander over to the floor-to-ceiling bank of windows, giving myself over to the champagne buzz in my head and the thrill of the view from fifty stories up. The twinkling lights of the buildings on either side of the Mississippi double themselves in the mirror of the river and the glow of the sky.

I let the scenery blur and focus instead on my own dim reflection in the glass, backlit by the chandeliers. A coil of hair has escaped from my chignon and snakes around my neck. I twirl the long, loose pieces around my fingers.

The sweet scent of baby shampoo wafts up from the recesses of my memory. The warmth of the bath towel Paul would wrap around my newly washed hair when I was done in the tub. Our first few years here, I didn't let anyone other than Paul or baby Izzy touch me. I stiffened whenever Aunt Evelyn made a move in my direction and ran away when Uncle Christopher tried to display any paternal sentiment.

An old-time riverboat, ablaze with lights, floats into view. A tourist attraction during the months that the Mississippi isn't clogged with ice floes. Back at Mt. Olympus High School, they made us study everything white settlers wrote about the Mississippi River, but nothing from the thousands of years of native history that came before. When my brother spray-painted *What about the Ojibwa? What about the Dakota?* across the concrete front wall of Mt. O, I was sure he'd get suspended, and of course, he did. Today he's wasting all that freedom-fighting energy on one tiny group of refugees in one tiny town. Why is he even there? He could come here, where thousands of Somali immigrants live and where actual services exist for resettlement. And people who care, not just hostile old locals who will never change.

My feet are throbbing now. I kick off my pumps and pad in my stockinged feet over to the nearby bar. After a quick glance at the post-party stragglers to make certain none of them are Grogan partners, I grab a leftover bottle of Dom that bobs, alone, in a bucket of melting ice.

Congratulations to me.

HERE'S WHAT I REMEMBER FROM OUR JOURNEY TO THE United States: Sobbing during the flight because the pressure hurts my ears. The whirring sound of pumped air, the cold snap of the seat belt buckle that Eddie shows us how to open and close, the musty smell of the blue fabric seats. My brother huddled against the window seat, pulling the oval plastic shade up a crack to see the white-blue sky, then down to plunge us into darkness.

I'm in the middle. Eddie sits next to me, his prosthetic leg jutting into the aisle. Christopher is in the seat a row across. Eddie tries to whisper questions to his brother, but Christopher keeps his baseball cap pulled low over his eyes and folds his arms. I peek across Eddie at the massive form that is Christopher King. I can see nothing but the rim of his cap and the bottom of his beard as his chest moves up and down with the slow breaths of sleep. Even in slumber, Christopher is a force.

MY BROTHER REMEMBERS THIS FROM OUR ARRIVAL: THE scratching sound of Eddie's key in his own front door while he turns it to no avail. Johanna has changed the lock. From inside the house, her voice is muffled, but he can tell that she's shouting. Furious.

Eddie carries me over one shoulder, a duffel bag slung across his other.

"Jo, just meet them," says Eddie. "They're good kids."

My brother knows enough English after weeks with our new guardian that he can piece it together. At six, he has a backpack all his own filled with new stories: *The Legend of Paul Bunyan. The Tale of Johnny Appleseed*. American heroes. Christopher—now Uncle Christopher—marveled at what he could procure through the embassy in Munich, where we waited until the official papers came from home that made it no longer our home.

"Learn about these men," he said, pointing to the drawings. A brawny giant with an axe. A tall giant with a sack. "This is your history now."

It's dark, late. We'd flown eleven hours to Chicago, then rented a car for the six-hour trip to Eddie's house in Thebes. Christopher has dropped the three of us off before continuing to the other side of town where he and Evelyn live. My brother says I slept in the back seat next to him the entire drive while he looked out the window at the endlessly long, flat stretches of road, unlike anything he'd ever seen in the mountains we were from.

Johanna is throwing things inside the house. Thud. Crack. Thud again.

"Fuck you for doing this to me, Edward!" Not so muffled.

"Let's talk calmly," Eddie says, leaning against the door. "They can hear you."

"So what? You go away for seven months and come back with this? A telegram arrives telling me—not asking me—telling me you're adopting two orphans from Bosnia?"

"I couldn't take them out of the country without making it legal. I had to bring them here. Let me in and I can explain."

Silence from the house. The rustle of strange leaves on strange trees all around.

HERE'S WHAT WE BOTH REMEMBER: JOHANNA HAS LEFT. We're living alone with Eddie. His kind eyes are hooded, his mouth downturned. We sit at the kitchen table after our dinner of franks and beans, heated up right in the red-and-white can in a saucepan of boiling water. Eddie calls it army cooking.

His stump from the Gulf War hurts all the time now. His artificial lower leg stays in the corner of the living room; he no longer puts it on at home.

He keeps a bottle of small blue pills on the counter over the kitchen sink. We fetch it for him and count out the pills. At first, it's two a day. Then four. More bottles appear on the windowsill like magic.

WAS IT A WEEK? WAS IT TWO? MY NEXT MEMORY IS THE afternoon my brother comes home from his new school to find me shaking under the living room sofa and Eddie unconscious. Christopher arrives to scoop us up, imposing and fearsome as ever.

We become Paul and Antonia King.

My brother is named for Uncle Christopher's brawny hero with the axe. No longer a folk song boy or a bearded dragon. I'm named for a fictional girl from Eastern Europe who migrated to the Midwest: a character in a novel Aunt Evelyn loves that I'm too little to read.

New names for our new life.

This is our history now.

Dawn

DARTH VADER'S THEME MUSIC FROM *STAR WARS* BLARES into my brain. My eyes open. It's dark in my motel room, some ungodly hour, and my head is throbbing. Before I can fully awaken and process what is happening, the theme repeats itself, all those ominous, self-important chords. The ringtone I downloaded for Uncle Christopher last week, after he cut me off. I'm tangled in my sheet and try to kick it off as I grope for my phone; instead, I kick a hard object that rolls off my bed and onto the floor. The empty champagne bottle I'd pinched from the party.

The Death Star blasts again from somewhere near my eardrums.

"Oh, please go away!"

The man in the room next door pounds on the wall. "Shut up!" he calls. I pound back in protest. Not the first time we've had this fight. His maximum-volume cop shows; my music.

I find my phone under the pillow. Christopher hasn't called or texted me since I told him I was taking the Minneapolis job, and I've been afraid to call him. Our only communication has been through his banker, closing my checking account and issuing the first notice of payment for what he referred to as my "student loans." Is he reaching out to yell at me again? To see if I'll apologize for my decision? Or maybe . . . possibly . . . to tell me that he loves me no matter what career choice I make?

I press Answer.

Ugh. Why did I press Answer?

"Antonia?"

My mouth doesn't work.

"Are you there?"

He's not yelling.

"The check is in the mail," I say stupidly.

"That's not why I'm calling. It's your brother. I can't reach him."

I check my bedside clock—4:30 a.m.

"Isn't he just asleep? Like I was?" I can't resist adding.

"Listen, we have a situation. Last night a bunch of renters were rabble-rousing. Protesting our Big Dig."

Renters: Christopher-speak for immigrants or refugees who've moved to Thebes in the past few years. All of whom just happen not to be white.

"I knew your brother would be there," he continues, "instigating against his own family and his own best interests. But that's him."

"You know activism is his passion . . ."

"Things turned violent. A cop is in the hospital."

Now I'm fully awake. "Was Paul hurt?"

"I don't know. But I do know he was part of the mob."

"He's a pacifist."

"Maybe he used to be. But those people he's mixed up with—they're no good. Your cousins think that you're the only person who can find your brother. Come home. We must keep this local. No Minneapolis involvement. It's safer this way."

"Safer how?"

"So we can find him before the police do."

"Is there evidence he did anything illegal?"

"My attorney has advised me not to say."

The knife twist: his attorney who isn't me. "Who knows what so far? Is there—"

"We can discuss this further in person. It's not smart to talk over the airwaves. Let's just say your brother has put this family at risk—and himself too."

I hang up the phone and immediately text Paul: *Where are you? Must talk ASAP.*

I need to hear my brother's interpretation of events. No matter what disagreements Paul and I have, he never lies to me.

My head is beginning to throb, whether from the conversation on the phone or the excess of champagne last night I'm not certain. I rub my temples and try to think. On the one hand, despite referring to modern telecommunications as "airwaves," Christopher isn't wrong about potential privacy issues when we aren't in person. On the other hand, it's too soon to assume that Paul is truly missing, both with his track record of disappearing and the pre-dawn possibility that he's just asleep. But an injured policeman is the kind of event that blows up fast these days. Everyone will be looking for someone to blame should the worst happen. If Paul is at risk of taking the heat, better for me to get out in front of the story and make sure his rights are protected. And maybe, maybe . . . this could be my chance to demonstrate the value of the path I've chosen. To show Paul that he hasn't cornered the market on dropping everything to come to the rescue of other people. And show my uncle that holding a job in his company isn't the only way to be family.

I knew I'd be drawn back into all the drama if I came back to Minnesota. I just hoped it wouldn't happen so soon. Am I making a huge mistake? Christopher can't see straight when it comes to my brother, he's still so hurt by Paul's rejection of all that he values. And I've added fuel to the fire by taking the Grogan job behind his back.

But Paul. What if he really needs me?

I flip on the harsh fluorescent overhead light, which does not help my hangover. I rummage through the pile of clothes I've dumped on the floor of the pint-size motel closet, my head pounding, trying to throw something reasonable into my gym bag. I find a sports bra I flung over a chair after my run yesterday morning, sniff it to make sure it isn't too disgusting, then pull it over my head and adjust myself into it. Bike shorts, flip-flops, and an oversized Harvard Law T-shirt. I check my phone quickly to see if Paul has responded. Of course not, he's probably asleep like a normal person.

Probably. But every one of my nerve endings pulses with worry that my brother might be in trouble.

———

I accelerate out of the dark and nearly deserted parking lot in my 2003 Chrysler PT convertible hatchback and swing onto the connector for I-94. I bought the car with money I earned as a second-year intern at Dewey, Baker in Boston to get me and my boxes to Minneapolis. I ignored the dents in the body and the rattling noise over sixty miles an hour in favor of a top-down drive across half the country that would keep the wind in my hair and the thoughts from my head. Despite blowing two tires and dropping a muffler along the way, the old car did the trick. I had every intention of trading it in toward something more alluring once my signing bonus came through, but now I'm just going to have to baby it along until I'm out of debt to my uncle. I need to get an apartment so I'm not camping out with angry wall-pounders at the Motel 6 for the rest of my life. That and my loan payments will be pretty much all I can afford for a while.

The sun is starting to rise over the Cities, bathing the eastern horizon with a golden hue and warming the sky from cobalt to slate to the palest pink. Northwest, where I'm headed, is still blue-black and inscrutable. I push the button that opens the convertible roof to let the chill dawn rush around me. Huge gulps of air help keep my queasiness at bay. Although now I'm not sure whether I'm queasy from what I drank last night or queasy about where I'm heading this morning.

When I connect my phone to the portable MiFi device charging in the cigarette lighter, its display lights up with the date: June 21. Per's auspicious summer solstice. The longest day of the year.

This is the solstice, the still point of the sun.

Unbidden, the first line of a poem Aunt Evelyn quoted on this morning each year comes into my head. Evelyn, a cooling mug of coffee in her hands, staring out the kitchen window at the tree line beyond the house, watching the pale sun begin its long path. When I was little, I'd watch her in profile as the light played across her face. She seemed deep in thought, far away from all of us, from Uncle Christopher. From the state of Minnesota itself. What pinged around her mind and heart on those summer mornings? What did my aunt wish for that she couldn't find in Thebes?

Evelyn wasn't much for talking—she preferred to parent through indirection. When I was dark and mopey, I'd find a novel left on my nightstand, its spine cracked open to mark a page where a girl in some nineteenth-century novel about orphans learned to love her new life. Scraps of inspirational poetry, copied onto Post-its in Evelyn's perfect, round cursive, dotted the bathroom mirror the day of a big test. *Be Yourself—Everyone Else Is Taken. Don't Sweat the Small Stuff.*

The light on my dash blinks to tell me that Bluetooth is now online.

"Text Paul," I tell my phone.

"Hey, call me when you wake up," I dictate, deliberately keeping my tone casual. Like someone who isn't worried at all about her brother. "I'm on my way to the house, I need to know what your deal is before I get there. What happened at the dig site?"

Christopher has been amassing resources and support for his Big Dig ever since I can remember. His plan: turning downtown Thebes into another row of Starbucks, Gaps, California Pizza Kitchens, and Abercrombie & Fitches. All with an eye toward hooking the choicest fish that swims the famous Minnesota lakes: Target. Homegrown big box magic. Christopher has been talking about attracting a Target to Thebes forever, and he's convinced that smaller chain retail will provide proof of concept.

For the past decade, he's been glad-handing for contracts, building his case, and working to have eminent domain declared. Still and always: Uncle Christopher plotting to save the town of Thebes and everyone in it—well, everyone he's willing to see as a "true" resident—as long as there's a pretty penny for him along the way.

Harrison has kept me up to date on the whole thing. Poor guy, he's been trying to prove his business acumen to his father since forever and he still gets shoved aside. After college, Harry returned to King Family Construction all excited to manage the public relations department Christopher had created to make a place for him. As far as I can tell, other than showing up for local media events, Christopher ignores Harrison's suggestions on the regular.

I keep reminding Harry that his father tends to dismiss anyone who's gay in the same way that he dismisses anyone who doesn't fit his mold. I've been in rooms where Christopher's work buddies crack homophobic jokes and seen him laugh along as if his own son didn't matter. When I've called him out on it, he says "It doesn't mean anything—that's the construction business. Anyone who can't take it needs to find another line of work."

Harrison doesn't want to hear me.

"I get him," he says. "He pushes me so I'll be able to stand my ground when it counts. You and Paul too. You just don't understand, and you don't even want to try."

Last month Harrison emailed me the *Thebes Oracle* cover photo of the Big Dig ribbon cutting—Christopher and Evelyn, he and Izzy, wearing King Construction hard hats and holding on to the handles of a giant pair of foam-core scissors while flanked by the mayor, the town selectmen, and dozens of balloons.

The ceremony was the same day as my graduation from law school. I was wearing my robe and mortarboard when the email came through.

The irony was not lost on me that my Harvard law degree was its own kind of hard hat. I was alone in Cambridge—not one member of my family sat in uncomfortable folding chairs for hours while "Pomp and Circumstance" played on a constant loop, waiting for their chance to hand me wilted flowers and tell me how proud they were. They were too busy holding fake scissors in Thebes. And my brother was doing whatever my brother was doing, probably already planning the protest that got him into this situation.

Christopher used to tell us stories about his childhood as a farm kid—old-timey, sepia-tinged stuff about pies and community. But then small agriculture dried up, manufacturing boomed and busted, and all the farmers' sons either had to go to work for the factory owners who lived in much wealthier Athens, or they ended up on the dole. The only other decent option was the military. Most of the boys who graduated from Mt. Olympus High School in his era enlisted during the Gulf War, including Christopher and Eddie.

Christopher's favorite story, the one he repeated like a mantra, was the story of the pact that he and Eddie made when they were seventeen and eighteen, down at Twin River Falls.

A tradition for every Mt. O senior class, including mine twenty-five years later, senior skip day at Twin River Falls, an hour south, celebrated freedom from the oppression of grades and teachers. Two months after Christopher's graduation, he and Eddie went back on their own—the last day before the brothers had to report for duty.

"A brutally hot August afternoon," Christopher would recall. "Eddie and I pushed through the rapids to stand under the falls just to cool our skin down enough to think straight. That's when we made our pact. No matter what happened to one of us over there, the other would take care of him. And the family. Forever."

Christopher's eyes welled up then. "I didn't know what hot was till we landed in Baghdad. On the worst days, I imagined us back at Twin River. Me and Eddie, jumping off Big Boulder and yelling like a couple of fools. Then came the explosion. His leg. I was the one left to uphold our pact. It all came down to me."

My uncle's story made me squirm every time. I wanted to paper over Eddie's presence in my life as fast as I could. Or at least, as fast as my guilt about Eddie would allow me.

"I made good on my word," Christopher would continue. "Eddie comes back from the Gulf with a stump leg. Who would hire him? I found the opportunity with Barrington, took him along with me to Sarajevo to make money and help him forget about the war. I tried to protect him again when the shit hit the fan in the Balkans. Let's get out, I said. But then we found you and your brother. Eddie had to save you, no matter how much red tape there was to navigate. Okay, I said. But you'll be the dad. I've got one of my own and one on the way. Well, guess what: Eddie couldn't handle it. Any of it. But here I am, still true to our pact. Family first. Forever."

I KNEW MY ROLE WAS TO EXPRESS GRATITUDE. BUT I didn't know how. It felt like Paul and I were burdens thrust upon Christopher by the death of his brother, who threw away Christopher's loyalty and generosity in favor of the comfort of a bottle of pills. I kept my head down in those moments and said nothing.

Sometimes, though, usually when other people were around to hear, we were trophies instead. Proof of both our uncle's personal benevolence and the righteousness of the United States government.

"Americans spreading our way of life around the world," Christopher declared during the trophy moments, his rooster chest all puffed out, when various local cronies came over to our house for functions. "And rescuing orphans from those terrible circumstances," he added, attempting to pat me or Paul on the head if we were nearby.

Our game was never to be nearby. I would shove Harrison in front of me to gaze up at his father, wielding his freckles and slicked-back blond hair. Uncle Christopher's hand stayed in hover mode when he saw I was replaced by Harrison. Not the child he needed to make his point, so not of use. Poor Harrison's little face was so crushed when his father pushed him aside to get to me. By then I would have dashed over to Izzy and pretended to be thoroughly absorbed in her Barbies or whatever other girly thing she was messing with in the corner of the great room.

"Look at those light and dark little girls!" I remember a woman gushing over the two of us. "Like Snow White and Rose Red!" A statement that prompted me to smile beatifically at Izzy as I simultaneously detached the head of one of her dolls and threw it across the room.

Paul was the bookish one back then, hiding, as usual, behind a volume of old and boring-looking philosophy. Before Izzy could rat me out to her mother, I skipped away and nestled against my brother, feigning innocent interest.

"What are you reading?" I whispered up to him, feeling safer in his physical orbit always, despite his dramatic, irritated sighs when I disturbed his solitude.

"Sartre," he answered, not looking away from the page. "He says hell is other people."

———

As I drive, I switch on my Marvin Gaye playlist and let his soaring voice wash over me and the highway. Classic Motown, nothing better. No one I know in my generation listens to Motown, but I can't be bothered with bubbly pop nothings. Marvin's powerful voice helps me forget. Not as much as diving into a bottle or two of something strong. Not as much as a night in the sack with a boy who leaves as soon as I tell him to. But it helps.

"*We got the right foundation . . .*" I'm singing along on the empty highway with Marvin and Tammi when the song is interrupted through the car speakers by "Call from Melanie Dwyer." Seven a.m. on the dot. On a Sunday morning. Welcome to Grogan, Dwyer, and Lenz. She's probably been going strong for hours, working out with her personal trainer at 5:00 a.m., drinking her green smoothie at 6:00.

Okay. Focus. Time to transform into my role as Antonia King: Brilliant Corporate Lawyer. Which of course I will juggle seamlessly with my role as Antonia King: Saving Her Do-Gooder Brother and Earning Her Uncle's Lifelong Respect. As long as I can hide my hangover.

"Morning, Toni. Time to get to work."

"I'm all yours."

"Here's the deal. Olufsen has a peccadillo we need to contain. It's potentially a nothing—but you have to keep it that way."

"Um . . . a what?" I might be hung over, but I think she just assigned me to booty-call cleanup duty.

"The eligible bachelor thing is good for his brand," Melanie continues, "but he needs to be discreet about the volume of his extracurricular activities, or it all goes south. This is where we come in. He admitted off the record to me that there was a rather unfortunate incident a few days ago. He took a jaunt to some small town, as he does when he wants to be under the radar, and he wound up drunk at a party somewhere he can't remember. With some local woman. He claims whatever happened was consensual."

"Claims?"

"Exactly. If there's evidence to the contrary, we need to contain the damage ASAP."

"Melanie, I thought I came on board to help manage his financial dealings. Isn't this basic PR stuff? Something that someone without a law degree can handle?"

"I'm asking you to handle it, Toni."

I know I should bite my tongue. I know I should just take the assignment, no questions asked. But really? Has all my striving for a bigger, more important life added up to this? Looking for clues about whether my client received some squalid hand job—or whatever?

My mouth opens, and the words come out of their own accord.

"I hear you, Melanie, I do. And I get it. But . . . but didn't I help you land the biggest account in Grogan's portfolio? I mean . . . Per said I really impressed him, and he wanted to work with me . . . with us . . . but also with me . . ."

"Yes, that's true. Your social skills are quite remarkable." Melanie's voice has turned acid. "But make no mistake: Grogan's excellent reputation precedes your very recent arrival. A portfolio like Per's isn't won by an unseasoned junior associate who knows how to exchange pleasantries over a cup of coffee."

Major misstep. Fuck. *Fix it, Toni.*

"Of course not, I wasn't trying to imply—"

"You have to pay your dues like everyone else. You will execute this assignment and you will execute it perfectly. You're not the only first-year in the pit trying to move up the ladder. If the work I give you is beneath your dignity, why, I'm sure there's another associate happy to take my call."

I take a breath. "I'm sorry, Melanie. Truly I am. You're one hundred percent right and I'm all over it."

She sighs loudly from her end of the phone. "All right. Per's files will be uploaded to our server by nine. Do the research; I need a report on my desk in twenty-four hours. No paralegals or assistants; this is for your eyes and mine only. Use the encryption code to access the information. Work remotely until it's done."

Lucky day. I might have almost messed up my job at Grogan, but at least I don't have to find a reason to be out of office tomorrow morning or tell Melanie about my family drama.

"Discretion is key. This is our first task for Per, and we'll be setting the tone for his trust, or lack thereof. You know my philosophy with clients—the more they trust us, the more money they make us."

"I'm on it, Melanie. You can count on me."

"Deliver, and I will." And with that, she hangs up.

I glance at myself in the rearview mirror: Hangover bags under my eyes. Hair a windblown nightmare. Ugh. I need to make better choices if I'm going to remain her protégée. With one hand on the steering wheel, I use the other to locate the Advil I keep in my bag (a lesson learned from other bad-choice mornings) and pop off the lid to swallow three without water. The hair is a lost cause; I'll have to resort to a ponytail when I get to Thebes.

Ninety miles to go.

At least I have a good two hours before Per's files will come through. If all goes well, maybe I'll have finished my business with Christopher and Paul by then and I can dive in and prove to Melanie that I'm the best lawyer to handle a real deal for Per. It's a test. I know how to ace a test.

"Check texts," I ask my phone. Still no response from Paul. Is it possible that he's just being self-righteous now? Ignoring me because we always argue? I'm on an even tighter time frame to earn his trust and save his ass than I was before Melanie's assignment.

"Paul!" I yell into the speaker. "I can't help you if I don't know what you're up to. You suck right now! Send Text!"

Wrong. That was probably not the kind of good choice that will lead me to my future life as the next Melanie Dwyer. I ask my phone nicely this time to reach out to him.

"Okay, Paul," I dictate in a calm, measured tone. "I'm sorry. I know we haven't spoken in a while and I know you kind of hate me right now and think I'm a corporate tool, but this is different. We have to be on the same side. Call me, please."

Coming Soon to Northwest Minnesota! A billboard appears around the bend out of nowhere. *Wind Power Farms brought to you by King Construction Company.* Well, that's new. I know without a doubt that "coming soon" means "coming never." Uncle Christopher is smart enough to advertise green, but I'm certain his display of environmental concern is so he can tease the state into believing he's offsetting his carbon footprint to get those big contracts. Another of Harrison's fantasies about hanging in to become the next generation leadership of King Construction: he plans to turn Christopher's green policies into something more than a ploy for good old green dollars. He sends me articles from marketing websites about how millennials want their brands to be eco-conscious and that this is the key to the future. *Good luck convincing your father,* I think. The millennials flocking to Thebes these days are Somali. Not Christopher's market of choice. And his cherished Big Dig isn't going to help matters.

Paul went on and on about Christopher's wrongheadedness the last time we spoke.

"Just because the exteriors of the apartment buildings aren't fixed up yet, Christopher thinks he can condemn the Somali neighborhood," he said. I was packing up my apartment in Cambridge, getting ready to start the drive to Minneapolis the next day. "This Big Dig is the worst idea he's ever had. He's going to displace the Somali community, and for what? A bunch of generic chain stores."

"Uh-huh," I said, wondering if I would have enough space to stack everything in my car for a few weeks or if I'd need to spring for a storage container somewhere until I found a place.

"My friends here have the real jobs of the future. Tech jobs. Christopher thinks retail is the way to go? He's living in some fantasy that it's twenty years ago. But we have a plan. We'll make him sit down and hear what we have to say."

"Paul," I said, shoving a box out of my way and grabbing my phone off the floor. I stared into its row of icons as if I could project the intensity of my need. "Forget Christopher. Come with me to Minneapolis instead. People from all over the world are there: Somalia, Syria. From Bosnia for fuck's sake! You can get your GED and go to college. You're too smart to waste yourself in that dump of a town we grew up in." He sat silently on the other end of the phone, letting the discomfort between us build until I couldn't take it anymore and hung up.

Looking back, I can see why he felt I was disrespecting him and his choices. But now, as I drive farther and farther away from civilization, closer and closer to our childhood home, the air thickens with futility. Nothing is possible here. Change will never take root—this very air we breathe in Thebes is a twister that descends on progress and sucks the life right out of it.

My phone lights up again.

Paul?

Not Paul. The ringtone from hell kicks in.

"Why aren't you here yet?" Christopher's voice fills the car speakers.

"Traffic is terrible. Must be an accident." I look ahead at the nearly empty stretch of highway, now fully bathed in summer morning light.

"Everybody is waiting. We have decisions to make. And quickly."

Oh, Advil, please work your magic. And quickly. I find my sunglasses on the passenger seat and slide them on. Better. "I'll be there in an hour. Have Aunt Evelyn brew another pot of coffee. Or how about mixing up a Bloody Mary?"

"This isn't a time for sarcasm. Hurry up."

No sarcasm intended. A Bloody Mary would help matters tremendously. I learned that from a pro.

"TELL ME THE STORY AGAIN," I'D WHISPER.

This was the best time, the time when all our squabbles melted away: after my bath, in the safety of my brother's room, certain that the comings and goings of Uncle Christopher and Aunt Evelyn no longer required our attention. My still-wet hair dampened the flannel on the shoulders of my red plaid nightgown. Paul ran a comb through my snarled mane, spraying detangling mist on the knottiest parts.

"Once upon a time," he would say, but I would always stop him.

"No," I said. "Start with the other part. About our father."

He put the comb away and settled back against his pillow. He began again.

"At night when I was little, and when you were too young to remember, our father read us the story about the great Dragon of Bosnia, Husein-kapetan Gradaščević."

The long name rolling off my brother's tongue felt familiar, like a lullaby.

"How did he tell us?" I wanted Paul to include every detail.

"He set me on his knee. And he held you in the crook of one arm. He read to us from a book of stories that had smooth pages and giant full-color drawings."

I had no memory of our birth father. Paul recalled a rough moustache, a mole on his neck, and his scent of stale cigarette smoke mixed with a warm spice like nutmeg but not quite nutmeg—a spice he could never find here in Minnesota.

I sighed with pleasure at Paul's revised opening. "Okay, now start back with the 'once upon a time' part. And tell it exactly like he did."

Paul still needed me to need him back then. *Take care of your sister,* the air around him whispered in our parents' voices. We heard it, in languages both spoken and forgotten.

"Once upon a time," he continued with infinite patience, "more than a hundred years ago, a boy was born to a wealthy and noble family in the north of Bosnia. His family was the ruling class, but they were kind, and this boy, Husein, was the kindest of them all. Compassion flowed from his fingertips when he wrote letters to serfs to thank them for their work. It shone from his eyes when he rode his horse to look out over the city of Gradačac. He was so intelligent that his teachers could no longer teach him anything new by the time he was ten years old. They recommended an education no one had ever had before—apprenticeships with the elders of every religion in the city. Husein was Bosniak, like us, and he studied at the Husejnija Mosque, but also with the Christians, both the Catholics and the Orthodox. And even with the Dervishes, who schooled almost no one from the outside in their mystical ways. But Husein was so kind and smart that everyone trusted him with their secrets and their heritage. He learned the ways of the world from every religion that practiced in Gradačac, and he learned the ways of the heart from his mother, who loved him very much."

I knew the part that came next.

"And our father would tell us that our mother loves us very much too, just like Husein's!" I shouted.

"Shh," Paul said. "Yes, he did."

"And then he said that we will be a family forever," I whispered. "Even later when we were living in a tent with our majka. Even now."

My brother's eyes darkened. "Don't think about all that, Andela. This story is about Husein."

I mimicked locking my mouth shut and throwing away the key, a gesture Aunt Evelyn taught me and Izzy and Harrison when we were being too whispery in church. Paul was never whispery with us. He was very adult and sat straight and quiet while the three of us squirmed.

"Husein helped everyone in the city, so when the Turks closed in and the war began, Gradačac united across all the religions to support him. He was eighteen years old now, and a captain in the Bosnian army. His older brother was killed, so Husein became the leader of Gradačac even though he was still a young man. Husein fought for the freedom of all people, no matter what religion they practiced. He was famous for saying 'In Bosnia, the sound of church bells never bothered the call to prayer of the muezzin.'"

I whispered Husein's quote silently to myself along with Paul when he said it in the sing-songy way of ancient truth.

"Soon Husein became the head of all the Bosnian rebel forces. Christians across the country heard of the Muslim who respected them too, so they marched behind him to save Bosnia and rise up to defeat the Turks! Husein was given the honorary title of the Dragon of Bosnia and became the civilian leader. He created unity and peace across all religions. In Sarajevo there were Muslims and Christians and Jews worshipping in different places on the same street. Then they would all come out to the market and drink coffee together."

Tugging on Paul's collar, I asked, "What did our father say then?"

Paul looked out into the dark of his bedroom as if looking up into our father's eyes. "He said, 'The Dragon of Bosnia would have compassion for us becoming Christians in order to survive. He loved all religions the same, and freedom most of all.'"

PAUL GREW UP TO LOVE FREEDOM MOST OF ALL.

And his love of that freedom took him away. From me.

Early Morning

TURNING OFF HIGHWAY 75, YOU WOULD ASSUME THEBES was beautiful. The route bypasses the decidedly unlovely downtown in a semicircle, meandering instead along Middle River. So many Dakota skipper butterflies dot the purple coneflowers on the banks that you can practically see them fighting each other for the best pollen. North of the river, you wind through bluestem prairie grass fields and tiny streams galore. If you didn't know that almost all the old-growth forest had been decimated by my uncle's company after he bought thousands of acres of land for cheap during the Great Recession of 2008, the baby fir trees lining the roadside for miles and miles would appear charming and make you think of Christmas Future. It all looks Dickensian to me for other reasons. Orphan reasons.

Thebes is not only the place where my uncle reigns supreme; it's the place where I cringe to think I might run into James Hollings. Whenever I made an obligatory visit back to the King abode for Christmas during college, Harrison and Izzy couldn't understand why I refused to go into town with them to our old haunts. Too risky. He could be anywhere. According to my occasional indulgence in late-night drunken internet searches for ex-boyfriend activities, I know that James and his wife have two kids, and he still works for Roberts and Associates Law

Offices in Thebes. I also learned that he ran for, and won, a seat in the state assembly—a part-time government role that only fueled my competitive juices about heading to Washington.

I drive up Tributary Access Road—a shortcut through the North Bank fields. Pink lady's slippers, the Minnesota state flower, are just beginning to show their blush-colored petals on the edge of the prairie grasses. We spent a great deal of our elementary school years memorizing critically important information that all future global citizens must know, such as the state flower, the state tree, even the state drink. Which is milk.

Here's what I remember about the history of our flower: Back in the early 1900s, it was such a popular adornment for church altars that the enthusiasm of the good Christian ladies for surrounding sermonizing ministers with the bobble-headed orchids created a statewide crisis. In 1925 the state legislature decreed it illegal to pick, remove, or transport the native-blooming lady's slipper across state lines. Is this the kind of earth-shattering controversy that James debates in his role as an assembly member?

I'm close now. Oppressively close. I pass formerly working farms, one after the other, now cordoned off by barbed wire fences littered with rusty but threatening signs warning not to trespass on the private property of King Family Construction. Who are they trying to keep out? The occasional CAUTION, BEAR CROSSING notices seem far more practical.

As I drive around the horseshoe bend past the turnoff for Old Quarry Road, the rows of rotted, twisting wire abruptly give way to ornate wrought-iron curlicues and spear-tipped fencing. It starts about four feet high, and grows as I drive, both in height and in drama. Finally, the enormous gates of the King family compound loom before me, complete with the coat of arms my uncle established all the way back in the ancient days of the twentieth century. The crisscross backhoe-meets-lion emblem soars into the sky as if reaching for the gods themselves.

I'm back.

New since my last time confronting these gates of Hades—I mean home—just months ago: electronic security everywhere. Three video cameras point their all-knowing eyes from the tops of the various entries to the property. A large keypad box with a speakerphone has been installed at the end of the driveway several feet back from the gates. As I pull up to the box, I glimpse a glass-encased guard booth just inside, with a uniformed guard visible from between the iron pillars.

Either Christopher is becoming seriously paranoid about the outside world or there have been incidents I haven't heard about. Or, quite possibly, given this is my uncle, the show needed to get bigger and badder and more dramatic. At any rate, nobody bothered to tell me the gate code, or send me a key card, or whatever.

I stare at the box, expecting it to somehow welcome me. To acknowledge I belong. I guess my refusal to return to the fold as the company lawyer has resulted in the reality that I'm not expected to return, ever. Even though I chose it, I still feel a pang. I'm truly an outsider now.

I could back up my car right now and floor it back to the Cities. I have a killer job; all I need to do is turn around and take it, take what I've worked my ass off for the past seven years. Paul will undoubtedly survive without my help—he's always made that clear.

But I can't. I need to know the truth. And I need to face the fact that I did let my uncle think for far too long that he might persuade me to return. I resisted, I questioned, but I didn't say no outright. I'm not blameless where Uncle Christopher is concerned.

Was taking the Grogan job a choice? Or was it an instinctive leap in any direction but here? Now, looking up at the tons of twisting metal between outside and in, between who belongs and who simply never will, I know it in my gut: I can't live this life. Not anymore. Coming back to work for Christopher with his rules, his gates: it would end me. I'm not a child dependent on him for life or death anymore. I'm stronger now. I have a job, a purpose. Goals. I live in a world bigger than all of this, where I'm my own person.

The rearview mirror says otherwise. I look like I've been through a hurricane. I try to smooth my hair, but to no avail. I yank it back into a ponytail, then grab a baseball cap out of my gym bag. My clothes might literally have HARVARD written all over them, but my general comportment does not. I take a deep breath, hold it for three seconds like the yoga instructors on the videos that Izzy sends regularly tell me to do, then exhale.

Nope.

Yoga might work for Izzy-size anxieties, but not for mine.

The mini bottle of Dewar's I stashed in the outside compartment of my gym bag for emergency situations is more like it. Top o' the morning to everyone. The shot burns my throat and travels immediately throughout my chest and limbs.

That's better. I press the electronic call button.

"Can I help you?" a male voice crackles. I can see the guard on the other side of the gate holding the phone to his ear.

"It's Toni. I'm here."

"I'm sorry, I don't have a Toni on the list."

"Antonia. Antonia King. It's me."

Rustling of paper.

"I don't see any authorization for someone named Antonia King . . ."

"I'm your boss's niece. Look on the family list or something."

"Ma'am, there is no niece on the list. Please provide proper authorization for entry and an ID that matches."

I punch in Christopher on my cell.

"You want me here so badly you call before dawn," I say. "So at least tell your henchman to let me in."

"My error. What was I thinking?" I can picture him holding his cell phone up to the intercom to ensure I'm hearing him call down to the guard booth. Reminding me again that he calls the shots here. "Larry, let our guest through and instruct her to park her vehicle in the back lot."

Guest. Got it.

A buzzing noise emanates from the speaker, and slowly and with re-gal fanfare—fit for a King, of course—the gates begin to swing outward. The backhoe and the lion part ways and each takes guardianship over a different vista: backhoe, with its jaws of steel, ready to gobble up the land to the south; lion surveying the north on its hind legs, baring its feline incisors.

When Harrison and I were little, one of our favorite games was play-ing superheroes. I was Batman, Avenger of All Wrongdoing, because I got to wear the best mask. Harry was Aquaman, Prince of the Ocean, because he loved how the cartoon character's blond hair curled perfectly over his forehead, even underwater. Izzy, three years younger than Harry, was always in peril. We pretended that the lion and the backhoe were evil bad guys holding her hostage in a dank, dark cave and it was our job to resurrect her to her rightful place as a princess in a castle on the hill. The castle that my cousins live in to this day.

Sunglasses and baseball cap in place, I floor the gas pedal and gun it past glass-encased Larry and up the hill to the circular drive at the front of the house, screeching to a full stop at a forty-five-degree angle that blocks any other car from passing me on either side. I press on my horn long enough to rouse a family of Canadian geese out of the fountain that graces the entry. The birds flap around the marble statues of Zeus, Hera, and Apollo that spout rivulets of water out of upturned sculpted hands into the fountain's base.

It wasn't until I saw the elegant row houses lining Commonwealth Avenue in Boston that I understood the difference between their understated grandeur and the House That Christopher Built. My child-hood home boasts endless rows of Ionic columns, a massive stone stair-way leading up to the oversized wooden door, fussy and architecturally dubious sconces, window frames dotted with carved cherubs.

I quaff the rest of the Dewar's, toss the tiny bottle in the back seat, and swing out of my car to face the King Family McMansion and every-one who awaits inside. Before I lose my whiskey-fueled nerve, I march up the steps and ring the doorbell. Nothing. I ring again. All of this—ignoring my ring, pretending I'm not welcome, using his guard as a go-between—is Christopher punishing me for signing with Grogan. I can be just as stubborn as him, though, so I ring the bell over and over until the door finally opens.

Izzy falls into me with a gigantic hug that practically knocks me backward.

"Toni! You're here!"

I smell the familiar lavender scent of my now-taller-than-me cousin's arms against my face and for a brief second, I'm back in our childhood days, sitting on the marble bathroom floor while Aunt Evelyn soaps Izzy's back from beside the tub. Little Izzy thought I was the most fascinating toy in her house full of toys, special-ordered from the other side of the world and delivered to Thebes just for her amusement.

Izzy was, and still is, too oblivious to notice any cues from me. She hugs me like I've come back for fun, just to hang out with her, and of my own accord. The happy sleepwalk of the cherished.

I pull out of her arms.

"So, your dad finally allowed you to let me in," I say, to remind her that everything isn't flowers and hearts between me and Christopher right now. She puts her hands on her hips and eyes me up and down.

"You look like shit. I'm totally giving you a makeover," she says.

"And you look amazing!" She does. At twenty-one, she's a natural

Minnesota beauty. If the Miss America contest was still a thing that mattered, she would win. Big blue eyes, shining wavy blond hair. The perfect pink lip at eight in the morning in her own house. She's wearing a crisp tank top and bedazzled skinny jeans. I'm aware again of my disheveled appearance.

"You should have seen me last night," I say. "Cocktail party. I was killing it."

She looks at me skeptically. I can't say I blame her.

"If it's not on social, it didn't happen!" she says. "And I know you're not on Insta. We're fixing that. It's, like, a brilliant lifetime record of your best moments ever; you just have to use it right."

Along with loving only Motown, I defy my millennial label by having no social media presence. Paul and I both. Him because it's a tool of materialist oppression that's been co-opted by the corporate elite for nefarious purposes. Me because everyone else does it.

"There she is." Harrison sticks his head into the main entryway and waves. He's dressed for business.

"Harrison, doesn't Toni look like absolute shit?" Izzy asks her brother.

"Worse than absolute shit," he answers. "I'm so glad you're home."

Izzy squeezes my arm again to show that she is also.

"Fuck you both very much," I say. I really do love these two.

If it wasn't for Harrison, I would have never survived Mt. O High School without serious emotional damage. His effortless popularity ensured that the whispers of "How did that family end up with someone like *her*?" from clusters of Minnesota farm girls were kept to a minimum, or at least relegated to the girls' bathrooms out of Harrison's earshot. He kept me off the hit list of Mt. O's bullies for four years, and I kept the secret that his biggest crush was on Tank Mitchell, the hunky linebacker, not Barbie Johnson, the bouncy cheerleader Harrison dated all through high school to have an excuse to be at all the football practices. I also kept the secret that one night after a drunken party celebrating Mt. O's victory over archrival Athens High School, Harrison and Tank had an epic make-out session down by the riverbank.

My sophomore year at college, Harrison emailed a photo of Barbie's engagement announcement to Tank Mitchell. I FaceTimed him immediately, and we laughed until we couldn't sit up.

"Come in, he's waiting for you." Harrison gestures me toward the great room, his eyes filled with urgency. Izzy skips ahead of me and I walk slowly, slinging my gym bag over one shoulder, past a six-foot-tall arrangement of birds-of-paradise and ferns splayed open on the marble table in the middle of the room. I pinch a fern frond as I pass: plastic. But almost undetectably so.

Izzy spins back toward me and pulls off my sunglasses. She reaches for my baseball cap, but I place my free hand quickly on my head to stop her.

"Believe me," I say. "It's not any better under there."

She believes me.

And here they are, arranged in the great room like plastic birds in their own paradise. Aunt Evelyn in a pale pink dress, hair dyed the exact same shade as Izzy's and coiffed to the skies, sits with her legs demurely crossed at the ankle in a high-backed upholstered chair, holding a coffee cup with both hands. Uncle Christopher looms behind her, wired for action. His physicality makes him omnipresent, as if the room were a hall of mirrors, each of which reflects him in motion, a thousand Christophers following me with every step I take. I feel diminished—like a woodland creature that somehow mistakenly got inside the house.

"Antonia, we have to move quickly," my uncle says, shifting from behind Evelyn's chair to beside it. "Your brother's actions have brought serious trouble to our family."

"Nice to see you too, Uncle Christopher."

Aunt Evelyn's eyes dart back and forth between us. Her mental checklist, silent to others but transparent to me: Is Antonia okay? Is there a storm brewing? Since my childhood, this has been her back-channel parenting style. Avoid setting fires by keeping her mouth shut but track the glowing embers to ensure they don't burst into flame.

Once Izzy hit her teenaged years and lost patience with hours of sitting at her mother's feet having her hair brushed and braided and curled and beribboned, Aunt Evelyn's sense of purpose seemed to fade. By the time we were home from school she had a wineglass in her hand, replaced by a martini glass at five and an after-dinner liquor by eight. Not to mention the vodka supply we all pinched from on the second floor.

When we were little, she was always managing our activities, organizing our lives. But when things shifted, this glazed-over Evelyn was left behind. Was having four teenagers at once just too much? Plus, the strangeness of me and Paul, the ghosts we dragged in behind us.

My impulse is completely out of character: I bend down and kiss her on the cheek. Her foundation makeup leaves a slight powdery residue on my lips.

She stirs. Is there something she wants to say?

Then Christopher's hand comes down on her shoulder, gripping tightly.

"Sit down, Antonia," he says. "Over here."

My aunt turns back to stone. Stares down at her white porcelain coffee cup once again.

I fold into the matching chair to her left, tucking my knees into my chest so the heels of my sneakers are digging into the upholstery in the most retro adolescent pointless kind of way. Watching Christopher shut her down makes me angry at them both. It's as if the dark and lonely teenager I was when I left for college wanders this room, waiting for me to return so she can hurl herself back into my body. If Melanie Dwyer saw me now, she wouldn't recognize me as the sparkling woman in the red dress from last night's event.

My phone vibrates. I slip a quick peek in my bag: Ah. It's Paul at last. I relax just seeing his name light up on the screen. He doesn't hate me. He was sleeping, he must have been. But I won't answer, not yet. Keeping the news from Christopher that Paul reached out is the best form of control I have at the moment. I shove my bag behind me on the chair.

"Okay, I'm here," I say. "What's going on that you couldn't tell me about over the phone?"

Christopher clears his throat, nods to acknowledge that as resistant as I was initially, he sees that I've done as he asked. There's an invitation in his eyes, in the lines that have deepened around his mouth in just the few months since I've seen him last—he wants me to bend in and be part of the family and the business that he holds so dear.

All I need to do is follow the lead of my cousins and his acrimony will fizzle away. Harrison's patient navigation, Izzy's shrugging compliance— Christopher understands this as family love. Soften my edges, speak their language, and his approval will be mine.

It would be so easy. And yet, for me: impossible.

Christopher clears his throat. "The Big Dig is slated to start tomorrow. We rolled our machinery on-site to prepare on Friday. Then, last night, a group of renters decided to make trouble. Against their own best interests, a few of them made the misguided choice to chain themselves to the lead tractors. Including your brother, Antonia."

Harrison mouths *don't say anything* to me behind his father's shoulder while Christopher continues.

"This obviously would never have happened if you joined the business. Paul would have instinctively wanted to protect you, and he would have stayed out of the entire disaster. Now I'm asking you to make it up to me."

"Make what up to you?"

"Your brother's betrayal."

Betrayal. I've heard this word from Christopher as long as I can remember. The world is measured in droplets of loyalty and oceans of betrayal. As in: loyalty requires unwavering adherence to the principles and practices that he lays out before you, whether you are family, friend, business associate, or employee. But loyalty is fragile. One step in the wrong direction, one failure to comply, and you have betrayed him. And that's forever. You're considered loyal only until the first time you have an opinion of your own. From then on, you can try all you might to crawl back into his good graces, but it's going to be either a lifetime of trying or a lifetime of banishment.

He did rescue us more than twenty years ago. He and Eddie found us, orphaned and utterly alone, under that cot in Sarajevo. And Christopher brought us into a clean, well-fed, safe home when his brother's overdose left us alone again. I know this. I'm grateful. But how do I show it when his definition of loyalty scrapes up against my own?

I remain still in the face of Christopher's accusation—not because Harrison is imploring me to do so, but because I need to think. What's at stake right now? How can I get the information I need from Christopher before I talk to Paul and find out his side of the story?

"Silence can be a good lawyer's greatest weapon," Melanie told me on my first day at the firm. "When you're silent, your allies think you agree with them and your adversaries think you've got something on them."

And when you don't know if your own relatives are your allies or your adversaries, silence is nonnegotiable.

"Here's what we need to do," my uncle continues. His voice is calm, rational. He has a plan. "Because the rioters committed illegal action by chaining themselves to private property, the police had no choice but to get involved. Because the police were involved, it became a matter of record beyond a small local interest story about a few holdouts. Because a policeman was injured, it became news. And because your brother"—he glances at me, then shifts his gaze back to the room at large—"placed himself publicly at the center of this affair, it threatens to become a sensationalistic story about this family that could completely undermine the Dig. I moved mountains to get support at the highest levels of state government, and I won't have those contracts placed at risk because of Paul's naïveté."

I'm pretending with all my might to be Melanie Dwyer, but Christopher's grandstanding is just too much. Teenaged me has been waiting in silence long enough. It's her voice that flies out of my mouth.

"Seriously? Paul has as much right as anyone else in this family to have opinions and express them however he wants! How long are you going to punish us for just being ourselves?"

Harrison now has his head in his hands. Even Izzy looks up from her Instagram feed.

"*Us?*" asks Christopher. "Does that mean you've known all along what he was planning? Tell me, where is he?"

"I have no idea." I can say this with utter clarity and truth that I know he sees in my eyes because I haven't yet responded to the call from Paul. At least I'm still in control of that information. It anchors me. "But no matter. He deserves to be treated like a human being."

"You need to understand the gravity of the situation. There's a warrant out for Paul's arrest. I don't have to tell you that he'll be treated far more like a 'human being,' as you say, if he turns himself in peacefully."

A low moan from Aunt Evelyn surprises us all.

"Mommy?" Izzy seems confused, as if she forgot her mother could speak or move.

Christopher turns her way. "Evelyn. Is there something you wish to add?" Is there a hint of a warning in his voice? Or even fear?

My aunt and uncle look at each other—a gaze loaded with something potent. Marital. Inscrutable. Then Evelyn brings her pale hands to her chest.

"I guess I'm not feeling well," she says, eyes downcast. "I think I'll just go back to bed for a spot." Whatever silent battle waged between them is over. She lost.

"Isobel, take your mother over to the sofa so she can lie down." Christopher is done with this distraction. "Evelyn, you can't go upstairs yet. We need to sign the papers."

"Papers?" I rise to my feet.

Izzy slides past me to help her mother cross the room. Christopher is ignoring her and watching me. He's not sure what to do with me yet, or whose side I'm on.

"At the advice of my lawyer—a form of authority I doubt you'd disagree with—we're issuing a statement from the King family disavowing Paul's actions."

"Hold on: you want me to denounce my brother?"

"Not him. His activities. An officer has been injured. Our reputation in this town is at stake—and on the brink of starting the biggest project we've ever undertaken. Despite your recent career choices, we are a family, and we must stand together."

So this is why he's brought me here. He wants me to help him throw my brother to the wolves. It's my loyalty, not Paul's, that we're debating now.

I look past my uncle to Harrison.

"What do you think?" I ask.

He shrugs. "It's just about staying out of the media. Why would any of us have anything to say to them anyhow? We might as well agree to it."

"Is anyone other than me wondering where Paul is, and whether he's safe? Or are you just hoping he won't give you any more trouble?"

"We need you to find him, and convince him to turn himself in," says Christopher. "He's putting himself at risk until he does. Even you can't dispute that."

He's right, I know. But because I have a message from Paul waiting on my phone, I push. "What if he's hurt, or lying in a ditch somewhere? Don't you care?"

"You know I always put my family and their safety first. Including you and Paul. Don't you remember the gossip when I brought you both home from the Balkans? 'Those kids sent poor Eddie over the edge. Johanna broke their engagement because of them. They've cursed the King family forever.' It was my protection and my standing in this community that ensured we all survived Eddie's tragedy, and that you and your brother thrived."

My Eddie guilt. Christopher always knows how to get to me.

"Toni, let's focus on what we need to do. This is a way you can help Paul." Harrison, still trying. "Don't you think it's better for him if we make sure we aren't dragged into a media frenzy? Everyone is looking for controversy out there; why should we feed the fire?"

Harrison is a natural conciliator. More than once he stopped me from starting fistfights in the halls of Mt. O High School. He risked his own popularity to defend me against anyone who called me a loser or a stuck-up snob, who made fun of me for everything from my 4.0 GPA to my jet-black hair to my dropout older brother.

Uncle Christopher senses my hesitation. "If you can't hear my concern for you and your brother in this moment, surely you can hear your cousin's."

Izzy, from the sofa where she strokes her prone mother's forehead with one hand, holds her phone aloft with the other. "Nobody on my social feed is talking about any of it yet, so we still have time."

Oh, Izzy. As if the fashion bloggers are going to pick up a local story about protestors chained to machinery. What were they wearing? Everyone wants to know.

I check the time on my phone: 8:45 a.m. Per's files will be on Grogan's server in fifteen minutes. And all this drama is not helping dissipate the last vestiges of my hangover.

Christopher leans forward. His intense blue gaze finds me, holds me like it did when I was a child. Forward, forward; everything about my uncle is kinetic drive to get to the *yes* he needs. Now, though, behind the urgency is an emotion I can feel but can't quite name. A struggle. A darkness.

Despite myself, something inside me softens.

I sigh. "Show me the statement."

Christopher claps his hands together. "Excellent. Everything's waiting in the office. My lawyer is there to answer any questions." He gestures me to go ahead of him and flashes an approving little nod in Harrison's direction.

Fine. Whatever. I'll assess the language that Christopher's new lawyer who isn't me has prepared. Then I'll get on my laptop and access Per's files. Then I'll talk to Paul before I sign anything and see how I can help get him out of this mess. That way I'll have all the cards for both work and family, and I can decide which ones to play, and when.

Christopher's home office is on the westernmost side of the house. His own West Wing, he bragged when he had it added on after a windfall back in the early 2000s. A separate entrance with a separate driveway from the residence allows for business to be conducted in tandem with his family time, while ensuring that whoever comes to the house for work could be kept private from us. Christopher made certain we understood that what happened in the office was important and sacred, and he crafted the physical separation between work and leisure to maximize the point: His crew took down the biggest, highest, oldest tamarack tree on the property to craft the floor-to-ceiling double sliding doors that dominate the end of the great room. A craftsman from Duluth planed the wood and hand-carved the King family coat of arms that Christopher designed into the doors. The backhoe on one side and the lion on the other are joined by a wrought-iron door latch forged from the hinges on the barn doors of Christopher's old family farm.

"Go ahead, open the door. He's expecting you," says my uncle from behind me.

To this day I hesitate to touch the latch to the office. When I was little, I would sit on the floor by the edge of the door, running my fingers over the carved toenails of the lion, thinking it was a real lion that came to life at night when we were all asleep. I used to imagine this was my birth father, the man I don't remember, silently padding through the darkened rooms, maybe even nudging his way into Paul's bedroom where I slept every night, curled tight against my brother because it was the only way I could beat back the nightmares.

I force myself to grab the iron hinges. *Do this fast*, I remind myself. *Do this and get on with your life.* I push the double doors aside.

Nothing could have prepared me for the man I see sitting at the conference table.

His dark hair is shorter now. His cheekbones are more chiseled, and there's a deeper furrow to his brow. It's him, though, holding an expensive fountain pen in his left hand and twirling it between his fingers as was always his habit when he was impatient. He looks at me and I feel him taking me in—the oversized T-shirt, the baseball cap, the bare legs under my shorts. Can he see me flush, or can he merely intuit it from the other side of that table?

"Hello, Toni," he says.

Uncle Christopher's lawyer is James Hollings.

He flashes a little half smile, a sign to me that he remembers everything from that summer. Absolutely everything.

THEN

I WAS SIXTEEN. A LATE-SEASON BLIZZARD THAT YEAR had dumped thirty inches of snow at the end of April, and by June the land was so sodden that the rivers flooded around Thebes. You could even hear the pounding of Twin River Falls from sixty miles south.

Everything was mud and rain. One morning was so bad that Harrison, driving me and Izzy to school in his Jeep, hydroplaned down the road from our house and took a nosedive into the mudbank at the bottom of the hill. None of us was hurt, but the car stuck so stubbornly that Christopher had to call a King Construction industrial towing vehicle to come pull it back onto the road. The three of us stood in our slickers and boots and watched the wheels of the Jeep grind so hard without purchase that mud flew up in the air and showered down on the trees and shrubs like some kind of biblical plague.

Paul was gone. Hitchhiking around the country, dumpster-diving for food, and camping out at any protest site that needed warm bodies. Uncle Christopher was distraught and furious. Since I was the only one around to stand in for my brother, he took his misery out on me. He railed at me for being ungrateful and thoughtless, while at the same time musing that if I ever left the family like Paul did, he and Evelyn would never recover.

I was just as upset with Paul as my uncle was. It was supposed to be me and my brother against the world. Now he thought that random political causes and random people were more important than us. And in the summer of 2006, no shortage of protests seemed to require his absence from my life. Every so often I got an email: Paul was marching against the war in Iraq with a group in Nebraska. Paul was organizing against the war in Afghanistan with a group in Missouri. It was a bunch of blah, blah, blah to me, mired as I was in the mud of my own life.

School was a bore. I was phoning it in and still at the top of my class. I wore all black and refused to cut my hair. In Thebes, this was enough to make me the school rebel, the punk goth girl, whatever. I was counting the days till the end of the year when at least I could hole up alone in my bedroom. Then Christopher called me and Harrison into his office to inform us that we'd both be working full-time jobs this summer.

"Here's a list of the opportunities I've generated for you," he announced, handing us each a printout with five bullet points on it. I glanced at mine skeptically before saying, "I'll probably spend the summer canvassing Thebes for the Democratic Socialist Party." Since there wasn't a house in town without a PROUDLY REPUBLICAN, PROUDLY AMERICAN flag flying from its front porch, including our own, I was pretty certain that door-to-door socialism was not on Christopher's list of approved activities.

"You'll have a job precisely to keep you from rabble-rousing like your brother. This is for your benefit, Antonia. The summer after junior year is when Paul dropped out of school. I blame idle hands and an idle mind."

My brother never suffered from either. But his passions were unsanctioned and therefore didn't exist.

Harrison didn't even look at the list we'd been handed.

"I want to work for you," he said to his father.

I laughed. "Are you high?"

But Harrison didn't laugh back.

Apparently, he was serious.

"Well," said Uncle Christopher, "this is a surprise."

Didn't my cousin realize he was voluntarily stepping into a homophobic cesspool? While he wasn't officially out to anyone but me, he wasn't exactly "in" either. By his own admission, he was biding his time until we finished high school because he understood in his bones that no one at Mt. O would have a problem with a popular gay boy who didn't make a political statement. To come out, to publicly go against the norm, would automatically be a political statement.

"Why should I rock the boat?" Harrison said when I pushed him to be true to himself. "Things are good for me right now, I can wait. It's not like Tank Mitchell is going to suddenly announce that he's gay too and we'll make out in the hallway and live happily ever after."

"But what about the truth? Don't you feel like you're living a lie?"

"Toni, you're way more absolutist than I am. Can't the truth be a lot of things? Like, the truth that I'm happy the way things are?"

"Is that a truth, or is that a compromise?"

"What isn't a compromise? Look, I've got you to talk to, and hello, an internet full of porn, and I'm just not sad."

"But Harry, what about the principle of the thing? Are you really saying that you'll put up with homophobia as long as it's subtle?"

"Does everything have to be painful all the time? If you just let yourself chill for a minute, you could have friends and have fun too."

Okay, I granted him points for skimming over the hideousness of high school as best he could, even though I thought his decision was wrong. But working at King Construction?

My uncle looked unconvinced as well.

"I thought some of the media opportunities I arranged would be more to your liking, Harrison." Was this his way of protecting his son

from the toxic environment that Harry seemed hell-bent on conquering?
I found myself in the unusual position of being on my uncle's side.

"You're such a good writer," I said, "maybe there's something you
could do with that?"

Harrison just shook his head.

"I want to work for you," he said to my uncle. "I want to be part of the
family business."

Christopher stared at him for a moment. "There will be no favorit-
ism," he said.

"I expect none."

"Everyone in this company has to put on a hard hat and know what
it's like to work on-site. Even the people I hire to run the office."

"Understood."

"You'll make minimum wage."

"Yes, sir."

"And I will personally tell whoever becomes your supervisor that you
don't have permission to go over his head to me, ever. You're at the bottom of the chain of command, son, and that means infantry."

Oh my god.

My uncle smiled, just a little, at Harrison. A smile of pride. Harry
was looking mighty excited about the sickening prospect of joining
Christopher's infantry.

I dropped the printout back on my uncle's desk.

"I don't care where you stick me," I said, "as long as it's far away from
King Family Construction."

That's how I ended up as a summer intern at the Law Office of Leo
Roberts and Associates, in the heart of the bustling metropolis of down-
town Thebes, Minnesota. Mr. Roberts was a seventysomething Korean
War veteran and president of the local Rotary club. Thanks to whatever
VFW brotherhood this meant between him and my uncle, Mr. Roberts

was willing to take my miserable, uninterested teenaged self into his temporary employ.

"Excellent grades," he said when he looked over the junior year transcript my uncle sent him in advance of my first meeting with him. "You should consider becoming a lawyer."

At the time I thought he was a crazy old coot. I would never be a lawyer. All I could see ahead of me was getting out of the house, out of Thebes, out of the entire state of Minnesota.

The first week of my internship was every bit as dreary as I'd expected. I sat cross-legged on the floor in a windowless back room surrounded by bankers' boxes filled with paperwork from decades before there was an internet, and a yellow legal pad with Mr. Roberts's shaky scrawl instructing me how to determine which documents should be saved and scanned, which should be archived but not scanned, and which should be shredded. Four hours went by like four days. Piles of paper grew around me as I removed them from one set of boxes, then shrank as I refiled them into another.

I listened to deep tracks from the Motown catalogue on my iPod to stay sane and plotted all manner of bloody vengeance against Harrison's hideous supervisor, John Joseph, a brawny dolt who had gone to high school with Christopher. Mr. Joseph thought all boys needed to be hazed to become men and took quite literally the instruction from above that the son of the boss was to be treated like the son of someone he'd never met. Harrison would come home exhausted from a day on the job site and tell me that Mr. Joseph had told him to spend all morning with a hand trowel shoveling pebbles off a driveway that needed to be paved. Then when he came back from lunch, he found the trough of pebbles empty and Mr. Joseph yelling at him for slacking on the job. As soon as he started shoveling again, he heard his supervisor snicker with a coworker while they watched him on his knees, refilling the trough.

I had murderous fantasies toward John Joseph and my uncle. I tried to comfort my cousin by describing in graphic detail how I wished I could unveil my old secret identity as Batman, from our childhood game, and smash both their heads into smithereens on his behalf. But Harrison wasn't interested. In fact, he seemed exhilarated by his experience.

"Nobody will ever say I didn't pay my dues," he said from his bed where he lay while I brought him ice packs for his knees and pilfered shots of vodka from Evelyn's stash. Despite the obvious pain of his body, a strange light shone in his eyes. My cousin believed in what he was doing, and he didn't mind being surrounded by ogres while he did it.

I was in the stockroom, sorting through depositions for the 1987 *Carlsbad v. Carlsbad* domestic violence hearings. Of course, the husband won. While I was taking out my private revenge on all abusive ogres past and present by writing *fuck off and die* in red Sharpie on the documents going into the "to be shredded" pile, I heard a commotion out in the reception area of Roberts and Associates.

The noises were muffled from my windowless stockroom, but I could make out high-pitched giggles from the receptionist and the slow but recognizable low rumble of Mr. Roberts himself. I stood up and cracked open the door to see what could possibly have interrupted the otherwise staid and predictable sounds of my summer employer.

I first saw James Hollings from the back. He was tall, thin, he wore a khaki suit that fit, and his dark brown hair was longish, curling around the top of his jacket collar. Everyone in the office was leaning toward him like iron shavings toward a magnet. When he laughed, I realized that there hadn't been a male voice other than scratchy million-year-old Leo Roberts's in this building since I started. All of a sudden, I felt achingly thirsty. I slipped out of my cave and attempted to be invisible as I inched my way across the back of the office to the water cooler.

James—although I didn't know that was who he was yet—turned

around at the sound of the water gurgling out of the giant plastic jug. Oh, he was handsome! But in a way completely unfamiliar to me. This wasn't the half-bored, half-menacing face of a high school football player waiting for the admiration of a girl because it was his natural-born right. His features were made of sharper stuff: angular, clean. The light hit him differently from the others, as if he'd brought his own air into the room. I felt my cheeks redden and instinctively moved to hide my blush behind my long mane of black hair.

"Who's this?" he asked the room at large.

I was bent over the water cooler, my hair falling in front of my face and dragging into the cup I held under the dispenser. When I stood up, the ends dripped water down the front of my black dress and my legs. As the drops hit my toes, I realized, with embarrassment, that I was barefoot. I had gotten into the habit of kicking off my shoes when I sat on the floor filing papers.

James Hollings looked at me, slowly, from my bare feet up. And when I say looked, I mean he *looked*. I was momentarily frozen, other than the prickles that rose on my legs and arms as he took in the entirety of me before meeting my dark eyes with his green ones. I lifted my chin slightly. He lifted his in return. Without shifting my gaze, I brought my overflowing cup of water to my mouth, spilling a few more drops in the process, and drank in huge gulps. Nothing had ever tasted as necessary as that cold water. I barely swallowed before taking the next gulp, and the next.

After I drained the cup, I wiped my mouth with the back of my left hand. He was still looking.

"That's Antonia," said Wanda, the receptionist whose hips poured over either side of her desk chair and practically touched underneath the seat. "Toni King. Our summer intern."

James finally stopped staring at me to acknowledge Wanda, then raised his eyebrows at Leo Roberts.

"Any relation?" he asked quietly.

"Niece. Adopted."

I felt trapped, mired, subsumed by the double force that was Uncle Christopher and my own past. Nowhere in Thebes was there any escape.

"Antonia, meet James Hollings, our summer associate," Mr. Roberts said. "James started like you, as an intern. Now he's just finished his first year of law school at the U." I could hear the pride in his voice. He looked at James with warmth and delight, like he couldn't quite believe his luck that this person was real and in his presence. Like a father would.

"You made it possible," said James. "Your letter of recommendation, and all you've taught me." I could hear in his voice that the warmth went both ways.

My thirst was gone, but the dry lump in my throat remained. My big toe discovered a loose thread on the worn-out gray wall-to-wall carpet and I hooked it around the front of my foot, pulling it tight. Anything to divert me from the sensation that I might choke on the intensity of being in the presence of James Hollings.

He turned to me.

"Are you at Athens Community?"

Even this innocuous question coming from him felt like a dive bomb into my essential self. I scraped my toe back and forth across the frayed carpet fiber, letting the sharp ends bite into my flesh.

"She's in high school!" Wanda's habit of ending every statement with a peal of laughter was never more irritating than in this moment. As I continued to stare at James, I felt *high school*, in all of its embarrassing, infantilizing, miserable reality, grow between us like a thicket. He was falling away from me, blurring into a less visible outline.

"I'm thinking about going to law school," I blurted out. The sound of my own voice embarrassed me. As did my words. Although law school suddenly seemed less horrible now that I knew he was there.

"Well," he said, still from the other side of the brambles that *high school* had created, "I'd be glad to offer my perspective about applying. I'm a lot closer to that process than Leo here!"

Mr. Roberts chuckled. He liked being teased by James. So different from the barbs that traveled like poison-tipped spears across the great room of my own home.

"Can you believe that I was in the very first graduating class of William Mitchell College of Law? 1958. I went on the G.I. Bill after Korea. Things are different these days. You know, there are women there!"

James caught my eye again at this—he was brimming with suppressed laughter. I wanted to say something in my typically quick and witty manner, but I could only manage a tiny, rather wan smile, when:

"Ouch! Oh fuck! Oh no, I'm sorry I said *fuck*!"

I pulled my toe out of the tangle of carpet thread to see the silver head of a thumbtack sticking out of the bottom.

Everyone was staring at me. And my feet. A small trickle of blood dripped from the big toe with the thumbtack and landed on the carpet. I saw Wanda's thoughts as if she said them out loud: *Great. The barefoot idiot intern got blood on my carpet and you know who's cleaning that up.*

"Don't move!" James swooped over to me, picking up a small chair along the way and depositing it behind me. He gestured for me to sit, which I did. He dropped to his knees and cradled my dirty heel in one hand while removing the tack with the other. Then he pressed the ball of my big toe with his thumb. My foot looked tiny between his hands.

"Wanda, can you bring the first aid kit from the break room?" he asked. I swear I saw Wanda roll her eyes as she pushed herself up from her chair and did as he asked.

Leo Roberts came over to us for a moment to make sure that I wasn't injured in any manner likely to cause trouble. As soon as he saw that I would survive, he nodded and rubbed his hands together.

"Looks like you've all got this covered," he said, and retired back to his corner office.

James pressed his thumb hard against my toe pad. "This will stop the bleeding," he said. It was clear that this was no emergency, and there was unlikely to be a surplus of blood. Nevertheless, he kept my foot firmly in both his hands.

I bit my bottom lip hard to counteract my rapid breathing. Even with the pressure of my upper teeth against my own flesh to distract me, the heat from his hands turned my body nuclear.

With both Mr. Roberts and Wanda out of the room, he looked at me again with the same slow, all-encompassing stare that first jolted me out of my complacent dullness. He raised one eyebrow.

"Who are you, intern Antonia King?" he asked, ever so slightly letting the hand that held my heel lift to touch my ankle as well. "You don't look like the family that runs our fair town of Thebes."

He was intrigued by me. No boy from Mt. O High School—or anywhere—had given me the time of day other than to categorize me as someone who perhaps they had to tolerate. This was something new.

So I would be something new.

I pressed my foot back against his hand, just a tiny bit. And smiled.

Morning

THE GREEN EYES ARE THE SAME. THE SLOW BLINK, THE sidelong glint. The all-encompassing gaze that almost knocked me down the first time he took me in: it's the same. His power over me at sixteen was cataclysmic. I look at the pen in his hand as he sits behind my uncle's desk and recall those same fingers all over me years ago, teaching me how to be alive in my own body.

And now? The first time James Hollings sees me in eight years? I'm as disheveled and unkempt and taken aback as I was the day we met. Clearly my plan for world domination isn't quite complete.

He taps that fountain pen again. The light catches his wedding ring.

"I hear you landed a job at Grogan, Dwyer. Congratulations. Leo will be pleased to know that you're back with us in the Land of Ten Thousand Lakes as a full-fledged attorney."

"How is Mr. Roberts?" I ask, with a sudden wash of nostalgia for the dignified man, so of another era, who kept his Korean War medals and citations framed over the chipped wooden desk he refused to spend the money to upgrade.

He grins. "Leo is old. But he's still Leo. We're partners now."

So James is on the masthead. Roberts and Hollings. Like father and son.

"Is Wanda still there?"

The grin disappears. "Wanda died a year ago. Cancer."

"Oh. I'm sorry."

He nods. "She knew she was sick, and wasn't going to be working much longer, so she trained her replacement before she went. Someone I think you might know from your high school years." When he says *high school* I shiver, remembering how he knew me from my high school years. "Her name is Barbie Mitchell."

Barbie Mitchell!

Harrison's beard who later married Harrison's crush.

I shake my head. "This town is way too small. It's why I left."

James narrows his eyes. "Is it?"

His question makes me nervous, and I allow him to see that. He's getting to me too quickly. I need to pull things back.

"Let's talk about why I'm here, not why I left," I say, folding my arms across my chest. "Lawyer to lawyer."

"All right, Toni. Lawyer to lawyer."

I've amused him. Not my intention. But he straightens up in his chair and pushes a manila folder in my direction. He'll play along.

"As you've clearly surmised, I represent your uncle and the King Family Construction business. So technically, you."

"Not me," I reply. "I was cut out of the holdings when I refused the job that you got as my uncle's second choice."

James chooses to ignore my pathetic and juvenile retort. "Yes, it's true that you're no longer a named beneficiary of the company. However, I'm here in my capacity as family lawyer, and you haven't been legally excised from this family. Your uncle wants complete unity on the public statement. You're the wild card, Toni. Without your signature, Christopher won't sleep at night wondering what you might say to the media."

Right on cue, Christopher and Harrison enter the office, followed by Izzy and Evelyn. I feel like I'm falling out of my body. How can I be standing in the same room with the man who has been my secret for eight years and the people I kept that secret from, then and forever after? I shut my eyes. All I want is Paul. But not the Paul of now: the Paul from the old days when we were little. Before he reincarnated himself as the Dragon of Bosnia, savior of all regardless of race, religion, or creed, and left me alone to fend for myself.

When I open my eyes again, I'm vertiginous. The office is closing in on me now, tilting and keening like a carnival ride. I can't be drawn back into the past. They can't have me anymore. I need to do whatever it takes to get away again as fast as possible.

"Give me the statement."

James stands up, walks around from the other side of the desk, and hands me the manila folder. I take it, but he doesn't let go yet. Instead, he stands opposite me, not touching me but so close that I catch his scent, his essence—both the sensory experience of him now and my memories of him then.

"Toni," he says to me quietly enough that the others can't hear. "Just do this. Don't get caught up in opposing your uncle because you don't want what he wants. You're better off without a fight. There are no tricks in here; it's exactly as it seems."

Has anything in my life ever been exactly as it seems? Would I know what that was if I saw it? Everything throws shadows. No amount of hardy midwestern American bootstrap culture has ever lifted those shadows away. The four people behind me spent my childhood trying to convince me that the shadows didn't exist. Even this man, who became my escape from the chokehold of all that denial: he represents King Family Construction now. He is not here for me. I can't let myself forget that.

I look at James. Then I look over my shoulder at the family, the four of them standing close to each other, waiting. Waiting for me.

I let go of my half of the folder.

"Please, give me a second," I murmur. "Long drive. I need to use the restroom."

Uncle Christopher lunges forward slightly, but James stops him with a glance.

"Take your time," he says, as much to my uncle as to me. "We're not going anywhere."

Christopher is all barely controlled intensity. But surrounded by the others, he pulls back. Slowly, deliberately, I pick up my bag from the chair where I dropped it and walk across the office to the bathroom. I bolt the door behind me and exhale.

Even after so much time: five minutes in a room with James Hollings and he's happening to me all over again.

THEN

ALONE IN MY BEDROOM, THE NIGHT I MET JAMES, MY heart was pounding so fast I couldn't fall asleep. Who was he? Everything about him was different from anyone else I'd met in Thebes. Forget anyone my age. They were philistines, grunts, backwater hicks. The older men in town that some girls considered handsome looked like wrung-out sponges to me: beefy boring blond men with red capillaries dotting their faces from too many years of glugging Jägermeister and screaming at each other about hockey games.

James Hollings had the feel of a city about him. Was it the suit? Maybe he chose law school in Minneapolis to get away from the claustrophobia of this Northern Baptist Church–slash–King Construction–run town. Once I was certain the rest of the household was asleep, I tiptoed downstairs to the family room where the computer we were allowed to use only for homework sat dormant. We all snuck non-homework-related internet searches on this computer. Christopher was adamant that we'd have no unsanctioned access to the smut and filth we were guaranteed to find online. But he and Evelyn were so computer unsavvy that it was super easy for us to hide our search histories from them. It was also super easy for us to discover each other's. Harrison's trail of man-on-man porn was particularly educational. Izzy was boring—all about fashion and makeup. Sometimes I planted stuff for them to find—stories about giant squids and marauding bands of sharks. Izzy and Harrison shared a fear of all ocean creatures and I loved to freak them out.

But it was Paul's searches I returned to most of all—stories and stories about the Balkans. The wars after Yugoslavia dissolved. The Serbian conquest of Bosnia, and later of Kosovo. The United Nations declaration of the war as genocide against the Bosniak people—my people. The role of Islam in Eastern European countries in the 1990s. Srebrenica and the Death March, eight thousand men and boys murdered. And the articles that forced me to turn my eyes away from the screen—the discovery of rape camps where women had been brutalized again and again and again. All part of the plan to destroy and eliminate us.

Paul had been teaching himself about our heritage before he ran away.

Uncle Christopher would consider Paul's research as dangerous as Harrison's porn. How many times had we had it drilled into our brains that we were Americans now? That Americans had our own history. That learning about Bosnia would get us nowhere.

Paul was reprimanded for any expression of curiosity about our former language and former culture.

"It will only depress you, Paul," Christopher said. "Leave it be."

We never heard the word *genocide* in school, let alone learned anything about Bosnia. If I wasn't born there, I wouldn't have known it existed. The *Thebes Oracle* didn't even have a section on international news. And the television and radio news broadcasts allowed in our house were limited to WKNW, a local network known for its favorable coverage of economic growth engines such as the King Family Construction business.

Once Paul was gone, his abandoned internet cookie trail became one of my few connections to him. When nightmares jolted me out of bed, I found perverse, twisted comfort in staring at the blue screen filled with articles about crimes against humanity that my brother had collected.

Crimes against my mother and my father, although they were faceless, nameless victims among thousands of ghosts. Hideous as it was to read, at least it reminded me that something real had happened. The bogeyman wasn't only in my head and I wasn't crazy. I might not be allowed to talk about it because I was an American now—but here on the computer was the truth.

This night, though, I had a different goal. I scrolled through everything I could find about James Hollings until my retinas burned. It would be easy enough to explain away if Harrison or Izzy found it—why wouldn't I be researching for my new job? I could even say he had asked me to write up a bio of him or something in the unlikely circumstance of Uncle Christopher magically learning how the internet worked.

James kept his cyber nose clean. The *Thebes Oracle* noted his graduation summa cum laude from University of Minnesota Duluth, and his intention to attend U of M Law School. The only child of a nurse at Athens General. Single mother? That might explain Leo Roberts's fatherly interest. Despite his suit and his tie and his adult chumminess with Mr. Roberts and Wanda, he wasn't that much older than me.

I opened up a second window on the computer and googled "age of legal consent in Minnesota." Sixteen. Boom.

That search history I made sure to erase.

He was a Republican of course. Pretty much everyone from Thebes old enough to vote was registered Republican. What struck me the most was how different he looked in person from his official college graduation photo. I studied every aspect of the stiff, impassive stranger in the picture, his hair slicked down, parted sharply on the right. No smile. Red necktie. The perfect cypher. Who was that guy? The James Hollings I met had a spark to him, like he secretly thought everything was a joke and he was looking for someone to share the joke with him. I knew I could be that person.

Back in my bed, blinking hard to adjust away from the blue glow of the screen, I focused my eyes on the froufrou that surrounded me. Aunt Evelyn's idea of what a girl's room should be, none of it my taste. I was forbidden from covering the walls with Motown posters, so I resigned myself to cultivating internal irony about my white four-poster bed with its purple-and-pink paisley spread, the matching white dresser and vanity table, the fluffy white area rug shaped like a heart—a heart! Wall décor: fabric-covered capital letters hung to spell LAUGH! LOVE! JOY! PEACE! HAPPINESS! Instead of preventing me from ever having a dark thought, they had the opposite effect. They screamed from the walls, wagging their fingers at me like enraged headmistresses from my bookshelf full of nineteenth-century novels about orphans. Also provided by Aunt Evelyn. *Jane Eyre. Wuthering Heights. David Copperfield.* And a leather-bound edition of *My Ántonia* by Willa Cather—my seventh birthday present.

"I chose your name after this book," Evelyn said. "It was my favorite in high school." I was too young to get past the first sentence or two. Later, when my sophomore English class had to read it, she sat in the kitchen when I came home, waiting eagerly to talk to me about the book. But I'd been humiliated, labeled a freak once again. The fictional Ántonia, like me, was an immigrant. It just gave the mean girls in school another reason to make fun of me. My name, just like my circumstances, was simply too weird for the Brandis and Barbies of Mt. O High School. The last thing I wanted to do was discuss *My Ántonia* with Evelyn. I shrugged her off, grabbed an apple from the bowl on the kitchen counter, and ran up to my room. I felt disappointment radiate off her. But she said nothing.

Laugh! Love! Joy! At the time, I couldn't bring myself to offer any of the above to my lonely and well-intentioned aunt.

The night after I met James Hollings, I lay on my back on the bed Evelyn had decorated for me and twisted a strand of my long hair between my fingers as I stared at those commands on my wall. For once, "laugh, love, joy" seemed less like a taunt and more like a promise. At age sixteen, the first glimmer of what escape could look like lit me up from the inside.

Uncle Christopher might have found me a job to prevent me from running away like my brother, but he inadvertently opened the door to my own kind of rebellion, one that suddenly seemed not only natural, but inevitable. I resolved to apply my skills and resources toward a new summer project: losing my virginity to James Hollings.

————

Once I made up my mind, I had no intention of being subtle. At sixteen, I didn't know how. I trained my eyes on James all day Monday. Blushed when he came near me. Stood too close to him at his computer when he taught me how to access the company server to download files. Leo Roberts was clueless; Wanda was too busy with her own giggly flirtation to notice my serious one. But James noticed everything. I felt the heat rise between us with every brush of his hand against mine over the keyboard, every time he brought his face close to examine a decades-old document I emerged with from the stockroom that needed his exclusive and immediate attention.

I felt so feral, so full of longing when he was next to me. I wanted to bite his shoulder, right through the white fabric of his button-down shirt. Instead, I inhaled the crisp scent of dry-cleaning chemicals that mixed with a peppery hint of his own odor and imagined him dropping the papers, taking this crazy mess of need I'd become, and fixing it. Fixing me.

I didn't have to imagine for long. Tuesday afternoon, Wanda left early to babysit her sister's kids. Leo Roberts disappeared into his office, ostensibly to take phone calls, but truthfully to take the nap I already knew he snuck in every day. Within five minutes of silence enveloping the front of the office, I heard a rap on the stockroom door that I'd left deliberately ajar.

From the floor where I sat, surrounded by reams of ancient deposition transcripts, I looked up and saw exactly what I hoped for. His desire. His need. I leaned back, let my knees fall slightly open—that's how ready I was to have him on top of me.

Everything was a blur then. His mouth on my neck, his hands crawling all over me, removing my clothes, removing his. Until the sharp push that woke me, focused me. The pain that kept going, until it swelled into something better than pain. The starburst of sensation I felt from the inside out. *This*, I thought. *This oblivion. This abandon.*

James Hollings inside of me obliterated everything I hated about my life. Everything I feared about my past. And I knew I was going to crave this obliteration, so complete that I almost sobbed with relief, again and again and again.

Morning

HOW HAVE I ENDED UP BACK IN THIS HOUSE, CURLED UP on the floor in the bathroom, feeling exactly as powerless as I did when I left? When I went to Harvard, I was going for complete reinvention. I threw myself into the stature, the prestige, the intellect, the competition—all of it became my world. I wasn't the weird goth-girl loner I'd been in high school. I wasn't the teenaged intern who fell for a summer associate in her office. I wasn't the orphaned waif who could never be grateful enough for the generosity of her adopted family. I wasn't even the frightened little Bosnian girl hiding behind her older brother. When I left, I wanted it all to disappear. Scorched earth.

Yet here I am, years later, hiding in my uncle's bathroom like a child afraid of punishment.

I rummage through my bag and pull out my cell phone. I need Paul. At least he called me back. Now I can apologize for being so self-absorbed when I begged him to leave Thebes and move to Minneapolis with me. I'll explain. I'll tell him it was all my bravado, all bluster and bullshit—I was scared, so scared that I was turning away from Uncle Christopher's expectations, even though I felt in my gut that returning to Thebes and the family business would undo me. It has, Paul, it has! In a matter of minutes! Please forgive me. Andela and Mujo, us against the world.

No message. He must have hung up when I didn't answer a few minutes ago. I push redial.

"Hello?" A soft voice on the other end that isn't Paul. It's a woman.

"Who is this?" I ask, keeping my voice down to make sure no one outside can hear me. "Where's Paul?"

"He's not here," she says. She has the flat accent of a Thebesian, but I can't place her voice. Not Somali unless she's been in the States all her life.

"Well, can you get him? This is his sister!" I'm barely able to keep my voice from breaking.

"No. I can't."

"But I've been trying to reach him all morning."

Her sigh on the other end is audible.

"I know," she says, "that's why I called back. I thought you should know that he's gone, and we don't know where he is."

"We? We who?"

A pause. I listen intently, trying to pick up any information I can from the background noise. I think I hear the clatter of what could be pots and pans, a kitchen? Dishes being cleared after breakfast—or is the sound of metal against metal a concern: Weapons? A hostage situation?

"We're Paul's friends," she says carefully. "We care about him too. But there's nothing more I can tell you about where he is."

I don't know what to believe. Best to get as much information as I can though. I modulate my voice, both to keep my mounting panic at bay and to ensure no one outside of the bathroom knows what's happening.

"Okay, can you at least tell me why you have my brother's phone?"

"He handed it to me when things got confusing last night. Next thing I know, he's nowhere to be found and Bashiir is being arrested."

"Who is Bashiir?"

"Bashiir Abdi. We all share an apartment. The two of them were the organizers."

Paul had mentioned rooming with people in the Somali area of town to save rent. I realize I don't even know how Paul's been making a living since he returned to Thebes. Did he tell me when we spoke on the phone a few weeks back? Why didn't I listen more carefully?

"Where's Bashiir now?" I ask.

"In custody, I think. He's not picking up his phone. They must've confiscated it."

"Is there really a warrant out for Paul's arrest too? And what about the policeman who was injured?"

"I don't know anything more."

She's lying. I can hear it. I need to see Paul's phone, look at his recent calls and texts. I have to find out who he's been talking to, if there are any clues to where he might be.

"Can we talk in person? I'm only in town for a little while and I have to—"

"I left town. After last night… and Bashiir in jail… it's too dangerous."

"I promise I won't tell anyone where you are. Please, I'm just so worried about my brother. I'm on your side as long as you want to help him too."

I hear her strangle a little laugh, or maybe it's a sob.

"Of course I want to help him," she says, so softly I have to strain to hear her. "I'm his wife."

She hangs up.

I hit redial, three times in a row, but the call goes to straight to voicemail.

I stare at the phone in my hand.

My brother has a wife. And she doesn't want to talk to me.

Why? What's happening?

I slide down the bathroom door I'm leaning against until I'm sitting on the floor, knees drawn up to my chest. Have we truly drifted this far apart from each other, that he would have married someone and not told me? Part of my heart, a part I maybe didn't know I had until this moment, feels like a sword has been thrust through it.

It's my own fault. Maybe he wanted to tell me when we spoke. But I leapt in with my insistence that he didn't belong here, that he had to come to Minneapolis and live with me or else he'd be useless. It makes sense now: if Paul was in love, married, that's what would bring him back to Thebes and keep him here.

Minutes ago, I was certain beyond a doubt that the one thing I could count on in all of this mess was that even though Paul might disagree with my choices, he would never lie to me. Now that's gone too.

Unless she's lying about the marriage. Is it possible? All my instincts, professional and personal, tell me she's not. I heard the hard edge in her voice when I mentioned the injured cop, and the soft emotion when she told me she was his wife. Whoever she is, and whatever the circumstances, I was speaking to my sister-in-law.

My brother kept his marriage a secret from me. His wife is almost certainly hiding more than merely her location. I don't know if they need my help or want my help. I don't even know if I can help. One thing is clear, though: this isn't just another instance of Paul shutting me out when he doesn't feel like hearing me lecture him about his life, or of him being so caught up in a movement or an idea that he doesn't bother to connect. He's either off doing something, or something is being done to him. But what? And how do I find out? I already know that his phone is too ancient for the GPS program I have to track its location—I can't locate his wife without giving my phone to the police so they can do the tracking. I am a hundred percent not about to do that.

Bashiir Abdi.

I might not know where to find my brother's wife, or my brother's phone, but I know exactly where to find the town jail.

* * *

THE BATHROOM WINDOW SASH SLIDES OPEN WITHOUT A
sound. I peek outside—no guard on this end of the property. I drop my
gym bag into the little petunia beds dotted with cedar chips below, then
climb quietly up onto the toilet seat. Now I'm grateful for my bike shorts
and T-shirt. I squeeze myself through the open window, head and torso
first, and walk my hands down until they touch the ground. From there
I wriggle my ass through the window as I pull myself forward along the
ground. Once my feet are through, I press them against the wall and lower
everything until I'm belly flat on the new plantings. I jump up, grab my
bag, offer silent apologies to the decimated pink blooms, then run to the
front of the house where my getaway car, still parked akimbo, sits waiting.

Down the driveway, through the gates that open automatically for
departure, I blast by Larry, whose head nods forward as he sleeps in the
guard booth. I'm out before anyone inside realizes I've gone.

The slant of summer solstice light as I drive into the hot wind is so
familiar, it's almost as if I've dreamed myself back into it. Down the big
hill, I whip past the lines of trees again. When I come to the crossroad
sign—road to the highway, turn left; road to downtown Thebes, turn
right—I pause. The road marker is local, hand-painted in the same style
as the *Welcome to Thebes* billboard. *To the Highway* is no bigger in size
than its opposing directional: *To Downtown*. No need here to call either
by its proper, mappable name. Whoever painted the sign couldn't imagine a person from the outside trying to puzzle out the code. The roads
themselves declare their xenophobic loyalties.

It might be a bright June day here and now, all postcard-ready prairie
flowers and waving grasses, but I know the weather in these parts never
lasts. And the nights are black as hell. Oh, but you can see all the stars in
Northern Minnesota! That's what people who stay here and never leave

claim is so special, why cities are so evil. But they're full of shit. Seeing the stars is no recompense—they're not beautiful to me. They're just a reminder that from a place like Thebes, everything that appears magical is millions of light-years away.

I send one more longing glance to the left. Minneapolis, southeast, civilization. Then I gun the accelerator and peel out in a blaze of dirt and dust. To the right.

I blink to keep the tears of frustration from streaking down my face. With a hard wipe of my hand, I banish the ones that eke out too quickly for me to catch.

I have to know what happened to my brother.

PART II

Midmorning

MY UNCLE'S HOME AND THE HUNDREDS OF ACRES RULED over by the backhoe and the lion sit at the highest elevation of Thebes township. A couple of miles below, where the property line ends, the first houses begin to appear—old farmsteads, some abandoned and left with rotting barns and boarded-up houses, but a few restored and still active. June is mulching season. The tang of cow dung wafts through the air, signaling summer is about to begin. That restless ache we all had when school was almost done! Kids longing to bust out of hot, gluey class-rooms; teachers showing us videos every period while they stage-whisper on their phones about plans to get out on the lake with a case of tall boys as soon as the brats go home.

That sulfurous stench is forever twinned with my itch to leave, to go, to get the hell out and be anywhere else. Our last day of high school, Harry and I drove with all our classmates down to Twin River Falls for Mt. O's traditional senior class cannonball leap off Big Boulder into the deep rushing river. This was the one time all year when the cliques and hierarchies of high school lost their meaning. Everyone, no matter who we were, screamed with joy as we plunged into the freezing rapids. One day. The best day.

Everyone knew I was going to Harvard—their derisive, too-big-for-her-britches whispers followed me through the hallways at school. But at

Twin River, I wasn't scorned or mocked. Harry didn't need to defend me. All I had to do, just this one day, was screw my eyes shut and jump off the rock like everyone else.

Later, as the sun crawled low and wide behind the stand of tamarack trees that dotted the basin and the water became too cold for even the most beer-soaked among our class to tolerate, Harrison pulled me aside. We were both shivering in our towels, dripping wet.

"Let's make a pact of our own," he said. "Just like my dad and Uncle Eddie did. Right here. Family forever, Toni. You and me." This time I didn't push my cousin away or roll my eyes. I wanted to believe Harrison that I was, and would be, his family forever. So I let go. Of Paul, of my guilt about Eddie. Of my nightmares from a dim past. Of the Bosnian family I was born into and survived out of. Instead, for that moment, I allowed myself to be nothing but a King.

Now, the stench of Thebesian summer mingles with the wind as I drive. Past familiar front porches, some of them dressed up with hanging baskets of begonias or wreaths on the doors. There's Cathy Mason's house. We took figure skating classes at the rink in Athens together when we were ten. Begonias and a wreath both bedeck her porch. Probably still smells like chocolate chip cookies in there.

Next, the tract-house communities built in the boom after World War II emerge. Split levels, aluminum siding, entire neighborhoods carved out of former farmlands, one after the other. Numerous FOR SALE signs line the street, pegged to clusters of mailboxes shaped like cows or painted with flowers. Even with the wind rushing in my ears, I can hear the whistle of spring peepers from the ponds that dot the landscape. The chorus of my past: thousands of tiny brown frogs hiding and singing. Little Izzy was obsessed with ferreting them out from under the slippery rocks and clusters of lily pads. She brought one home from day camp in her backpack to start her own terrarium—but there was chocolate mint ice cream waiting. Poor frog breathed its last breath smothered under a damp Minnie Mouse beach towel, found with a shriek by Aunt Evelyn when she emptied the pack to do Izzy's laundry several hours later.

We could hear the peepers whistle during silent prayer on Sundays. I fly past the turnoff for Northern Baptist Conservative Church, up the hill to the left next to Upper North Pond. Services don't start till eleven, but the conga line of cars is usually backed up to the road by ten. It always mattered who got there early enough to be inside first, to be in the position of greeter to the rest of the congregation. Closer to the minister, closer to the front—it all meant closer to absolution by the God worshipped here. Northern Baptist isn't a fussy church. In fact, if you show up too fancy, you're suspect. Worship must be modest, and clothing for worship shouldn't cause excessive attention to your body, your face, anything. There are rules, and the people of Thebes love their rules.

When we were little, church was the place we could count on front-and-center placement from Uncle Christopher. You'd better believe he hustled all of us out the door so we could be the very first in the vestibule. And here, at services once a week, my brother and I were presented as living, breathing evidence of the King family's Christian charity.

"The orphans," I heard people murmur as they approached. At first, I was so young that I barely remember anything other than the whisper of skirt hems brushing against nylons as I stared at the knees of the ladies parading by. Paul and I clutched hands the entire time, standing arm to arm so I could lean against him for support when my small legs felt like buckling. He had told me how important it was to stand up during the meet and greet, not to give in to my desire to fold. "It was what our mother told me when you were just a baby," he said. "Do everything they do in church but do it even better than the others." That was how our parents tried to say alive in Sarajevo, converting to Christianity. Could our mother ever have imagined that Paul would be here, hewing tightly to her words, in a place so far away from where we began?

Christopher beamed with pride at Paul's ramrod-straight back, his firm handshake. At the time I was too young to understand much, but I liked church. When Paul was showcased, I felt important too. He was so much a part of my being that I didn't differentiate what happened to him from what happened to me. I willed myself to be strong and stay upright by his side as we greeted our neighbors, even while I sent longing glances to the back of Izzy's stroller where Harrison sat comfortably at his mother's feet.

Paul was Uncle Christopher's superstar. Brilliant, obedient, a model of gratitude and politeness. And handsome too, in his little blue Oxford button-down shirt, dark hair combed and shining. Christopher would laugh and clap Paul on his narrow shoulders as the line of people coming to services invariably paused to pay respects to the most successful businessman in town.

"He's smart enough to run the whole company someday," our uncle would brag. "Can you believe that the boy I picked up from a bombed-out apartment in Sarajevo would turn out to have more potential than my own son?"

Harrison, blissfully unaware that he was being offered up to the masses as a failure, sang softly to himself and played with the bows on the front of his mother's shoes.

Oh, the bitter disappointment that Christopher felt as Paul grew older and began to reject the role laid out for him!

At fourteen, my brother simply stopped going to church. Uncle Christopher threatened him. Cajoled him. Grounded him. Everything short of drawing a gun on him and forcing him into the Escalade with the rest of us, although I'm sure he considered it. Paul refused to engage, holing up in his bedroom whenever he was home.

Finally, after many muffled conferences with Evelyn behind closed doors, Christopher conceded defeat.

"Good to see you, good to see you." My uncle would continue to glad-hand the community like every other Sunday morning, pretending nothing was different even though Paul was no longer by his side. I was eleven, and for the first time, I felt horribly exposed and alone. I didn't realize until then how much I still leaned on my brother—perhaps not physically any longer, but in every other way. Even his silent anger was a shield for me. I could go about my business being a sass, whipping around and mouthing off because Uncle Christopher thought that only Paul mattered. Paul's sullenness, Paul's defiance. Paul's sudden refusal to complete any homework and his resulting plummeting grades. Paul this, Paul that. I was free.

Until my brother became a pillar of stone, withdrawing into himself. Casting around for someone to blame, Uncle Christopher found me.

I doubled down at school, getting nothing but perfect grades so I could sit smugly across the table from my uncle at dinner, daring him to call me out as a failure at anything at all. Was I also trying to prove I was Paul's worthy successor as the object of my uncle's hopes? Yes, that too.

Late nights though, alone in my room, I missed my brother with a hard knot in my stomach that wouldn't release. Why was he shutting me out along with the rest of them? Without Paul, I had no source of connection back to my mother and father. My nightmares flared. I took to creeping out of my bedroom at two or three in the morning, padding silently down the dark hallway, and curling up on the floor against Paul's locked bedroom door. I tried to make myself imagine I could hear his even breaths through the wooden barrier, that it was the same as sleeping next to him to be this close. I leaned against his door until my body finally began to droop again, then tiptoed back to my own bed for a few more fitful hours before the morning came.

———

My phone rings.

Melanie.

9:09 a.m.

I pull over to the side of the road. I need to focus.

"Are you in the portal?" she asks. "Did you access the Olufsen files?"

Think fast.

"Perfect timing. I'm trying to log in, but my ID is giving me trouble."

"First time using it to log in from offsite, right?"

"Yes, first time. I was going to reach out to the weekend IT emergency service, but with what you said about confidentiality . . ."

"Overly cautious is the correct way to be. Stay on the line."

When she puts me on hold, I grab the law firm laptop out of my bag and quickly plug my Wi-Fi device into the charger in my car. *Please have a signal*, I pray. *Please, please, please.*

The bars light up in the right-hand corner of my computer just as Melanie comes back on the line.

"Okay, Toni, are you at your computer?"

"Yes, of course," I say in my most professional-sounding voice.

"I just got you level-two clearance, the problem might have been that level one wasn't working remotely. Try now."

I tap in the ID number and password that I've been pretending didn't work. Oh, what a surprise, I'm in.

"That did the trick, thank you!"

"All right. As soon as you have anything we can use, call my cell. Don't send it through email because Jackie picks that up. And don't forget—follow the money. Everything costs something. There's no reason I shouldn't hear from you by this afternoon, right?"

Ugh. I have to give Melanie a bit of information about my whereabouts, just enough to offset anything weird happening, like finding myself in a zone with no cell phone service.

"Yes, you'll definitely hear from me today. This is my number-one priority. But just so you know, I'm working from pretty far outside the city right now. Everything's fine, just a small family situation I needed to head up north to manage. I'm taking care of Per's thing first and then I'm here so I can do what I need."

Melanie's silence communicates her displeasure. She can't tell me I shouldn't have gone—it is Sunday, so technically my lawyer boss knows I'm not required to be within some local radius of her person—but we both know I'm in new associate purgatory these first few months. It's an unspoken rule that first-year associates should avoid family situations.

"I promised you earlier, you have my guarantee that I'll get this right," I remind her in the silence she's created. "There's no way I'm going to let the first job I do for you and for Per be anything but stellar."

I hear her sigh.

"Just stay hungry for it, Toni."

"Melanie, I'm fucking starving."

This makes her laugh. "Okay, that's the woman I hired."

I've bought myself a couple of hours. Hours I need to find this guy Bashiir, grill him about my brother, learn the truth. And make it right.

THE CURVES OF ROUTE 35 DOWN TO THE CENTER OF town are as familiar as my own body. Past the Erikson farm on the left, around the hairpin turn, and down the straightaway till Hopper's Hardware appears on the right, the first business on the stretch before the intersection that marks the commercial zone. Paul bought a beat-up truck for $300 of his salary at Hopper's the summer before he left. Christopher had cut him off for his shitty grades and general refusal to behave as planned, thinking that money would bring him back around. But Paul turned out to be as clever at mechanics as he had been at philosophy. He tinkered with the engine of Mr. Hopper's rusty 1953 Ford when his shifts

at the store were over until the truck roared to life. Mr. Hopper, an ex-
cessively whiskered man with a beach-ball belly and yellow tobacco stains
on his beard and fingers, was delighted at Paul's ability and sold him the
truck on the spot.

Paul adored that vehicle. He spent the last few months that we lived
under the same roof restoring the rotted parts, oiling the dry parts, taking care of the truck like he used to take care of me. I came out to the
garage to sit cross-legged on the drop cloth he spread on the ground by
his truck and handed him tools while he worked, peppering him with
questions about the mechanics of the thing just to hear him talk again
about something he loved. It was the only time he didn't chase me away.

One day, just before he took off for good, my brother let me drive.
I was thirteen, almost fourteen, and small. Because the bench seat still
couldn't move forward or back due to excessive rust, I had to stand up to
put enough weight on the brake to slow the truck on the downhill curves
so the bumps wouldn't pitch us off the pavement. Paul held on to the back
of my jeans to keep me steady while I stood on the pedal and steered the
behemoth like I was riding the back of a monster in an arcade game. It
was pure joy, whooping my way down the road with my brother by my
side.

I TURN THE CORNER ONTO ASHFIELD AVENUE. A STOP-
light now hangs above the intersection, new since the last time I was in
this part of town. It's blinking yellow, which as far as I can tell means
"ignore me" in street sign, so I decide to drive faster. The houses are close
together here, with blinds drawn over the windows.

A door opens to one of the houses on the right side of the street—a
thin middle-aged white woman dumps a plastic grocery bag on her front
porch. The clank of glass on the floorboards gives away its contents.

Post-Saturday-night clear-out time. The woman catches sight of me driving by and gives me and my convertible a once-over. Apparently satisfied that I'm not an immediate threat, she turns back inside and lets me pass.

If only I still wore my borrowed Nordstrom outfit—I need that suit of armor back to shield me from the feeling that this place, this tiny world, isn't as far in the rear view as I need it to be.

Down the block, two pale, freckled boys are sitting on a dried-out patch of front lawn with an overturned bicycle between them. One of them is fiddling with the chain. The other sees me and yells, "Hey lady, I'm gonna steal your car!" Because they're kids, I don't give them the finger. But I think about it.

The scent of dung. The itch to bolt.

I swallow hard and keep on driving.

Accompanied by the sound of a dog barking from somewhere nearby, a church bell begins to ring. First Methodist, which tends to the downtown worshippers as opposed to Northern Baptist, where those who live in the outskirts and in the bigger houses, like my family, go. I turn left onto Main, ready to see the throng of churchgoers pressing up the stairs. But it's surprisingly unpopulated. A few older couples slowly make their way to the entry; parents here and there urge their foot-dragging offspring.

Town hall, however, looks to be overflowing. Here are the hordes, or what passes for hordes, I was expecting to see at both of the churches. Why is it even open on a Sunday? I slow down to see what gives. A sign made out of a bedsheet hanging between a streetlamp and a tree announces in red spray paint: END THE INVASION! SAVE OUR TOWN!

Invasion?

Everyone amassing in front of the building is white. I'm sure I went to high school with all of their children—who are probably in the growing crowd before me too. I pull my baseball cap low around my face. Now I wish I had raised the top of my convertible before I came through. From under the brim of my cap I take in the handmade placards bobbing over the heads of the growing crowd: *Somalis, Go Home. Keep Thebes Thebes. Only English Spoken Here. We Built America, You Can't Have It.*

I don't study the faces of the people holding the signs out of fear that I'll know them. How can Paul believe he could do anything meaningful here? The minds are too small and the hatred too big. When I find out where he disappeared to, and how to get back in touch with him, I have to convince him and his wife to leave. What I'm seeing here right now can't be fixed.

Still low in my seat, I take a right onto Oak Street, even though it's the opposite direction from where I'm going. I can't look at the scene unfolding on the town hall green for another second without screaming, and I don't want to be any more noticeable than I already am. *Eyes on the prize, Toni. Find Paul and get out.*

My detour takes me right past the Law Office of Roberts and Associates—the one building I'm least excited to see right now after my unexpected morning reunion with James Hollings—but I can't avoid it without doubling back past the gathering at town hall. The office appears on my left, and to my surprise, it's the one location in downtown Thebes I've passed so far that looks almost nothing like it did seven years ago. Pickle's Sandwich Shoppe and the Wash-o-Mat still flank it, each with the same peeling signs and tired façades I remember. The law office, however, now rises twice as high as it used to between them. Shining brass raised letters across the top show that it's now ROBERTS, HOLLINGS, AND ASSOCIATES. The scrubbed exterior has Corinthian columns—clearly meant to evoke the Supreme Court—two on each side of the large marble-plated door. The faux grandeur of it jars against its neighbors' workaday entrances.

Once upon a time I saw James Hollings as the pinnacle of city sophis-tication. He was the future of Thebes, and the man who would change the world. I wonder what he thought when he realized I was gone, just minutes ago, leaving him and his fountain pen and his paperwork in Uncle Christopher's office. I wonder what he thinks about this mob of philistines. I wonder what he'd do if I came back to the house, sneaking through the same window I used to escape, tiptoed into the office, shut-ting the heavy door behind me to keep them all out, and straddled him in that swivel chair.

I should be disgusted at myself for even having the fantasy. But I can't help wondering what it would be like now, so many years later. And I can't help the flood of memories that pours back over me—the memories I've tried to avoid by staying out of Thebes.

THEN

STATE REPRESENTATIVE JAMES HOLLINGS TURNED ME
every which way that summer. We spent sticky hot July afternoons on the
stockroom floor while Leo Roberts napped on the sofa in his office. The
old man never suspected how eagerly we awaited his daily siesta. James
would send Wanda out for complicated lunch orders from restaurants
miles outside of town, and we would practically run to the stockroom as
soon as the door closed behind her. We kept a box of condoms hidden in
the bottom of the banker's box labeled "To Scan." A box Wanda would
never deign to investigate.

Sex and laughter, sex and laughter. Some pro forma document filing. And lots of knowing looks, secret signs. I lived fully in the present,
no room at all for Andela and her scared, lonely eyes reminding me that
everyone leaves us. James could touch me, fuck me, co-opt my thoughts
as well as my body, and I could forget the rest. He was a tsunami; I was a
twig.

I woke up each morning excited, happy. The days passed by in a haze
of sexual exploration so intense it obliterated my nightmares. Finally, for
the first time since Paul told me he was too old to have his little sister
crawl into bed with him, I had found a solution that let me sleep long and
deep into the night.

Harrison's summer, on the other hand, was taking a different turn. John Joseph's crew hid Harry's work boots and replaced them with a pair of clown costume shoes the morning he had to walk three miles along the rocky forest edge to stake out the perimeter for the crew's next clear-cut. My cousin's feet were a mess of torn skin and blisters.

"How can you stand it?" I asked him. "The way they treat you is criminal, and that brute who is supposed to be your supervisor doesn't lift a finger to protect you!"

"Toni, you don't get it," Harrison said, once he could speak again after the sting of the antiseptic-soaked cotton I was patting on his raw soles subsided. "This isn't criminal. Every guy on the crew went through the same hazing their first time on the job site—ouch! Go easy!—It's normal. How would it look to the men if Mr. Joseph gave me special treatment?"

"Now you're just quoting your dad. It's abuse. I don't care if it's traditional abuse or brand-new, special Harrison-only abuse. Why does the fact that everyone else suffered make it right?"

I couldn't help assessing his experience at work from the perspective of my own, secret and illicit though it was. Each day at noon, I found a new angle, a new rhythm, to sate the now-constant pulse of desire that accompanied me everywhere. Rapacious, that's how I felt. Even after James and I had satisfied my physical needs, I could sense the cycle of want, its slow build starting again almost immediately. I desired desire itself. When I woke each morning hungry for more, I practically wept with gratitude. I slept every night without visits from the past, and a few hours hence, my daily dose of self-medication would happen again.

Although I couldn't tell my cousin why, I understood the release and the triumph that physical exhaustion could gift a person all too well. I just couldn't understand enduring it under his circumstances.

"Harry, you're going back to school in a couple of weeks. Then college.

You're not going to be on their crew ever again, so what are you getting out of all this torment?"

"I'm earning their respect. You'll see."

But I couldn't. Seeing the world through Harrison's eyes would have pried the lid off the Pandora's box of perspectives I needed to shut out. My cousin didn't have enough influence over me that summer to show me what I was avoiding. Or pretending to avoid.

Even my usually oblivious family noticed I was different.

"Aren't you rosy these days!" Aunt Evelyn said to me one morning about a month in. I was startled that she said anything at all to me about my looks. After years of lame attempts to dress me like her light and lovely Isobel, only to realize that ribbons and lace turned to cobwebs on my bony frame, she wisely chose to ignore my appearance by the time I reached high school. But she caught a glimpse of what was happening to me: for the first time I saw myself through the eyes of someone who found me exciting and intriguing. No surprise—I loved it, and it showed.

Uncle Christopher glanced up from the *Thebes Oracle* to give me a once-over.

"Hard work," he said. "Good for the body and the mind."

"Oh, yes," I said. "I'm working hard. In fact, I'm the queen of the stockroom. You have no idea what I rule over back there in that law office."

His eyebrows shot up. He sensed I was toying with him somehow but didn't take it any further. After all, I was out of the house and accounted for every day, which was all he needed to know.

"Well, keep it up," he said.

"I do," I replied.

I reported our breakfast conversation to James later that afternoon on the stockroom floor and he shook with laughter.

That's the memory that sticks with me the most from our summer.

Maybe because in retrospect, it embodies the happiness I felt being someone new, someone I chose instead of someone I was pushed and prodded
to imitate.

Or maybe because it happened the day before the *Oracle*'s announcement of the engagement of James Hollings of Thebes, Minnesota, to
Denise Juliette Larson of same.

MY AUNT LEFT THE NEWSPAPER ON THE KITCHEN TABLE
that morning, folded open to the Weddings and Engagements section.
She marked the announcement with a canary-yellow Post-it Note, my
name a curl in her round cursive. *News from your office*, with a tiny arrow.
I picked up the paper and studied the full-color photograph of Denise
Juliette Larson that accompanied the article. Of course, she was blond. A
homegrown Minnesota state flower, all pink and white like the lady's slipper itself. Making her the ideal wife for a young, ambitious lawyer-to-be.

Izzy wandered into the kitchen, still sleepy-eyed, in her baby doll pajamas. At almost fourteen, she wore braces on her teeth but had already
sprung a set of D-cup breasts that she didn't yet know what to do with.
She peered over my shoulder at the photo.

"Wow, she is so pretty," my very helpful cousin announced. "I totally
want to be her."

I handed Izzy the paper. "Dream big."

If I had been the heroine in one of those nineteenth-century Vic-
torian novels that sat on the shelf in my bedroom, I might have fainted
delicately. Or, if I were the hardier type, rushed outside and run to some
craggy hill, wind whipping my hair around my face, then fallen to my
knees and clutched my breast as I cursed the heavens. Instead, I went
into the office that morning as usual. I filed and archived and scanned
documents for Leo Roberts without comment. And then, at lunchtime

when Mr. Roberts shut his office door to take his top-secret nap and Wanda left for her hour-long break that would extend to two hours because her junior boss had a craving for an Orange Julius, obtainable only at the mall on Route 35 but necessary if he was to finish his important work that day, I practically threw James Hollings into the stockroom and straddled him.

A switch had flipped for me. I not only wanted to fuck the living daylights out of this man, I wanted to do it my way. He was startled, to say the least. The first weeks had all been his mastery and my discovery. But that day I was fury and fire. When he tried to initiate any touching or movement, I slapped his hands. All me, all in my control. When I came, it was with a roar.

"Damn," he said when we finished, both of us rife with sweat and still panting. "What happened to you?"

This was the moment I could have told him about my morning reading the newspaper. When I could have stood up and declared him a cad and a scoundrel and cried and threatened to tell Miss Lady's Slipper all about her perfect fiancé's afternoon activities at the office. That's what a wronged girl was supposed to say. It was even what I rehearsed in my head before lunchtime as I was sorting depositions.

Except that I didn't want to say any of it.

He was looking up at me from the floor with something more than his usual lust and amusement—he was looking at me with admiration. A new understanding of my own power was dawning on me. Look what I could do to a man like him: more than just lying back and letting him teach me, I could take the lead. And take over. My capacity expanded a hundredfold.

"Nothing happened to me," I said. "I happened to you. And I'm not done." I rolled off of him onto the floor, placed my hands behind his head, and guided his face between my legs.

* * *

THAT NIGHT THOUGH, ALONE IN MY ROOM, I COULDN'T
drift off in the haze of satisfaction I'd grown used to. Sleep wouldn't
come. I threw off the covers and stood under the air conditioning vent to
feel the shock of cold on my face and neck.

The rules of Thebesian society dictated that someone like James
Hollings must be adorned with a lady's slipper. Her perfect engagement
photo in the *Oracle* was a reassurance to all that the order of the universe
would be preserved. Bosnian orphans who cause upstanding citizens to
overdose on opioids by ruining their lives, then hide under sofas instead
of helping said citizens, have no place in this picture.

Everybody leaves us, Andela whispered to me again as I began to
shiver under my cotton nightshirt. *Everybody always will*.

A soft rap on my door. I turned to see a creamy envelope slip through
the sliver of hallway light that shone below. Heavy paper, with *EK* in raised
letterpress on its back flap. I sat on my bed, turned on the small lamp, and
opened the folded notecard to read a quote, copied in in my aunt's hand,
from the book by Willa Cather she named me after fourteen years ago:

> *This is reality, whether you like it or not. All those frivol-*
> *ities of summer, the light and shadow, the living mask of*
> *green that trembled over everything, they were lies, and*
> *this is what was underneath. This is the truth.*

On the back she wrote:

> *Dear Antonia, Keep a brave face. You are destined for more*
> *than what is here in Thebes. You won't need a man to make*
> *your way in the world. Yours in confidence, Aunt Evelyn.*

I ran my finger over her words.

Aunt Evelyn knew about James. Or at least, she guessed how I felt about James. She left that *Oracle* article open for me to read as more than a nod to my workplace.

I slid the card back in its envelope. Then I went to my bookshelf, pulled down the leather-bound edition of *My Ántonia*, inscribed to me from my aunt on my seventh birthday. I inserted the card between its pages, and reshelved the novel in its place.

Midmorning

A BEAM OF SUNLIGHT SOUTHEAST OF THE LAUNDROMAT rises from behind a nearby tree and warms the side of my face. I check my phone: 9:45 a.m. The morning is creeping forward.

Time to throw Melanie a quick bone.

I refresh my laptop and hit Enter to start diving into Per's files. This time, though, the Wi-Fi bars blink between none and one before flatlining completely. Oh no. I forgot to plug the MiFi in when I left the city, and I must have drained the remaining power by leaving it on when I was driving through town. Now what?

I look up at the façade of the Law Office of Roberts, Hollings, and Associates. If Barbie Mitchell is the administrator now, what are the odds that she's done nothing to update any of the computer systems she inherited from Wanda, including the internet password? Knowing her capacity for sophisticated thinking back in our Mt. O days, I'm going with enormously high. I hover over the Wi-Fi dropdown menu, click on the network "Roberts," type in my ID as "intern" and my password as "starsandstripes."

I'm in. Thank you, Barbie. May your closeted husband bring you a thousand years of marital bliss.

Their system is slow, but on Sunday morning, I'm the only one using it. I can download everything I need from the server to my laptop.

"Going through the files now," I text Melanie. "Lots of detail to comb through. More soon."

Almost immediately she texts back a thumbs-up emoji. Any expression of approval from Melanie, no matter how slight, sends a rush of pleasure and accomplishment through me that feels like medicine. *See,* I tell Uncle Christopher in my head, *I'm not a screw-up.* Melanie Dwyer thinks I'm good. It's the same conversation I imagined throughout college, every time I got an A on a paper, or a compliment from a professor. *See? See? Can you see me yet?*

Senior year, when my advisor asked about my ideas for the future, I had only one. I was going to law school. Four years at Harvard had introduced me to forms of power I never imagined existed back in Thebes, but I knew from looking at who held that power and how many generations back it went that those avenues would not be available to someone like me. I'd been exposed to two kinds of power growing up: the domineering, in-your-face power of my uncle, and the cool, analytical power of lawyers. I could gain access to only one of those without going back to the world of Christopher King. Law school merely required everything I already did well: ace tests and make grades.

I set my phone alarm to ping at eleven as a reminder to send Melanie an update. Then I log out of my identity on the borrowed internet server. They really should be changing their passwords every six weeks, not every seven years. Maybe I'll offer that nugget to James Hollings as some parting advice from the desk of a big-city lawyer.

With Melanie placated for now, I can turn back to the task at hand: Bashiir Abdi's information about my brother.

I pull out of my parking space and I'm about to head around the corner to the police station when I pause. Before I meet Bashiir, I should know more. Instead of turning, I keep going straight, toward the other end of town. The area where Bashiir and Paul and Paul's wife have been living. I'll see for myself if there's anything there that could lead me to my brother—or any information I can use as leverage, if need be.

Two blocks down, the houses begin to look more weather-beaten, with peeling paint exteriors and slatted blinds drawn over the windows. The stores here are closed. The farther from the center of town I go, the more boarded-up buildings appear in between the few businesses scattered about: auto repair, hardware, pizza place, gas station. I'm the only person out right now and it's beginning to feel eerie.

I turn right, and I immediately see why.

Police tape is everywhere, binding off the entrances to the side streets. Stray electric-yellow ribbons reading CAUTION! DO NOT CROSS! litter the sidewalks, some with muddy shoeprints marring the words. Just beyond the barricade, a small fleet of King Family Construction vehicles sits dormant: backhoes, tractors, transport trucks, the works. The jowls of one of the bulldozers gape wide open.

The Somali neighborhood.

I can't get any closer in my car, so I park where I am and cross the street, lifting a tangle of police tape up so I can duck underneath. I walk slowly through the deserted area. A large warehouse-like building covered by pale green aluminum siding dominates the block, facing off against the row of machinery. Black *X* marks have been spray-painted on the bottom third of the walls about six feet apart; I recognize the pre-work of my uncle's crew when a building is slated for demolition. Windows with smoky glass panes line the upper third of the warehouse. There are no doors or indications of use I can see here. I continue walking up the block, picking my way past somebody's lost right sneaker, a Vikings cap, and a deep blue headscarf with gold fringe threaded through. Signs of chaos, people rushing about, trying to leave? I stop in front of the cap and nudge it with my foot. If only I knew what I was looking for. Any of this could be evidence. Any of it could tie back to Paul.

A quick Google search shows little of use: *Trouble at local construc-tion site, details unclear* seems to be the consensus across the few Thebes-focused online news patches. Someone's dark and blurry cell phone camera footage, no faces, and a lot of ambient noise.

My uncle appears to be as good as his word: Paul's name is nowhere to be found—at least for now. Not helpful for my personal search. But after seeing the fury on the faces of the sign wielders at town hall, I wonder if Christopher might be doing right by my brother after all. Protecting him.

I put away my phone and walk around to the next corner, farther off the main street, where the warehouse continues. Here is where the build-ing reveals itself. Murals swirling with color dance up the wall, *Peace* in perhaps a dozen languages and alphabets, painted in the shape of a giant heart. A globe surrounded by hands of all hues holding each other in a circle. In another setting I would brush it off as kumbaya art, but the con-trast to what I've seen so far gives the murals a remarkable glow. Finger-prints of humanity for the first time.

A white cloth banner hangs over the door of the building: SOMALI-AMERICAN COMMUNITY CENTER, and a bulletin board is mounted to its right. I come closer so I can read the proliferation of fliers thumb-tacked here: English conversation classes 5:30 p.m. Tuesdays and Thursdays. Women's basketball league. Bocce courts open daily 9 to 7. Communal supper schedule. Most appear to have the information printed in both English and Somali. A smaller sign at the bottom of the bulletin board says, ENTRANCE FOR MASJID AROUND THE CORNER. So this is an all-purpose building: house of worship, cultural center, gym. And this is the building slated to be destroyed first in the King family Big Dig.

"Hey, lady! You're not supposed to be here." A deep male voice ap-pears out of nowhere. I whip around, my heart pounding.

It's John Joseph. Crew boss for King Family Construction and former tormentor of my cousin Harrison. He's wearing an orange security
vest over a white T-shirt that barely contains his brawn.

"Don't you know there's a police-ordered evacuation of this area?" He
strides toward me, then stops when he sees who I am.

"Yes, it's me," I say. "Are you with the police now or are you just acting
in your capacity as a concerned citizen?"

John shakes his head slowly. "Do yourself a favor and leave," he says.
"I don't know why you're in town, but I know what your uncle told me
to do and that's keep this area swept. There's a twenty-four-hour curfew
in effect."

"Seems to me from the business over at town hall that's a pretty selec-
tively enforced curfew, Mr. Joseph."

"Curfew is for the police action area only. For the safety of the
residents."

"Well, I think everyone in town would be a lot safer if there was a
curfew on the people waving hate signs, not on the people trying to pick
up a little bocce game on a beautiful morning."

He's implacable.

"If you don't walk away, I will be required to alert the police. If the
police find a disturbance, they will probably extend the curfew. That will
be on you, Miss King."

I can see why my uncle relies on John Joseph for his biggest jobs. This
guy is the perfect henchman. I would keep pushing him just for the joy of
doing battle, but I believe his threat about calling the cops is not an idle
one. I doubt that my arrest would be a good look for Melanie, especially
when I'm already trying to work my way back into her favor after my gaffe
this morning.

"Lovely to see how well the citizens of Thebes take care of each other,"
I say as I turn to leave.

"We take excellent care of the citizens of Thebes," he replies. "Our actual citizens deserve nothing less."

I force myself to keep walking away from him, to keep my feet moving one step at a time until I'm back behind the wheel of my car. Only when I've put a stop sign and a flashing yellow light between myself and John Joseph do I fully exhale.

What frightens me about his parting words isn't his anger. It's his complete lack of anger. This isn't an emotional issue for him, it's a deeply held value.

———

Thebes's police headquarters gleam. Its scrubbed white clapboard front, the preponderance of yellow pansies dotting the entryway with their overwhelming cheeriness, evoke the elementary school that it used to be rather than an edifice of law and order.

The gray cinderblock town library next door looks like a jail.

I pull my car into the police station parking lot, right next to the only patrol car—the only other car at all—parked there. This Bashiir guy might be locked up inside, but the surround doesn't exactly look like a deterrent for hardened criminals. It would be far more dangerous to try to escape from the library by the looks of the moldy, sodden wooden steps leading up to its front door. A row of abandoned scaffolding hangs off the side of the library building. As I get out of my car, I see the hand-scrawled sign taped to the library door: *Closed for the summer.*

WELCOME! says the printed sign on the police station door. WE ARE HERE TO SERVE THE PEOPLE OF GREATER THEBES. Perhaps the kids come here to hang out since the foreboding library clearly doesn't want them.

The sun is higher in the sky now. Another reminder that the clock is ticking on my work for Per.

I push open the door of the police station and a delicate little bell jingles. So genteel. I had to go to Boston police HQ several times as part of my clinical work in law school. Now that was a place to be reckoned with. You knew there was a system at work. Whether it was corrupt or benevolent, it was formidable.

A small entry desk, like a teller station at a bank, welcomes me.

"Hold on, be right there!" a female voice calls from somewhere in the back.

I hear the tinny sound of a radio station coming from the direction of the voice—some cheeseball pop music that bounces around like what I imagine the soundtrack to Izzy's thoughts would be. My phone buzzes—a text from Harrison.

Where did you go?????

Before I can reply, the woman whose voice I heard emerges, holding a plastic bin filled with hanging file folders. She's wearing standard-issue police blues, the shirt stretched across her chest in that unflattering way of clothes designed for men and adapted for women. She looks about fifty, with broad shoulders and a teased helmet of very red, very dyed hair.

I shove my phone back in my bag and stand up straight in my best lawyer posture.

"Good morning, Officer"—I look at her badge—"Schmidt."

Schmidt. Mrs. Schmidt who taught home ec at Mt. O? Whose daughter, Brandi, was in my class?

She squints at me.

"Why, it's Antonia King as I live and breathe!" She sets her folder box on the countertop and puts her hands on her hips. Her shirt buttons strain even more with the shift.

"Hello, Mrs. Schmidt. I didn't know you were on the police force."

"Strictly overtime front desk assistance. Do you remember my daughter? She graduated from the police academy a few years ago and works for

Sheriff Ringwald now. She got me into a training program and onto the job—can't do anything on a part-time teacher's salary anymore, you know."

When we were juniors, Brandi regularly stole her mother's key ring from out of her purse and invited anyone with access to alcohol, including Harrison, to party in the home ec room after school was closed. One time, Harrison convinced me to come along. The image of Brandi, stripped down to her pink bra and a miniskirt, standing atop one of the sewing tables with a fifth of whiskey in one hand and a Coke bottle bong in the other singing "Hit Me Baby One More Time" doesn't exactly scream future law enforcement officer.

"And how is Brandi?"

Mrs. Schmidt purses her lips and nods, exactly the way she used to when holding up some exemplary pillowcase or banana bread made by one of her students to show the rest of us how it was done when it was done right. "Every mother deserves a daughter who grows up and makes her home nearby," she says. "Isn't your aunt ever so lucky she has her darling Isobel!"

And I'm having more and more fun with every Thebes reunion.

"Yes, she is, Mrs. Schmidt. And I'm ever so lucky to see you right now. I'm here to visit someone being held here—Bashiir Abdi?"

The self-satisfied look dissolves: a wary, disapproving frown replaces it.

"Well, I know you aren't a family member. Only family members are allowed. What business do you have with him anyhow?"

"I'm his lawyer." The lie comes out of my mouth before I can stop it. But I haven't come all the way to Thebes to be stopped from finding out what happened to my brother by the woman who taught me that you mix dry ingredients separately from wet ones. Although that is, I must admit, useful information.

Her eyebrows shoot up in the air. I see her take in my absolutely unlawyerly outfit.

"Well, now, dear . . . I'm not one hundred percent sure—I'm only a desk officer—but I do think I can't let you in without proof that you're really here to represent him . . ." She says *him* as if she's talking about an alien. And I don't buy her fake self-deprecating "Oh, I don't know" crap for a second. She wants to give me a hard time. I'm not going to give her the pleasure of my concern.

"Of course! You are so good at your job, Mrs. Schmidt. I totally understand, and how could you look at my outfit and think, *This is a serious lawyer?*"

I can mince and be girly with the best of them.

Mrs. Schmidt audibly sucks air between her teeth as she gives herself permission to let me see her judge my T-shirt and shorts.

"Now that you mention it . . . you're not exactly dressed for success."

Internally I roll my eyes eight thousand times. Externally I sparkle. "I know. I just had to drive back to Thebes from the Cities so quickly this morning. Now, where is that thing I'm looking for . . ." I make a big production of rummaging in my bag, like I'm a bit scattered and silly, just the way I remember Mrs. Schmidt likes girls to be. "Aha! Here we go!"

I place my membership card to the Minnesota Bar on the desk counter. "Mrs. Schmidt, does this work for you?"

Mrs. Schmidt takes her sweet time perusing the card, turning it over front to back, looking for anything that might seem irregular.

"I'm not usually in charge of lawyer visits," she says, "but there's a lot going on today. One of ours was hurt last night. As you know since you're here for . . . him."

"Yes, I am, Mrs. Schmidt. And as you know, the law states that we're all innocent until proven guilty in our country."

She cocks her head and narrows her eyes.

"I always wondered, dear—do you see this as your country? I mean, your uncle and aunt are saints to have raised you and your brother like they did, but is someone who wasn't born here ever really an American at heart? I mean, your brother has made his loyalties clear . . ."

I visualize Mrs. Schmidt's face melting down her neck into a bubbling pool of liquid ignorance that leaves nothing behind but her shockingly red hairdo while I remind myself that she is the gatekeeper, not the goal. I have not returned to Thebes to create a problem—I've returned here to solve one.

"I'm an American," I manage to say. "And I have a client inside your building. May I see him please?"

She reviews my bar admission card again, just in case there was something she missed the first time I suppose, such as "Provisional License Only, Due to Murky Eastern European Heritage Designed to Confuse Sheltered Dingbats" but seeing nothing on either side that gives me anything other than legitimacy, Mrs. Schmidt waves me through the metal detector. After a cursory bag check, I'm in.

THE SINGLE JAIL CELL IN THEBES'S POLICE STATION HAS long been used as a way station for staggering drunks after midnight, when the only bar in town, the Meister Brew, announces last call and the gentlemen find themselves wandering up and down Main Street until a patrol car picks them up. We all knew that even as kids. When any one of the guys was employed by King Family Construction, Uncle Christopher would get a 6:00 a.m. wake-up call from the station.

"Isn't he kind to take care of everyone like that!" Harrison said after one particularly heavy morning-after when three King Construction workers had been hauled in after beating each other up on the town green. "He always pays their bail."

"Oh, very kind," I responded. It was the summer of my internship and I was armed with all kinds of stockroom-floor secrets from James

Hollings. "You do know that the money comes out of every single employee's paycheck, right? He calls it 'buying in to health care benefits' and takes it off the top. In fact," I continued, still convinced I could sway Harrison to see his father through my eyes and wrest my cousin from the lure of the family business, "look at your own pay stub. If you haven't."

"You're wrong," he muttered at the time, but I never heard back from him on the issue to the contrary, so I assume I was right and he was avoiding telling me so. And avoiding what it might mean to his vision of a future working for his father.

Soused belligerents. Oxy addicts wandering the streets in the cold, looking for shelter. The occasional teenaged shoplifter getting a life lesson from their parents. That's who usually ends up here. Anyone who commits a crime deemed more than a nuisance violation is taken to Athens. They have a real jail there, and, I assume, real police officers as desk minders, not high school home ec teachers making an extra buck on the weekends. This reassures me as Mrs. Schmidt buzzes me through the back door toward the wing with the jail cell. The warrant out for my brother's arrest could result in nothing more than a slap on the wrist. And if this guy Bashiir was going to be charged with anything more dangerous than disturbing the peace, it hasn't happened yet. Either they're holding him here until they can prove something they haven't proven, or the issue is lack of bond money.

So when I turn down the corridor toward the cell, I'm surprised to see a police officer—a real police officer this time—sitting on an orange plastic chair next to a gray metal door. He's armed.

"Good morning," I say, determined to make the probably highly unusual appearance of a poorly dressed young female lawyer visiting her client in jail on a Sunday morning seem routine. "Bashiir Abdi, please."

The officer, paunchy and pale, with sand-colored hair sticking out in all directions from under his cap, doesn't bother to move from his slouched position in the chair. He barely even glances up at me, but I note, uncomfortably, that his right hand has shifted from his lap to his weapon.

"That's the only one we got in here," he says. "Can't miss him." He absently rubs his thumb and forefinger over the shining metal handle of the gun in its belt holster.

"Okay. May I see him, please?"

The officer lets out a long sigh, as if I've disturbed him during a very important meeting. With himself. Slowly he takes his hand from his gun, places it on his knee, and groans as he leans forward to stand up. A small shower of crumbs falls from his uniform onto the floor at his feet. The remains of a blueberry muffin.

A large ring of keys hangs from the left side of his belt. He shakes his head as he unhooks it and riffles through the assembled options until he lands on a large square key.

"That's a bad one there," he says—whether to me or to himself I'm not sure. But I sense an opportunity, so I jump in.

"How so?" I ask.

This time he looks directly at me. "They say he was one of them who got rough with the sergeant. You can't trust any of these Africans to follow our laws."

"Oh really?" I ask, still using my innocent girl voice. "I came in from out of town. I don't know anything about what happened."

"They bit the hand that fed them is what happened." He spits like the words are another round of muffin crumbs he wants to shake out of his system. "The whole lot of them started a riot in town last night. It got ugly real fast. Or that's what I heard. Wasn't my shift but Sarge and Pfeffer were on so they took it. All I know is that Sarge is in the hospital and they brought in this one," he gestures his head toward the gray metal door, "so I'm guessing he's the thug who hit Sarge in the gut with a bat."

"Wow," I say. And I mean *wow*—as in: Wow, the local cop really shouldn't be saying all of this to someone he doesn't know, because he's revealing what could be extreme prejudice against my fake client, and if I were really his lawyer, this guy could be ruining any chance of an indictment. But I leave it at that and assume he will draw his own conclusions about my meaning. Which he does, clearly, as his next words to me are a warning.

"Be careful with that guy in there," he says.

I keep quiet, as per Melanie's reminder that silence can be a lawyer's greatest weapon. Let him think I'm hanging on his every word if it means he'll turn that square key in that big lock and escort me behind the gray metal door.

He does. He gives me significant looks from beneath his sandy hair as he opens the door. I glance at his name tag, and whisper "Thank you, Officer Hansen" in a sweet-as-pie-at-Sunday-supper voice. He holds up a warning finger in response. I nod with so very much appreciation. My true appreciation comes when he gestures me in, and I hear the door shut behind us. I know once he brings me to Bashiir, he'll be watching on the video monitor I saw outside on the table near where his chair was placed, but I also know it's permitted for him only to watch, not listen. I can live with that.

The outer cell area still looks like the former kindergarten classrooms that long ago took up the space here. I was one of the students in Class A—which I recognize as the left side of the visiting room, where a plastic table and four chairs and a water cooler now reside. Harrison was in Class B, to the right. That's where the holding cell is now. Its door is shut and only the row of small rectangular windows at the top of each let in any light. The cinderblock walls around me and the doors itself are all painted industrial green. Twenty years ago, the walls were lemon yellow, and always covered with masking-tape-hung sheets of construction paper decorated with handprint Thanksgiving turkeys, or cotton ball–bearded Santas, or pressed wildflowers from the prairie in spring.

I see myself, just turned six, alone in the corner of Class A sitting on the floor, tracing patterns with my finger on the frayed edge of the red-and-blue polka-dot rug that marked the border between the "group time" area and "time out" area. Aunt Evelyn started me a year later than most of the other kids so I could make up for the first three years of my life speaking no English. I was labeled "slow" because my past was unknowable. I didn't help matters by refusing to speak to anyone the first few months of school. I was far from slow—I understood everything and was already five steps ahead of not only the others in Class A but the teacher as well, an old lady named Mrs. Firth, with blue hair and frosted pink lipstick that crusted into large horizontal flakes on her wrinkled lips and shed onto her blouse in distracting patterns.

The good side of Aunt Evelyn's decision to hold me back was that I was the same year in school as Harrison, who is six months my junior. When Class A and Class B came together for recess, Harrison always found me and stayed valiantly by my side during what would otherwise have been unbearable experiences like Duck, Duck, Goose or Red Rover, Red Rover. The other children became accustomed to calling Harrison to "come over" to their Red Rover line and seeing him grab my hand and make me run across the playground with him. These games were utterly senseless to me, but I could tune out the noise they created in my head by just knowing recess was when Harrison and I were together.

"Batman and Aquaman" he'd whisper to me. Sometimes it helped.

Back in Class A, Mrs. Firth learned that I wouldn't cause any trouble if she ignored me. It was the best option for both of us. My spot in the corner was my refuge. Large blond children wandered over to stare at me at first, but after some time, I was an anonymous, if odd, fixture in the firmament, like the one fluorescent ceiling light, three from the center, that buzzed and crackled and flickered on and off no matter how many times the bulb was changed.

I turn away from my dark, hunched, six-year-old self with her knees drawn into her chest and look at the green cell door. The guard is still checking me out to make sure I'm capable of handling myself in the face of a hardened criminal or whatever he thinks is happening here today. I play the part.

"I'm ready, Officer," I say, looking demurely down at my feet, then squaring my shoulders as if I'm bracing myself to have my delicate sensibilities shattered.

Hansen loves the authority he believes I've given him. He nods and places his hand back on that gun for the clearly extreme danger the situation presents. At the holding cell, he raps on the door. Without waiting for a response, he unlocks the door and pulls the large metal handle open to expose a narrow room, painted the same industrial green as everything else. A small metal sink and open toilet occupy one corner. A tiny window hugs the ceiling line, sealed off by iron bars but large enough to meet federal standards for humane treatment of prisoners. In the other corners lie three metal cots the length and width of coffins with a thin vinyl-covered camp mattress adhered to the top of each. At the farthest possible point from the door, the back of Bashiir Abdi curls away from us. He leans against the wall, knees drawn up on his narrow cot. His head is bowed forward between his shoulders, exposing a sliver of bare neck above his shirt collar.

My kindergarten self recognizes his stance immediately. He could be me. I'm looking in a mirror across time.

"Abdi, you got a visitor," Hansen shouts, even though he's about ten feet away from Bashiir.

Slowly, Bashiir unfolds himself, his legs emerging first to plant on the floor, the knobs of his elbows straightening. He's long-limbed, skinny, taller than I thought he would be from the way he took up as little space as possible in the corner of the bed. Finally, he turns to look at the policeman. His brown eyes are ringed by dark circles. Lack of sleep? He blinks.

When Hansen steps back from the door, Bashiir sees me. His expression remains unchanged, but his body language shifts—he sits up straighter, braces his hands against the side of the concrete slab. He recognizes Paul in me, I can tell. He knows who I am. A small chill runs down my spine. Never before have I been seen first as belonging to someone, as a family member who looks like I'm part of the group. More than myself. Always the first reaction to me, wherever I've been, is a question. *Who is she? Where is she from? How did she get here?* Bashiir is reacting to me like I'm not a question, but an answer.

"Hi," I say. I instinctively want my brother's housemate to like me. "I'm Toni."

A quick, small nod from Bashiir. He's handsome, despite the heavy look about his eyes and the unshaven stubble dotting his chin. Medium-dark skin, close-cropped hair, heavy eyebrows. If I saw him walking down the street, I'd look twice. I swipe at my still-impossible hair, wilder than ever without the cap I left in the car. He looks better after a night in jail than I do right now.

"Do you wish to receive this guest?" The officer is reciting off of a script now.

"Yes," says Bashiir.

"Stand up." Hansen pulls a set of handcuffs off his belt and gestures to Bashiir to walk toward him. Bashiir is a good six inches taller than him at least. He puts out his hands willingly but averts his gaze over Hansen's head and away from me as he submits to the humiliation of having the cuffs snapped on his wrists, the clink of metal gear teeth closing as Hansen turns the key to lock his hands together. I'm embarrassed for Bashiir that this is happening, and that his friend's younger sister is a witness. He's perfectly calm though as he allows himself to be led to the plastic table in former Classroom A, and he doesn't flinch when Hansen reaches up and pushes his shoulders to indicate he should sit in the folding chair beside him.

I slide into the chair opposite Bashiir at the table and look back at the officer.

"Okay, thanks!" I say with a falsely chipper inflection.

"You're welcome," he responds. Then he pulls out a chair at the head of the table, plops himself down, withdraws his gun from its belt holster and places it in front of him, barrel aimed squarely at Bashiir, although the weapon lies sideways, and the safety stays on.

This is not what I had planned.

"We're all set, Officer," I continue. "You can leave us now."

He shakes his head. "I don't think so, miss. This is for your own safety. You never know with his kind what risk you're taking."

His kind. I flash a quick look to Bashiir to make sure he knows that I have no delusion about my safety and who is in fact at risk here. His almost imperceptible shrug and slight half roll of his eyes tells me this drill isn't new to him.

Time for me to stop playing girly for this jerk and start being the lawyer I am. I pull out the Minnesota Bar Admission card and place it on the table by Hansen's gun. Ante up.

"Seeing as I'm Mr. Abdi's attorney, I have the right to privileged communication with my client."

I sneak another glance at Bashiir to see how he's receiving the news of his representation. I've surprised him. And it doesn't appear to be the good kind of surprise. He glowers at me from under his eyebrows, but he doesn't say anything to the contrary. I take that as a small victory.

Hansen's doughiness quadruples in irritability as he looks from me to

Bashiir and back again. I can hear the burbling stereotypes ricochet from one side of the empty cavity that should hold his brain to the other: *But she's a white girl! And he's a terrorist! Does. Not. Compute.*

"Antonia King, associate, Law Offices of Grogan, Dwyer, and Lenz, Minneapolis." I add my business card to my bar association membership. I see your gun, Officer, and I raise you two legal affiliations.

"Abdi," he shouts again, even though this time all three of us are seated around a small table together. "Is this your lawyer?"

Bashiir is weighing his options, I can tell. But how many does he have? He's in handcuffs. And it doesn't look like anyone else is waiting in line with Mrs. Schmidt to see him on a Sunday morning. *Please,* I think silently, holding Bashiir's gaze. *Please, please, please . . .*

"She's my lawyer."

I smile broadly at Bashiir. He does not smile back.

I'll deal with that next.

"You heard my client, Officer. Kindly leave the premises."

He has no choice, and he knows it. He takes back the gun and stands up.

"If you say so, miss," he says. "But don't you worry, I'll be right there on the other side of that door if you need me. Right there!" He points with two fingers at the hallway. I can only imagine he'll be glued to the visual monitor looking for any signs of proto-terrorist behavior so he can swoop in and save my life.

"Duly noted."

Hansen backs out of the room until he reaches the door and has no choice but to turn around. The door clangs shut.

————

Alone with Bashiir. Finally, I'm through the Thebesian obstacle course of small-town gorgons I had to slay to arrive at this moment. A thick silence settles around us. Bashiir's eyes are lowered, looking at his own hands in cuffs on the table in front of him.

I want him to speak first. I want him to be relieved to meet me, to see me—now that we're alone I'm ready for him to pour out all the information he has about my brother and tell me he knows where Paul has gone, what he's doing. More than anything, I want him to tell me that Paul is safe.

He remains quiet.

The longer he says nothing, the more anxious I grow. I don't have time for this. I have to get out of here and find my brother and then I have to get back to work. This is Paul's world now, not mine. While seeing his roommate in custody tugs hard at my sense of the injustice wrought upon him by this backward town, feeling sorry for Bashiir won't get me what I need.

I lean forward across the table.

"Bashiir," I say. "I regret having to meet you under these circumstances."

He looks up. This close to him I can see his eyes are bloodshot from lack of sleep. But his gaze is strong. And it isn't warm.

"You're not my lawyer," he says softly. His English has a faint musical accent.

I hate having to begin with an apology, but here we are. "I'm sorry for lying," I say, "but it was the only way I could get in here to see you and the only way we can talk in private. I need to know what happened last night for real. I need to know where my brother is and what he's done."

Bashiir's shoulders slump a bit, but he keeps his steady gaze on me.

"Paul warned me about you," he says.

Warned?

"What do you mean?"

He shakes his head slightly.

"Toni," he continues, "do you see where I am? Do you see what's happening? I am literally in chains in front of you. I have been arrested on charges that I know to be unjust. Honestly, what I could use the most right now is a good lawyer."

"So here I am," I practically leap out of my seat toward him. "You've got exactly what you need."

Bashiir continues to shake his head.

"A good lawyer would come in here to represent me. You have no intention of doing that. You used the circumstance of being a lawyer to bypass the law. Your goal is getting what you want, not giving me what I need. Paul was correct."

"Correct about what?"

"He said you were self-absorbed. That you forget where you come from and only care about where you're going. And he did warn me. He warned me not to trust you."

His words are a slap across my face. Now I'm the one slumping in my seat. Paul and I have had a version of this argument since I left for Harvard, but I never thought it was between anyone but us.

"Excuse me," I say. "I understand that my brother is your friend and housemate. But you and I have only just met. You sound pretty judgmental for someone who's known me a total of five minutes."

"And the entire five minutes have been about you manipulating the police officer to get what you wanted. Impressively, though, I do have to add."

Well, there's that.

"Let's be real: he isn't exactly a tough target."

Bashiir is amused, just a bit. "True."

He has a sense of humor. I can move him. I know I can.

"Maybe I was being manipulative," I concede. "But maybe there's something useful for you in it as well. What if we can help each other? And what if I'm pushing hard because I'm genuinely afraid for my brother?" My voice cracks when I say that out loud. At this point, I am afraid. With a single word, Bashiir could either calm my fears or confirm them. But he isn't giving an inch. His face is stony, his shoulders stiff. Whatever he knows about Paul, he isn't going to trust me until we can make some serious headway. My hopes for a five-minute info-gathering visit are down the tubes.

Regroup, Toni. Make it work.

"Okay, I'm going to be direct with you," I say. "I came to Thebes because our Uncle Christopher called to tell me Paul was missing. At first, I wasn't sure if the situation was serious. He's been picking up and disappearing since I was a teenager. But lots of things look fishy now that I'm here. I don't know what or who to believe. Paul might have problems with my decisions—I definitely have problems with his—but when it comes to trust, I guarantee he'd take me over Christopher any day. So that's what I want: Paul's side of the story. And you're the only one I know who might have it. So please . . ." I hear my voice starting to break a bit again. "Bashiir, please. How can I help you so we can help each other?"

Bashiir is silent. Only the buzz of the air-conditioning unit in the corner window fills the void. I can tell that he needs me to be silent too, so I hold my tongue.

Paul used to say that I used up all my quiet in childhood, leaving me with nothing but opinions and the will to have them known. I would prove him right by smacking back with some retort like "At least opinions don't get me suspended from school. Graffiti on the walls though? Maybe you'd be better off with more opinions and less desecration of property." The same fight, always. Who was making a real difference in the world— the one who talks or the one who acts? And now: all this trouble over a few chain stores coming to town. How bad could it be, really? There are jobs at stores. Did Paul think about that? Not that I'd ever tell my uncle to his face, but I do give him some credit for caring about the local economy.

Bashiir is taking his time. While he does, I use the opportunity to look him over a bit more. Who is this person living and breathing a daily life with my brother? His clothes give away nothing. A tan short-sleeved collared shirt with a black windowpane check. Jeans. Tennis shoes. He wears three bracelets on his left wrist—a twine braid, a row of black beads, and another colorful braided one, all of which are tied closely so the ring of the handcuffs runs up and down over them when he moves. A longish scar on the inside of his right forearm that looks like it's from some time ago by the shiny pucker and mild discoloration. Aside from the overnight stubble, he wears a very neat, small beard just at the bottom of his chin. My first impression holds. He's handsome.

"Here is the thing," he says at last. "What if I don't have what you want? What if I don't know where your brother is right now any more than you do?"

"Were you with him last night? At any point during the protest?"

"I was."

"Then no matter what, you have more recent information than I do. Maybe with what you know about Paul, and what I know from my uncle, you do have something I want?"

Bashiir goes silent again.

I'm starting to get antsy, but I remind myself to stay calm. This is not a person who responds to pressure, that much is clear. Despite my irritation, I respect that about him.

"Okay, what might I have that you want?" I ask. "What if I actually offer to be your lawyer for real? Like you said, it sure looks like you could use one. Don't you want to get out of here? Have they officially charged you with anything yet? They only have thirty-six hours to do so before they have to release you, but what if I can help you get out sooner?"

He's shaking his head again.

"I definitively do not want you to be my lawyer."

"And why not?"

He laughs. "You seem to have a fundamental lack of understanding about why I'm here. You don't know anything about me. You don't know anything about my community, despite the fact that your brother is my roommate. I'm not a criminal, I am a human being who participated in a peaceful demonstration against what I believe is a heinous and deliberately aggressive act of destruction against that community—and that's an act committed at the hands of your family. Why would I trust you to represent me?"

"Paul is part of the same family and he's on your side."

"Paul renounced everything to do with the King family and King Family Construction. He lives by his word."

"I have nothing to do with them anymore either. Christopher tried to get me to come back and be the attorney for the company, but I refused. And he cut me off financially because of it!"

"Not the same. You're on the outside because you refused what they wanted, which was to have you on the inside, advocating on behalf of all that they do. Paul is on the outside because he objectively assessed the way that the King family runs its business and decided it was counter to his deeply held beliefs. He chose to live in Thebes and fight on behalf of his beliefs. You traded one fancy lifestyle for a different fancy lifestyle. Fine. That's your right. But the person who makes that choice is not the person I want to be my lawyer. I've done nothing wrong. I know as well as you do that I cannot be held here beyond the legally allotted time. I would rather wait in that cell for another day than compromise my values by giving you the power to speak on my behalf."

Ouch. I liked him better when he was silent.

My phone alarm vibrates from my bag. Time for my next check-in with Melanie. Every minute I'm not working on the Per Olufsen case is another minute that I'm risking my precarious first-year associate status, another minute closer to the time when Melanie taps another new lawyer to take over my research and do it better, faster, smarter . . .

I sigh and fold my free hands on the table across from Bashiir's cuffed ones.

"Tell me about yourself," I say.

His skeptical affect doesn't change.

"Look," I continue, "you don't have to like me. You don't have to retain me. But we both love my brother."

He softens. Got him.

"I'll start," I offer. "Okay, here's something that nobody in the world knows about me other than Paul." The old kindergarten room takes me right back. "From the time I was three until I was six, I pretended that I barely knew how to speak English. But I did. I understood everything."

"Ah," says Bashiir, "you learned how to manipulate people quite young."

I laugh. "That's one way to look at it."

"I bet that worked well for you."

"They all thought I was stupid, until I was ready to show them I wasn't."

"The immigrant's secret weapon."

"Really?" I'm genuinely startled. I thought it was just my own ornery personality asserting itself young in a family where I instinctively knew that self-protection would serve me.

"When I started at St. Cloud State, I was nearly fluent. But other Somali upperclassmen taught me a good trick to get through paperwork for university services and financial aid and the like was to smile and shrug when they asked you any questions, as if you didn't understand. The staff

were so accustomed to us—and none of them bothered to learn any Somali, of course—they would rubber-stamp us through the processes."

"I only know English. Paul remembers a little Serbo-Croatian. But I
was too young, none of it stuck with me."

"Do you remember anything?" Bashiir asks.

The boots. The sleeve. Night terrors. Shaking outside of Paul's bedroom door in the dark.

"No." I can't help the rigidity that comes back into my voice. Bashiir
takes note. I feel him trying to will me to meet his gaze. But I can't. I
won't. We fall into silence again. This time, though, it feels more compan-
ionable from his end, less contentious. Now I can take the time to breathe
myself back to the present. I'm a lawyer. I'm this woman, not that girl. I
am in a police station here in Thebes, not in a kindergarten classroom,
not under a dirty cot in Sarajevo. I'm in control.

"What about you?" I ask Bashiir. "How old were you when you left
Somalia?"

"I was twelve. My mother, my older sisters, and I fled Mogadishu in
2001 because of the war. We traveled on foot to Kenya." His voice is calm,
as if walking to another country to escape his death was just a childhood
story. "We lived in a refugee camp there until my oldest sister got a student visa to go to Germany in 2004. My middle sister married a Kenyan
man and brought me and my mother to live with them until I got a visa
to come to the U.S. to attend St. Cloud State. So, I'm eight years here in
Minnesota."

"No other family in the U.S?"

"None. But the Somali community is family. We open our doors to
each other always. I haven't been alone since I arrived."

"Why did you move to Thebes?"

"I got a job in Athens. There aren't many of us here compared with
the Cities or even St. Cloud, but we are enough to make it a home."

"What do you do?"

"Computer systems engineering. I went to St. Cloud to study it in particular. I even got my certification before I graduated."

"I have no idea what that means in real life."

"It means a lot of things. But for me, I create computerized video surveillance programs. My company supplies most of the local businesses between here and Athens with programming and monitoring." He gestures with his chin up to the blinking green light over the door. "I wrote code for the program that records what that camera is looking at right now."

"Ironic."

"Very. I programmed the video system your uncle's business uses as well."

The new cameras installed around Christopher's property. This isn't some random brag about the work he does in Thebes. He's given me an opening, a connection. Whether on purpose or not.

"Two-minute warning!" Officer Hansen's voice cracks over the intercom.

"Bashiir," I say. "You might not trust me. But please, don't be short-sighted. I can help you, and I know you can help me." I rustle around in my bag for a pen. All I can find to write on in the mess of junk I managed to bring with me is an old grocery store receipt from who knows when. I smooth out its crumpled edges and quickly write my cell phone number on the back. I push the receipt across the table.

"Take it before that dumb cop sees you. Call me if anything changes. Like your mind. Or your circumstances."

He looks at the piece of paper like it's an insect of unknown origin—will it bite? Sting? Fly away? Open its wings to reveal some magical pattern imprinted by nature in glorious colors?

"One minute!" Hansen's voice weighs in again.

"Just take it," I say.

He reaches out with his cuffed hands for the receipt and, with a sigh, shoves it in the front pocket of his jeans.

I lean toward him. "So?" I whisper.

He shakes his head.

"You are not my lawyer."

"But Paul. What about Paul?"

Officer Hansen bangs through the metal door.

"Time's up."

I reach one last time across the table, but as soon as Hansen unlocks his wrist from the table, Bashiir stands, turns his back to me. He walks back to his cell unbidden.

The only person who can help me find my brother would rather be locked in a jail cell than partner up with me.

THEN

THIS IS WHAT I REMEMBER FROM STORY CIRCLE, WHEN Class A and Class B would come back from recess and were still all together: Sitting in my chair, looking down at my swinging feet, while Mrs. Firth told us tales about Our Local Heroes. The loggers who felled the first tamarack trees to build houses. The brothers who founded what she called the "real" twin cities of Minnesota: Thebes and Athens. And one afternoon: Christopher King, founder of King Family Construction, the hero who returned from defending our country in foreign lands to build the biggest company in Thebes and single-handedly lifted the community from ruin to prosperity.

"We are very lucky this year, boys and girls," she said that day, nodding to all of us in our circle of chairs, "Because Mr. King's own son, Harrison, is one of our classmates! Someday, he will be a hero like his father and continue his family's great traditions for our blessed town."

"And Toni!" Harrison piped up from his seat on the other side of the circle. "She's a King family hero too! She's Batman!" Twenty blond heads swiveled in my direction; twenty pairs of blue eyes stared at me like they had never seen me before that moment. They couldn't all have been identical, could they? But that's how I felt at the time: dark, small, with the entire world looking just like my cousin and nobody but Paul looking anything like me. I tried to will myself to disappear into my chair.

"Thank you, Harrison," said Mrs. Firth. "Antonia is also a very lucky girl. She is an orphan, but now she is receiving the kindness of your father and has the good fortune to be raised here in the greatest country in the world. Now, let's all finish story circle with our prayers for the hero we learned about today."

Everyone knew their cue. Heads bowed, hands clasped.

"Dear God," twenty tiny voices spoke, "thank you for bringing us the heroes of Thebes. Thank you for blessing us by making us Americans. May Thebes be our peaceful and happy home forever. Amen."

Only I was silent. They didn't know I understood English well enough to join them.

The immigrant's secret weapon.

But the distinction between me and them, the absolute shamefulness I was supposed to feel for being different, the forced gratitude for the great hero of Thebes: I understood everything.

School or jail. This room has always been a prison.

Late Morning

THE SUN IS CLIMBING OVERHEAD AND THE BLAST OF heat on my skin after the institutional air of the police station is both a relief and an oppression. The atmosphere has thickened. The northern Minnesota air, choked with humidity, is rising off the 300 million lakes everyone brags are so marvelous, so special, so . . . Minnesotan. I feel like a coating of Thebes itself is settling over my skin, attaching itself to me like cellophane.

The longest day of the year is getting longer every minute.

I check my phone: a voice message from Harrison and a text from Izzy. Nothing from Paul's wife. And, fortunately, nothing from Melanie.

"Toni, are you still in town?" Harrison's voice sounds like he genuinely hopes I am. "I don't know why you ran out, but Izzy and I just want to hang. We haven't seen you since last Christmas and then you were only here for a day. Don't leave until we can catch up. Please?"

My cousin can still tug on the one heartstring I have left.

I open the text from Izzy. A GIF with some teen queen, a Disney Princess type, made up and coiffed beyond her years, someone I'm probably supposed to recognize but don't because of my social media illiteracy. The girl's shoulders move up and down in a slow-motion shrug while she mouths: "What the fuck?" over and over again, her words subtitled below her plumped-up lips and furled but perfectly shaped eyebrows.

Okay, I have two heartstrings left.

I text Harrison: *Still here.*

Immediately a typing bubble appears, followed by: *Where r u? Onsite?*

I'm not ready to tell him where I went or who I saw. My instincts are telling me to keep that quiet.

Not far, I text back.

Izzy and I want to see you, he replies. *Just us. Just catching up.*

Not at the house. I don't want to be ambushed by Christopher.

Lunch at the Parth? he suggests. The Parthenon is a diner just outside the main part of town. It's the place we used to go after school for french fries, the crinkle-cut ones, clearly industrial but slathered in so much fry oil and salt they might as well have been shredded paper for all we cared. My only happy memories of family life after Paul took off are of sitting in vinyl booth seats at the Parthenon with Harrison and Izzy. I could use a happy memory about now.

I text that I'll meet them at noon. That gives me time to poke around on the Per Olufsen case enough to send Melanie a new status update.

I RAISE THE TOP ON MY CAR—BOTH TO BLOCK OUT THE sun and to hide from inquiring eyes—plug my laptop into the car charger and, with apologies to the environmental-protection gods, turn the car on idle so I can work in air-conditioned and power-corded isolation.

As I unzip the compressed files I downloaded from the Grogan server this morning, my screen lights up with document after document. Oh, this is heaven. I love exclusive access to information, especially information about powerful people that everyone else knows only from the outside. My fingers are tingling, like they used to in law school when I came upon the perfect legal precedent and started writing my brief for class, knowing I'd cracked the problem and all I had to do now was write and reason it out to its logical conclusion. Research. Discovery. It's what I do best.

I start flying through the documents, feeling my breath even out. I can sense my blood pressure dropping. Here's where I'm my best self. Here's where the improbabilities and miseries and emotional black holes of Thebes can't touch me. Data doesn't care whether it trusts you or not. Data doesn't get engaged without telling you or reject your help in favor of a jail cell. It gives you exactly what you need, when you need it. Data can lead to the truth. You just have to figure out how to break the code.

Time logs from Per's digital calendar open in one window; route information from his limo's GPS open in another. I start toggling between them to see what evidence we have of Per's back-and-forth over the past two months. What patterns of motion can I establish? I need to build a foundation of what is routine so I can note what is exceptional—and therefore, where the points of weakness are should opposing counsel ever subpoena his records and calendars.

Quickly it becomes clear that world travel is routine for him, as anyone would expect from the head of a global aviation company. Air Trek lists Per's own plane as Air Trek One. It wasn't unusual to see AT1 leave Minneapolis–St. Paul airport three times in one week during the time he was negotiating the new hub—a jaunt to London and back for two days, a quick trip to LA, then out to Oslo for three. Air Trek Industries has locations in ten cities, so no surprise to find that Per has a hotel suite on standby in each of them.

He's a runner—we talked about running at the cocktail party last night, and he showed me his watch, where he logs in his runs, their coordinates, the mileage. I poke around the cloud apps I've accessed with his assistant's passwords and I add his Garmin data to my screen. He's religious about it: five to eight miles, six days a week.

I'm tapping out my spreadsheet, cross-referencing all the locations, travel times, meeting logs. Where does he go for leisure? Where does this well-known international playboy play? *Follow the money*, Melanie said. I open another window: small accounts. Personal banking.

It looks like the logical conclusion is that the majority, if not all, of Per's dalliances take place in his homes. He isn't trying to hide his womanizing—goodness, it's part of his brand. But the clever man aligns it with his philanthropy. A quick scan of his media coverage files shows many photos of Per in one elegant tuxedo after another at a parade of charitable galas with a different woman every time. I'm impressed with the strategy. What high-profile cause wouldn't want Per Olufsen at their benefit when the paparazzi know that the big news ensuring their big paydays will be all about which supermodel is on the arm of *International Business Magazine*'s three-time winner of Most Eligible Bachelor that night? The highest traffic and the most shares and retweets came from a benefit for La Scala in Milan last December when Per brought the same woman—an Israeli glamour queen—he had been seen with a week before at the dedication of a new hospital wing in Madagascar. The tabloids exploded with "exclusive" revelations for a week: Per is secretly engaged! Per had a secret wedding! Is that a baby bump from a side-angle view of the Israeli beauty or did she just have high-sodium soy sauce with her sashimi for lunch?

When the next benefit event just three days after Milan—a New York City fundraiser for End World Hunger—shows Per with a gorgeous Ethiopian woman by his side, the tabloids don't even bother to retract. They don't care that the previous week's headline was lies and camera tricks. It's all entertainment anyhow.

I can imagine what Paul would say if he were sitting next to me in the passenger seat of my car.

What are you doing, Toni? Looking for loopholes to allow this corporate asshole to get away with having whoever and whatever he wants? This is your grand plan to use your power and education to make the world a better place?

Bashiir's voice echoes in my head. *Paul doesn't trust you.* My brother's image fades away, replaced by his roommate, turning his back to me as he returns to his cell.

I close my eyes, shake myself back into the moment. Then I open them and focus again on the screen.

That's when I see it.

A small note on the calendar. Almost undetectable. But I detect it because, I realize as I double-check the date, I was there.

June 19, 2014. Just two days ago.

"Retainer agreement. GDL Offices. 6 p.m."

That happened, just as noted. Melanie and Per in her office, the notary public on standby, me in the pit with the rest of the newbie first-year associates, pretending to grind away at some deposition review but quietly gloating about my pivotal role. Basking in the jealous looks from the other first-years as Per blew me a kiss when he and Melanie walked through the pit to the elevators, and at Melanie's thumbs-up as she came back to her desk.

A few minutes later, she IM'd me. We celebrated in her office with bourbon and Thai restaurant delivery till around ten, finalizing details for the cocktail party for Per that would take place the next evening. That night I decided for sure that I wanted to be Melanie Dwyer when I grew up, and that I was no longer resentful that she pulled me out of Boston and brought me back to Minnesota.

Per's calendar for June 19 says: "Dinner. M. Dwyer. 8 p.m."

That never happened.

Sure, it could have been a plan that he canceled. But I spent the evening deep in a bottle with Melanie and she did not seem like she was on the back end of a dinner date gone south. I tab over to the GPS log of Per's driver—I know he used his official car to come to our offices on Friday because, in my eagerness before he arrived, I was peering out the front window bank of the lobby of our building, pacing back and forth until his cream-colored Mercedes limo with its Air Trek vanity plates pulled up to the portico. Melanie had asked me to personally escort him up to our offices.

There we are on the mileage log: The IDS Building, arrival time 5:57. And there's the departure at 6:43. From there, the Mercedes doesn't return to Air Trek's offices in St. Paul. Nor does it go to Per's penthouse. It doesn't even go to the airport. It goes to St. Cloud, sixty-five miles away. GPS pins arrival at 8:14. Cross-checking with Per's Garmin data confirms that he is in the car.

What is Per Olufsen doing in St. Cloud when his calendar says he's at dinner with my boss in Minneapolis?

Then I sit straight up in my bucket seat. Little prickles of discovery run up and down my spine. The GPS shows Per's car leaving St. Cloud at 12:35. More than four hours after it arrives, having gone nowhere.

Is this the four hours I'm looking to seal from the record? Could the GPS log be the key to bulletproofing Per's alibi for . . . whatever he was doing with some woman not famous enough to enhance his public image?

The hole in the GPS I see now might be the smoking gun. Should I call Melanie to clue her in? Or should I take care of it myself to keep her hands clean and call her with "It's handled"? Surely I can find a legal loophole that allows me to bury this information so deep in some computer database that it would take thirty paralegals and a tarot card reader to discover it again.

Slow down. Triple-check. This is my hallmark as a researcher—I will always be more thorough than anyone who comes before or after me. I go back to the Garmin. Sure enough, there's more data for the night of June 19. And it's a lot.

By 9:00 p.m. the information shows that Per was on foot—somewhere forty-three miles away from the spot where the car stopped in St. Cloud.

I don't care how dedicated an athlete the man might be—he did not run forty-three miles in less than an hour. He had to have left his car behind and taken another.

What was he doing that required him to switch vehicles? A lawyer's nightmare: somewhere out there exists a car that can be tracked back to this time and place. I might be able to bury the in-car GPS I know about, but Garmin data in iCloud—that's beyond my skill set.

I zero in on the coordinates from Per's watch: 45.32 degrees north, 93.86 degrees west. I type it into Google Maps . . .

My blood freezes.

Two nights ago, between the hours of approximately nine and eleven, Per Olufsen was here.

In Thebes.

Midday

"TOOK YOU LONG ENOUGH!"

Harrison sits in our old booth across from Izzy and taps his watch three times when I walk through the door of the Parth. Izzy, of course, has her face in her phone.

My head is on fire with what I just discovered about Per. I was too freaked out to share it with Melanie—I sent her a text saying I'd narrowed my research down to a four-hour time frame and would continue to mine the data. All true. I just didn't happen to mention that the time frame and the data placed him in my hometown.

I need to figure out what I'm going to do next. I also need to eat. All I've had since last night is a mini bottle of whiskey.

Izzy and Harrison have food. And maybe they have information as well.

The Parthenon Diner is the same fluorescently lit palace as it was the last time I set foot inside. Ceiling fans turn lazily across the restaurant in their overmatched attempt to move the output from an inadequate number of air conditioner vents around the room. Regulars know which booths have the best temperature control, summer or winter, and strategize the times they eat based on likelihood of booth availability. Tables in the center are a free-for-all. Napkins blow off the tables under the fans while diners engage in a dance of sweaters on, sweaters off, ordering water with extra ice that melts before they can polish off a glass, or constantly straining over their shoulders to see if Mitzi—the lone waitress as long as I'd been coming to the Parth— happens to be on a coffee refill run and they can snag a little warmth.

Mitzi's husband, Rocky, runs the kitchen. Of all the residents of Thebes, he is the only descendent of actual Greeks we ever knew. That seems to be his main qualification for running a Greek diner. It definitely is not his cooking. When we came on a day with few customers, only regulars, Rocky would come out from the kitchen and he and Mitzi would drink diet sodas behind the counter and entertain us with stories about their past life following the Grateful Dead around the country, selling tie-dyed T-shirts to make enough money to buy weed and tofu. They were at a concert in the Cities when an acid-fueled revelation came to Rocky— the ancient Greek goddess Athena. She told him it was time to stop following Jerry Garcia, who was a false god from a heritage not his own. He came to, sold their remaining tie-dye inventory and their Winnebago to an enthusiastic younger Deadhead, found the "other twin cities" on the map—the appropriate-to-the-vision towns of Athens and Thebes—and bought what would become the Parthenon.

Mitzi tells the story differently. "He was on a bad trip," she says in her gravelly smoker's rasp. "He took a tab in exchange for shirts from some shady guy and he was bugging out. I held his head all night and told him I was done. That he had to get his shit together and find us a new gig or I'd be on the next bus back to Cleveland. And then the next morning: poof! He wakes up and frigging 'Athena' has visited him in a dream and told him to open this crap diner."

"It was Athena!" Rocky grumbles at this point. "She wore a toga."

ROCKY AND MITZI HAVE LINED THE WALLS OF THE PARTH with photos of their personal heroes—Jesse Ventura, Hulk Hogan,

Anthony Quinn—and one black-and-white image from their own Dead-head past: the two of them, forty years younger and collectively one hundred pounds lighter, both with long dark hair and puka shell necklaces, barefoot, leaning against the infamous Winnebago. Rocky's arm is casually draped over Mitzi's shoulder, and her head is tilted toward his. I pored over this photo many, many times when I was young. No adult I knew had anything like it in their known past and I was fascinated.

Has Bashiir eaten here? Do any of the Somali community of Thebes? I scan the room. Other than my cousins, only two booths and a table have any customers: all old and all white. Did any of them drive out from downtown, having worked up a hunger after all their racist sign waving?

I imagine Bashiir walking into the Parth next to me. Would heads swivel? Would Mitzi be hustling over to me like she is now, squeezing my shoulder in greeting on her way to deliver two sweaty glasses of iced tea to the booth in the back, or would she throw us a look of warning?

What am I thinking? There is no "us." Bashiir hates me.

And Paul hated the Parth, even when we were kids, so I'm sure he never brought his roommate or his wife or any of their friends here.

It was always Harrison's, Izzy's, and mine. Here's where we hid from their fancy-pants parents and my self-righteous, angry older brother and reveled in our little band of three. As I walk over to our booth to where they sit, so familiar, so reassuring, actual good memories of life in Thebes prod at me. Making Izzy laugh so hard with my imitation of her ninth-grade biology substitute teacher trying to use a microscope that she snorted chocolate milk out of her nose. The three of us ordering mozzarella sticks and fries and onion rings but asking Mitzi to bring them out separately, only after each one was done, because we wanted to extend the time we had at the Parth as long as possible. Harrison came out to me here, one frozen winter afternoon.

I slide in next to Izzy.

"Put that thing down," I say, grabbing the phone from her hand.

"We already ordered all the things," says Harrison. "You do know that noon happened many minutes ago."

"Sorry, I had to catch up on a work issue." My head starts to reel again. Do I need to grill them about Paul, or do I need to grill them about Per? Worlds colliding.

I'll start small. "So," I say, "what's been happening?"

"Ooh, me first!" Izzy squeals. "Guess what?"

I bite. "What?"

"I'm officially an influencer."

"You are?"

"Yes! On Instagram. And YouTube. I reached enough followers that now I'm sponsored by my first business."

"Good for you." Maybe Izzy has an actual plan to gain independence from King Family Construction. "Who is it?"

"Blushing Flower Spa. It's where I get my mani-pedis, in the strip mall out Route 9. I know, hyper-local. But Mrs. Evanson who runs it just got bought by a franchise and the owner is from Miami! I could go national if things go well. And all I have to do to get her to promote me to the owner is make her daughter into a YouTube star."

"Izzy, this sounds complicated. Her daughter?"

"No, it's great! You saw Michelle—that GIF I sent you this morning was her. We shoot videos of her and then I edit them for WTF moments. Isn't she cute? I styled her myself."

Still Thebes-centric. But maybe there's some ambition here. I'll support it.

Harrison is distracted by the television mounted in the corner of the room behind Izzy's head. He keeps glancing up at the blurry local newscast—it isn't even a flat screen, but one of those bulky old-school boxes. He's barely looking at us in between checking the muted broadcast and tearing fringe along the side of his straw's paper wrapper. I reach across the table and tap the back of his hand.

"Hey, what's up with you?"

"Huh?" he replies, as if suddenly remembering I'm not the usual daily company. "Oh, just . . . nothing."

"Is something about the Dig on the news?" I ask. "The protest? Paul?" I stop myself before I ask about Bashiir.

"No, Dad has that under wraps for the time being. WKNW is giving us till the 10:00 p.m. news before they go out."

"Wanna tell her why they gave us that sweet deal?" Izzy says, teasing Harrison. He blushes.

I glance back over my shoulder again at the screen. The news anchor looks exactly like she's supposed to—red rayon form-fitting dress, beauty pageant makeup, glossy brown hair shellacked into a pouf. Her mouth is moving silently; somehow, she manages to maintain her white-toothed smile while she reads from the teleprompter.

Harrison moves from his straw paper to his napkin, continuing to create enough fringe for a rack of cowboy vests. He doesn't meet my eyes.

"Um, well, I'm kind of involved with a producer there."

I clap my hands. "So great, Harry! How did you meet? What's his name?"

"It's Matthew. I don't want to say much though. We're not ready to go public yet . . ."

"He's the head of the station!" Izzy stage-whispers to me. Harrison gives her a death stare, then sighs.

"Okay, but please keep it quiet. You know it's shady that I asked him to hold the story."

I wave my hand dismissively. "That is about the least shady thing any member of the King family has ever done. Or, at least, admitted to doing."

Now Harrison meets my gaze with the full force of his blue eyes.

"Toni, we only have till ten tonight to keep our name out of the press. Unless we all sign the nondisclosure and agree to the statement, they're going to run a 'Family Divided' story. They'll label Paul a fugitive from the law."

"Right. I wondered how long it would be till we got back to this."

"Toni..."

My lawyer-self kicks on automatically. "Okay fine, if you want to talk business, then tell me where Paul is."

"I don't know."

"Then your father knows and you're covering for him by choosing not to know."

"That's not fair."

"Hey, hey!" Izzy interjects. She puts a hand on each of our wrists. "We're finally back together. Don't ruin it for me by fighting."

"Come on, Toni. We're all concerned about Paul," Harrison says. "If he doesn't turn himself in or you can't find him, we'll take the next step and start looking. But you know there's nothing we can do about it till then. Having it all over the local news will only hurt him, not help him."

"You father has access to everything that happens in this town. Why does he really need my signature on those documents? Is he still so bitter about Paul leaving the family that he expects me to turn against my own brother or he won't let me back in?"

Harrison is shaking his head.

"Toni, you were angrier at Paul for leaving than anyone. We all know that's the reason you hate coming back. We all had to get over him, not just you. But he came home. Maybe not to live with us, but at least he's been here in Thebes. Frankly, you're the one who's gone for good. Now we've had to get over you."

I let the sting of his words settle between us, allowing the familiar sounds of the Parth to rise: the clatter of dirty plates in the plastic bin where Mitzi dumps them to wait for slow times when she can load the dishwasher.

The sizzle of grease on iron that hums from the kitchen, the clang of metal spatula against stovetop. The *thwap, thwap* of overhead fans.

Harrison pressed on a bruise, and it hurts.

"Fried mozzarella sticks and an order of stuffed grape leaves on the house because Toni is the only one of you who likes 'em and, good gravy, here she is!" Mitzi sets two platters down on our table and air-kisses near my cheek.

"Hey, Mitzi," I say, grateful for the interruption that breaks our awkward silence. Harrison is too, clearly.

"What brings you here all the way from Boston?" she asks, resting her hand on my shoulder for a moment before handing us silverware.

"Actually, I'm working in the Cities now."

"What? Nobody told me, and I know about everyone who comes and goes between here and there!"

"It's new," says Harrison. "We weren't even sure whether she'd be coming around because it's such a huge job. Associate at a major law firm. Of course, they're lucky to have her."

I flash a half smile of appreciation and reconciliation at my cousin, and he reciprocates. Dear Harry—a lover, not a fighter if there ever was one.

"Mitzi, wait!" I sit up. "Do you really hear about everyone who comes to Thebes from the Cities?"

"Honey, we get one or two new folks a year max if the blizzards don't kill us in the winter and the twisters don't kill us in the summer. It's not like any of 'em are building their lake homes around here." She laughs her gruff, tar-filled laugh at her own joke.

"Has anyone come around asking about a man who was here a couple of nights ago? Blond, really good-looking, around forty. Probably wearing an expensive suit."

"Do I look like a girl who would kiss and tell?" Mitzi laughs at herself again. "Someone like that shows up, I might have to leave this dump."

"But did he? That you know of?"

Izzy, who had checked out when the conversation stopped concerning her, checks back in.

"Wait, Toni, who are you talking about? Do you have a boyfriend too?"

Harrison's eyes get huge at the indirect allusion to his situation. He mouths "Shut up!" at Izzy across the table.

I, however, sense a good cover and jump on it. "Maybe," I say. "I'm not sure yet, but there's definitely something there." It's so much easier to let Izzy create stories about my life—it allows me to keep asking questions and avoid explaining what I'm after.

"Keep us posted, darlin'," says Mitzi, filling my water glass from a sweating metal pitcher. "Meantime eat Rocky's grape leaves and tell him how much you like 'em. Everyone else who comes here is scared to order from the 'exotic' side of the menu." She waggles her eyebrows like air quotes around *exotic*.

I pick up one of the oily green logs and stuff it in my mouth. Flavorless, gooey rice and chopped meat that's probably scraped from the bits that remain on Rocky's grill after the burgers are all cooked mix with the slimy texture of the store-bought grape leaf wrap. I'll be chewing for a while, but I wag my eyebrows back and give Mitzi an okay sign.

"Good girl. Stop me before you head out and tell me what you think of the new recipe. He's adding sugar and lemon juice now."

I finally swallow but before I can follow up with any more questions about Per, Mitzi moves to her next table.

"Harrison, you need to chill. You and Matthew are an adorable couple." Izzy is unfazed as ever by her brother's anxiety. "It's 2014. Rainbow flags are totally in."

"Yes, but you know where we live, Izz. Nobody around here is flying those flags."

"Speaking of flag waving," I say, "I passed quite the interesting scene at town hall earlier."

Harrison nods his head. "Yep, I heard about the demonstrators. Just business as usual. The new religion is walking around with signs."

"'Stop the Invasion'? That's some serious race baiting."

"They're like bees, Toni. Ignore them and all they'll do is buzz. But stir them up and they'll sting."

"Did you see them today? Is it more than usual because of the protest last night, or was that a bunch of buzzy bees too?"

He pauses, takes his time to cut a piece of gooey fried cheese. Chews, swallows.

"The Somalis have a right to protest our Dig," he says finally. "The locals have a right to protest the Somalis. We can make it all go away by not giving either of them any reason to get louder, or to point fingers at us."

I put my fork down.

"Who is 'us'?"

"The family."

Meaning his father. "So hush-hush about racism and xenophobia," I say. "Hush-hush about same-sex relationships. Then everything will be fine?"

"Actually, yes. If we can negotiate instead of fight, I believe it will."

I hate Harrison's position. But I can't hate Harrison for it. The same little boy who believed that all he had to do was hold my hand at recess and the kindergarten know-nothings would embrace me like they embraced him, who turned his sunny face up to his father time and again for approval and never lost hope when approval didn't come, is the kind man across the table. Naïve, but kind.

I sigh. "I believe it won't," I say, "but that can't surprise you."

"Toni, you are a total force of nature. You were made to go out in the world and change it. Me—it was my fate to be born here and maybe it's my fate to stay here to . . . I don't know, keep the peace? Make more peace? All this conflict gives me heartburn."

"Fried mozzarella gives you heartburn. Conflict forces you to choose between right and wrong."

"Didn't Paul used to say something like that, but about truth and lies?"

Paul, twelve-year-old Paul, wrapped around dusty philosophy textbooks he brought home from the library, hiding out in the corner of the great room while the three of us argued over whatever we were playing or doing: card games, freeze tag, trying to stand on our heads the longest. I always wanted Paul to arbitrate our competitions, declare a winner and loser in every situation. His opinion mattered to me above all.

"Paul, who's the best at cartwheels? Me, Harrison, or Izzy? I want to know the truth."

"I'm the best at cartwheels!" Izzy, age six, spun around in a circle, pigtails flying out to the side, until she fell down, dizzy and giggling.

"That's not cartwheels, it's spinning!"

"It's cartwheels to me," she said.

"No! Cartwheels look like this!" I executed a perfect cartwheel. Harrison followed, crashing into the coffee table.

"I win!" Izzy said.

"You do not!"

"We all win!" said Harrison.

"Only one person can win! Paul, who wins?"

"Nobody wins when the truth cannot be known."

"So tell us the truth!"

He looked up from his reading and sighed. "Plato says: Use your own eyes to see and your own heart to know. Why does anyone else's opinion matter?"

"Ugh! You and that stupid book."

He shrugged. So I threw myself on top of him and tickled him until he had no choice but to laugh and try to wrestle me off.

At the time I considered that a victory. Now I can see he was already halfway gone.

"USE YOUR OWN EYES TO SEE AND YOUR OWN HEART TO know. That's what Paul used to say."

The three of us pause for a moment, each reflecting on what that means. At least, Harrison and I do. Izzy seems pretty sure already—three quick taps in her phone and she turns it around to show us a photo of Harrison seated at a desk in what must be a news studio, what with the background filled with screens and mic equipment, looking up at a curly-haired man about ten years older than us with a moustache and his shirt sleeves rolled up focused on a set of papers. By the expression on Harrison's face, I gather this is Matthew.

"I see with my eyes what your heart knows, Harrison," says Izzy. "And being in love is the most important truth in the world."

My cousin. She can be such a surprise!

Harrison is blushing, but he doesn't take his eyes off the phone.

"You have to let me post this on my feed!" And the regular Izzy is back. "I'll put a rainbow heart filter around it and add hashtag-love-is-love. It will totally go viral!"

Harrison gestures to Izzy to bring her phone with the photo closer to him. When she does, he snatches it out of her hand and deletes the image.

"Harrison!"

"I can't risk it."

"What do you mean?" I ask. "Are you afraid Matthew will break up with you?"

"No, it's . . . it's different. Toni, you haven't lived here for a long time. You don't remember what we have to do to make things work."

Something about the tone of Harrison's voice makes my stomach clench.

"What things?"

His fingers are working the shredded napkins in front of him again, crumpling and uncrumpling the pile of paper.

"Family things. Business things." He leans forward. "Okay. I'll tell both of you this, but I am swearing you to secrecy. Promise me."

Izzy and I exchange a quick glance. We both nod.

"Dad has promised me that I'm next in line to take over as CEO of King Family Construction, once he retires."

"Harrison, that's amazing!" I can't believe it—is Uncle Christopher truly going to do right by his son?

Izzy claps her hands. "Yay, Harry!" she says. "But why do we have to keep it a secret?"

He looks down at the cheese grease on the plate in front of him. "Dad says we need to maintain the trust placed in us by the people of Thebes for the past twenty years—that we've always placed traditional Thebesian values at the heart of how we work."

This is not going to be good.

"So, he asked that I make a public declaration before he makes one in return."

"It's Paul, isn't it!" The words explode out of me. "Did he send you here to convince me to sign your documents in exchange for allowing you to run his company?"

Harrison looks up from his plate, genuinely startled. A sad look crosses his face.

"Toni, for once can you please not assume everything is all about you?"

Now it's my turn to look down. Guilty as charged.

"Sorry," I mutter. "Go on." Izzy quickly squeezes my knee under the table.

He sighs deeply. "Dad has asked me to take on a role that will help consolidate the King family's legacy in Thebes. He's requested that I announce my engagement. To a woman."

I'm frozen in my seat. This is utter madness. Even Izzy, next to me, can't think of anything to say, so completely unexpected are these words.

"It's merely practical. Dad and I discussed it thoroughly and as long as all parties involved understand the ground rules and there's no deception, it isn't wrong."

"But . . ." Izzy finally finds her voice. "What about love?"

Harrison shrugs. "We can all pursue love in lots of ways. I'm not pulling the wool over anyone's eyes. I'm a gay man. I'll just be a gay man in an asexual, consensual marriage to a woman."

My head is throbbing. "Forcing you into a marriage? It's fundamentally unjust, Harry."

"No one's forcing me. And my world view—by necessity—never assumed that marriage was love's endgame. Does yours, Toni? If you're being honest?"

"I'm not like Izzy. I don't believe marriage is an endgame at all."

"And can you honestly tell me you don't know a single hetero who hasn't made the same decision?"

I'm silent, wondering about James Hollings and his lady's slipper. Can't say that out loud.

"Then don't judge me," Harrison continues. "And Izzy, if I do this, I get to have love and more. Matthew understands. He's the one who suggested Charlene."

"Who's Charlene?" I ask, at the same time Izzy's mouth falls open and she says, "Charlene Daniels?" Harrison's look confirms it. Izzy nods toward the television behind us, where the talking-head baton twirler still yammers on mute.

"Wait, Charlene Daniels is the news anchor?" I ask. "On the broadcast station your boyfriend runs?"

"We get along," he says. "And the arrangement benefits her and her girlfriend too. Dad says he'll build us a house and buy us a condo in Athens; we each live wherever we please. It's for show only. The construction business—you both know how it is."

"You'll have to compromise your identity, your actual truth!"

"Seriously, Toni—I have to call bullshit. You're sitting across from me accusing me of what, exactly? Working to create change from within? Finding a way to make King Family Construction a better, greener company—because you know I can—without upending everyone and everything like you and Paul always do?"

"Harrison, I don't even know who you are right now." Tears of anger and frustration sting the corners of my eyes.

"Is everything black and white to you? I'm not even sure why you came back here today—was it really to help find Paul or was it a chance for you to descend on us with your Harvard judgments and your big-city bias? You always accuse Dad of acting out of prejudice. Who's the prejudiced one now?"

I turn back to Izzy, looking for her support, but she's hiding behind her phone. I yank it out of her hand once more.

"Izzy, you think this is as crazy as I do."

"Well . . . I mean, I'm shocked about Harrison's marriage too, but actually, some of the other stuff . . . about you, how you act toward us . . . he's not wrong."

I gather up my things and push myself out of the booth. Tears blur my vision as I throw a few crumpled dollar bills on the table. I'm not letting King Family Construction buy me so much as a single stuffed grape leaf. I'm heading toward the door when Mitzi cuts me off by the register.

"He was here." Her voice is low, and she doesn't look me in the eye.

"What?"

"The man you were looking for from the Cities. He was here."

"At the Parth?"

"No, but around."

"Is there anything else you remember? Who told you he was in town?"

"Nobody told me. There was a table of guys here for lunch yesterday.

From your uncle's company. I overheard them talking about a bigwig in town and it sounded like your man."

"Do you remember who in particular?"

"Oh, a couple of his suits. They were from the accounting team, I think? Oh, wait a minute, I almost forgot: later on, one of your uncle's foremen joined them. That big guy, been working his crew forever . . ."

"John Joseph?"

"Yep. That's the one. And when he finished his Jell-O, he stopped over at the booth where James and Denise Hollings and their two kids were eating. I think he dropped a folder off. Is that helpful?"

Oh, Mitzi . . . how can I answer that question? Was the man I lost my virginity to who is now my uncle's attorney involved in some kind of mysterious dealings with the corporate magnate I now represent as a lawyer? And did he look like he was starved for good sex? With me?

"Thank you," I say. "It's helpful."

The spin cycle in my head is on super-fast. I double back to my cousins, still in the booth, and try to catch Harrison's eye to offer a peace glance, but he's not having it right now. He isn't the one I need at the moment though. I put my hand on Izzy's shoulder and lean close so only she can hear me.

"Hey, would it be okay if I borrow some clothes?"

Izzy grasps my hand in her hand and lets out a deep sigh of pleasure. "Oh, Toni. I thought you'd never ask."

MY LAST DAY AS AN INTERN AT ROBERTS AND ASSOCI-
ates, the staff hosted a farewell party. Wanda bought a cake from the
Supervalu down by Twin River (I had a pretty good guess about who
must have told her to drive all the way there to purchase it at lunchtime). It was chocolate iced, with sprays of yellow frosting flowers in
every corner. *Thank you, Toni,* said the cake. Leo Roberts gave a little
speech about my filing skills and handed me an envelope with my last
two weeks' pay.

I was about to bring a forkful to my mouth when Wanda, licking a
stray flower off her fingers, said to me, "I guess the next time we'll see you
will be with your family at James and Denise's wedding!"

My fork froze in the air. I looked at James. He appeared to be paying
a great deal of attention to the cake on his plate, but I could tell he was
attuned to my reaction. And I saw in that moment what we had been
doing. Through all the intensity of our physical relationship, the obliter-
ating need for each other's bodies to the point of wearing each other out
daily—we were pretending I didn't know what I knew. Or pretending it
wasn't real. The stockroom was our universe. If "James is engaged" stayed
outside of the four walls that held the entirety of our feelings for each
other, we could keep pretending.

I set my bite of cake back down on my plate untouched. Would he look at me? Send me any kind of signal?

He took another bite of cake, chewed and swallowed, and then said, "We have so many Thebes families on the list. We won't be inviting anyone's children."

Children.

I got it, James Hollings. My uncle is too important, too prominent, to exclude from your business meeting . . . I mean, wedding. You can't have a scandal on your hands, especially involving the adopted niece who arrived from nowhere with her rebellious brother and drove Eddie King to his death. You need a lady's slipper.

Something as definitive as the look that had initially brought us together my second week at Roberts and Associates happened then too: a quiet stilling of what, merely two hours ago, had been pulsating and more alive than anything I'd ever experienced.

I finished my piece of cake. I got through the chatter about James and his wedding. I took my check, and I went home.

BY MONDAY MORNING, I HAD MADE MY CHOICE. I SAT quietly in the back seat of Harrison's Jeep while he and Izzy in the front sang along to Justin Timberlake and pretended to sob about returning to school when, in reality, they were both super excited and had been planning their outfits for days. I, on the other hand, was steeling myself for a new mission.

Just as I had known when I first found out about James Hollings's engagement that I didn't want to end things between us, I knew why I wasn't red-eyed and despondent now. James had delivered an important lesson in the way he both coolly began our relationship and coolly finalized it. He showed me what real power looked like. I thought I had power over him because he wanted to have sex with me. But he had more. He had more because I not only wanted sex with him—I wanted to become him. I wanted to be the one with the cool-headed swerve between on and off. I wanted to be so self-assured that I could size up any situation and create who I needed to be in order to win. On behalf of anyone I loved who suffered at the hands of a cruel and unjust system, like Harrison on his knees scooping gravel while John Joseph laughed—but equally important, on behalf of myself. No one else would ever take care of me, so I'd better learn how to take care of myself.

You won't need to depend on a man, Aunt Evelyn wrote in her secret note. *Your destiny is more than Thebes.*

Had she foreseen the inevitability of this moment? Despite the ever-increasing number of hours she spent drinking, she appeared frighteningly sober about the state of my heart.

I'd heard nothing from James since Friday. Not an email, not a phone call. How did he know that I wouldn't tell Mr. Roberts—another lawyer no less—everything we'd done all summer as payback? Or my aunt and uncle, who surely would have no qualms about protecting me? Was it arrogance? Blind hope?

He didn't know I wouldn't tell. He couldn't know.

But I knew.

I learned something about myself that summer that had been lurking under the surface, waiting, I think, for me to understand. I had pursued James Hollings in equal measure to his pursuit of me, so even if the technical "fault" was his, because as a supervisor, I could claim he was abusing his power, for me to do so would be unfair. I'd been seething about unfairness for weeks: The unfairness of how John Joseph treated Harrison, even though, legally, he had the right to do exactly what he was doing. The unfairness of Paul leaving me behind to find his own way. The unfairness of Brandi Schmidt dictating who mattered at Mt. O and who didn't while she danced half naked on a table in the home ec room.

My summer with James Hollings brought all of it into focus. I would never make a choice that was merely legal if it was fundamentally unfair.

I walked into Mt. O High School that swelteringly hot August day with a straighter spine than ever before. In nine months, I'd be out, and I finally knew that I had a goal for the future. I was going to become better at being James Hollings than James Hollings was at being himself. My world would be bigger, the stakes would be higher. And I would become the one who called the shots, no matter what.

Early Afternoon

THE VINE THAT SNAKES UP THE BACK OF THE HOUSE below Izzy's bedroom is thick as a tree trunk. We all climbed in and out of the house this way during high school—usually with flashlights in our mouths and booze in our backpacks. Izzy has opened the sash and waits for me inside as I climb. She grabs my wrists and pulls me up so I can leverage my body weight and push myself through. They should just eliminate doors in this house all together.

Izzy promised that our old trick could get me back in without triggering security or revealing to Uncle Christopher and Aunt Evelyn that I was on the premises, and she delivered. Recent practice sneaking in a guy she met in Athens has kept her on her game. She told me where to leave my car, behind an abandoned silo a half mile from the house. From there, I picked my way through the twigs and leaves that covered the overgrown pathway from the unused farm to avoid detection. Izzy told me that there was no video surveillance trained on the back of the residence; Christopher is concerned only with recording the comings and goings of his business associates and protecting whatever precious information he keeps in the office about King Family Construction Company. And he never suspected Izzy would be anything but a virginal princess, so why would he worry about her? I'm impressed once again by Izzy's flare for deviousness.

I pull a few stray bits of nature off my shirt and chuck the mess into Izzy's bedazzled trash can.

"You might as well throw everything you're wearing in there too." She stands in front of her closet, its double doors thrown wide open.

"Nothing with sparkles," I say. "Or logos. Or deliberate holes where no holes are supposed to be."

"Is this outfit for business or pleasure?"

When I texted James to tell him I was ready to sign the papers, but only if I could go over the details alone with him first, he invited me to meet him at the office this afternoon, which would be empty on a Sunday.

We can talk, he wrote. *Lawyer to lawyer.*

I sizzle a bit all over again thinking about his text. How can I help it? He was my first. I've been actively avoiding him all these years because I was afraid of exactly this feeling. But now, the razor-thin opening that my past with James allows is the only path I have left to learn something real about Paul. Am I above using it? What other choice do I have?

"Definitely business."

James works for my uncle now. On the one hand, I must question his allegiance. On the other hand, he has access to the information I need. And who doesn't work for Christopher in this town? Even Bashiir installed his security system.

Bashiir. Those disapproving eyes of his cut through me like I'm made of paper. No way he would condone what I'm thinking about doing. But his disapproval started long before I walked into that jail today, because Paul told him I couldn't be trusted. *Fine, Mister Too-Principled-to-Take-My-Help Abdi. Sit in that jail cell. I'll get what I need without you.* I'm not sure what I'm willing to do in James Hollings's empty office today, but it's not going to happen without the exchange of some vital information on his part about my brother.

Izzy emerges from her closet holding an eggplant-purple pencil skirt in one hand and a pale peach V-neck silk tank with fabric buttons down the front in the other.

"Do you have anything black?" I ask.

She rolls her eyes.

"You said business, not a funeral." But she hangs the shirt back in the closet and replaces it with a lace short-sleeved pullover top. In navy. It'll do.

I give myself a quick sponge bath with a packet of Izzy's cucumber-scented face wipes while she throws a camisole, clean underwear, and gold hoop earrings on her bed for me. My flip-flops will have to stay—her feet are bigger than mine.

"Can I at least give you a pedicure?" she asks, surveying my toes with a critical eye.

"No time." Izzy's skirt hits me just above the knee—with her longer legs it must be a mini on her. But I'm glad for the extra bit of professionalism today. Antonia King, attorney at law, must show up for real.

Izzy is attacking my head with hairspray when her computer pings several loud chimes. Gone are the days when we all had to share the family computer—Izzy's screen is gigantic.

"Ooh, that's probably my latest batch of video footage," she says. "This guy I know from town, Brian, films Michelle for me. I review his clips to find the best WTF moments, and he makes them into GIFs."

I wave her off of me, grateful for the distraction before she can turn my hair into a pile of spun sugar. I look into her full-length mirror to pat it back down into something in between Izzy's vision and the way I showed up.

Andela stares back at me, shaking her head. *This is James Hollings we're talking about. Remember?*

As if I could forget. My biggest goal when I left for college was ridding myself of this man. But I startled every time a tall, dark-haired, slightly older man passed me in the Yard. Which happened a lot. Professors, graduate students, random strangers walking across Harvard Square—any man who had a certain lanky gait, who looked fly in a suit, whose fingers were long and tapered, had the ability to send me into paroxysms of longing. So, when my econ professor second semester introduced the PhD candidates who would be leading the small sections, a tall, dark-haired grad student who towered over the others became my fixation. His section was the only one that didn't fit into my schedule.

I changed my schedule.

I didn't stop there. Fall of my sophomore year I set my sights on another tall, dark-haired teaching assistant, this one in poli-sci. I became a prompt and regular visitor during his office hours twice a week. They were like candy, these men—so very easy to binge on, but none of them satisfying enough for a full meal. And I found that I was always ravenous.

If none of them was going to hold my attention for more than a night, I didn't want to waste my time anymore in pursuit of men just because they bore a passing resemblance to the one I left behind. That's when I turned to younger guys. Easier guys. Freshmen. Even seniors in high school staying overnight in the dorms as prospective students. You'd better believe they left campus with Harvard as their first choice. Nothing but sex, though, thank you very much. I made sure to keep my friendships, female and male, separate from my Saturday night party prowls. I just needed the booze and the boys so I could sleep through the night.

During the week, I studied instead of sleeping. In that regard, I fit right in. I was determined to show anyone who was looking over my shoulder that I belonged with the elite in Cambridge, even though privately I had no idea how to categorize myself. Was I a hick from northwestern Minnesota who'd never been out of the state? A refugee from one of the most well-known genocides of the post-Holocaust twentieth century? Alone at college, both identities felt equally strange to me. My family of birth was dead, murdered by unknown people before I could even remember them. My family of record now seemed like foreign objects to me—away from them for the first time, I viewed them as I viewed the glass-eyed Neanderthal family at the Museum of Natural History where I had to research for my intro cultural anthropology class. Immovable. Immutable. Over. And my brother, the only person in the world who could be a bridge between the two, the only person who seemed real enough to matter, had left me behind.

So: reinvention. With no one from family near enough to visit and only the bursar's office and the Harvard registrar in need of information about my whys and wherefores, I was free to make up a childhood that could blend into the background until I could accumulate enough on-campus experience to make talking about home a thing of the past. My imaginary family was boring. Minnesota, middle class. Two parents, a sister, a dog. A best friend who stayed in state for school. I made my father an accountant, my mother a teacher. How simple, how dull, nothing anyone could care enough to ask about, especially when there were house parties to attend, and clubs to join, and endless opportunities to show off my smarts and knowledge.

I filled my summers with on-campus jobs and internships. And after freshman year, I had invitations from New England students I befriended to visit them over holiday breaks. I accepted every invitation that came my way, and every opportunity to study the lives of others to see what I could make into my own.

I also scrupulously avoided taking any classes that touched on the events in the Balkans of the early 1990s. No genocide studies. Nothing that would invoke the wrist and the sleeve.

If I was going to be new, I would be new from birth.

BACK HERE, THOUGH, IN IZZY'S MIRROR, ANDELA AND I
blink at each other. She's been waiting for me. What is she trying to do:
warn me off or draw me close?

My phone buzzes. A text. Paul's wife? Bashiir? Melanie? My pulse
quickens at the thought of any one them weighing in.

Dear Antonia, I would like to speak with you.

It's Evelyn.

"Izzy, does your mom know I'm in the house?"

"No way. She and Dad don't get home from church for at least half
an hour."

There's something we need to discuss.

First Harrison, now my aunt. Christopher has activated his minions.
Well, too late—my own plan is in motion now. I'm not talking to any
of them again until I know what happened to my brother. I look at the
frazzled little orphan from Bosnia who stares back at me from the mirror,
with her borrowed clothes and borrowed moxie. *We can fix this,* I tell her
silently. *All you have to do is wait until I take care of business here, and then
you and I can go back to Minneapolis and be a successful lawyer.*

She looks back at me skeptically. Rightly so. I don't have time for her
reservations though, not now. I have to focus. If I don't have all of my wits
about me with James this afternoon, I'll never get what I need.

Yes, I text Evelyn. *Later.*

Behind my shoulder in the mirror, Izzy works at her computer. I
imagine my aunt in her early twenties when I look at Izzy, so similar are
they in coloring and expression. Imagine her face when she found out, at
that age, she had to raise four children, not two.

I add another text: *I promise.*

Light from Izzy's screen pulses across her face as she scans frame after
frame of slow-motion video featuring the beautiful girl whose image she sent
me earlier: the girl's hand outstretched to take a selfie in the center of a group

of teenagers raising red Solo cups. Teenagers holding beer bottles. Teenagers throwing their arms around each other in drunken glory. They flip by, inverted on Izzy's monitor behind my own reflected image in a blur that could be a replication of all of my own high school years: me, alone, uncomfortable and serious in the front while everyone behind me parties with each other in an endless loop of fun things I'm not invited to do. I'm done with the portion of today that's about wallowing in sad past lives, though. I've advanced from hideous outfit to mediocre outfit thanks to my cousin—hopefully it will be enough to give me the confidence to stand up and—

"Izzy! Wait! Stop!" I say.

Izzy pauses, hand on her computer mouse.

"What?"

Something in the corner of my eye from her screen leapt out at me. Something out of order. I run to her side.

"Scroll back," I say. "Again. Again. Once more."

There.

The frozen frame is another party shot. Nighttime, a string of lights dotting the periphery of the image, the kind that someone hangs on their back patio to make it look festive. Michelle looking straight at the camera surrounded by screaming revelers . . . and a blurry man stooping behind her, his face half obscured by the longish blond hair that sweeps across his eyes, his mouth locked on the side of Michelle's pretty neck.

"Izzy, do you know who that man is, the one all over Michelle?"

She squints at his image.

"No, I've never seen him before—but eww, gross! He looks old! This is not okay. How did I miss this? It must have happened when I was posting my behind-the-scenes stories."

I guess it makes a perverse kind of sense. Where would an internationally recognized playboy go to play where he could be anonymous? Some house party in a backwater town with a bunch of drunken teenagers who think only someone who's had a show on the Disney Channel could possibly be famous. I look at the time stamp of the image: sure enough. June 19, 2014, 11:23 p.m. It tracks with Per's visit to Thebes.

"Play the whole segment again," I say. "As slowly as you can."

As Izzy clicks her mouse, stop-motion Per drapes his arm around Michelle, kissing her again on the neck, then on the cheek. He's clearly drunk. She's smiling, a fixed, staged smile. For the video camera? Because of him? She moves away from his arm. He lunges forward—it could be a drunken stumble, or it could be deliberate—oh God, his hand is down her shirt! And now his back is between the camera and Michelle. A few frames later, he stumbles out of view. Michelle's frozen smile hasn't changed one bit, but her eyes have.

No. Oh, no.

Per's so-called peccadillo is more than off-brand: it's with a teenaged girl.

And he's my client.

A wave of bile brings the grease from lunch back into my throat. What am I doing? And what do I do now? I close my eyes—will the whole thing go away when I open them again?

It looks even worse.

Get the facts, Toni. Lawyer up.

"Izzy, do you know where this video was made?"

"It was here."

"Yeah, I know, here in Thebes. But whose house?"

"No—here. As in, here at this house. The back patio."

I look more carefully. The string of lights is temporary, the people and what they are doing is distracting . . . but yes, now that I adjust my eyes even more to the scene, I recognize the edge of one of the patio chairs, a sliver of the familiar sliding glass door leading into the three-season porch.

I rub my temples. My stomach does another flip. My client. My house. And . . . ick.

"Okay, why are a bunch of high school students having a party on the patio?"

"Because I staged it. I have to buy them beer to make sure lots of people will show up, so I need Brian to film at the house. I'm like a straight-up art director. But not for this—I have to make sure she's okay. I can't believe she didn't she tell me this happened. Oh no, what if she thought it was part of the plan? Ugh!"

"Why is Per . . . why is the older man here at all?"

"I think he's one of Daddy's business associates," Izzy is rapid texting as she speaks. "Daddy had one of his catered closed-door dinners on Friday—and Brian's video must have been running when I was off to the side posting—hey, wait!" She looks back up at me. "Why do you know him? Toni, this creep isn't your boyfriend, is it? The one you mentioned at the Parth?"

Too much is happening: Per is at my childhood home when he commits the act I've been dispatched to bury. Izzy feels responsible. But as disgusted as I am at this moment by the image of a drunken Per slobbering over a drunken girl, I also see, all at once, that it's expedient to continue my ruse.

I need the video. Not just to protect my client.

James Hollings's client needs protection from it too. I have something James will want. He has information about Paul that I want.

I swallow my bile, and my pride. *Yes, that's my boyfriend*, I force myself to nod.

Izzy puts down her phone to stand up and take me by the shoulders.

"Toni, I don't care how much you like this man—look at what's on the screen. You deserve better than him."

She is a bundle of goodness. And I'm about to use that goodness to save my job and give me the leverage I need to help find my brother.

"You are right. So right," I say. "Can you send me that video clip—and convince Brian to delete it from his phone? And delete it from your computer too? And make sure it's wiped out completely, not just sitting in the trash?"

"Yes. Brian has a huge crush on me. He'll do whatever I ask. And I definitely don't want Michelle to be afraid anyone will ever see it. But shouldn't we keep the video to prove he's gross, just in case? Like, as an insurance policy?"

"I need it to confront him myself. It's my relationship."

Izzy sighs. "As long as you promise you won't let him keep behaving like this. It's so sad. Harrison can't be public about who he loves, and you can't love someone who treats women right."

And I'm lying to my sweet cousin to keep her innocent about the real reasons I need that video.

Izzy has nothing behind her eyes other than concern about me. About my heart. No double-dealings. Her biggest secret is the occasional visit from some guy—and she's twenty-one so it's not even an ethically challenging secret. It's a secret of kindness to her old-fashioned father, who just doesn't want to know. Her hands are still on my shoulders. I reach up and cover her hands with mine, squeezing them hard.

Izzy's the one I don't deserve.

———

Evidence found. All sources neutralized. Video attached. File deleted everywhere else.

I text Melanie from my car behind the abandoned silo before I head back into downtown Thebes. I thought long and hard about what to say while I tramped back through the woods from the house, this time trying to navigate the path while wearing a purple pencil skirt. Do I bring up anything about Per's trip to my hometown? About his dinner meeting with my uncle at my childhood home? I decide to rely on my legal training: give exactly the information I've been asked to provide. No more. At least not until I've done all that I can while I'm here to dig up the rest of the story on my own.

Nice work, she texts back.

What is Melanie aware of and what not? Her reply reveals nothing. It's no surprise that Air Trek would be in talks with manufacturing companies around Minnesota. But Per himself at my uncle's house the day he signs the retainer with Grogan? I think back to Melanie's whispered reassurance to Per last night at the party: *she's exactly what you're looking for.* I must confront the very real possibility that I might have been sent on a fool's errand—or worse—by my boss and my client.

This time as I drive down Route 35, it's not memories that flood my thoughts but calculations. It's true that Per Olufsen got himself into a compromising position with a teenaged girl—one that could damage his reputation if there was evidence that could be leaked. It's true that I found the evidence. As his lawyer, I can't reach out to Michelle, but Izzy, who knows her, is ready to provide support. If this was a genuine search-and-destroy mission, I did my job quickly and well. It's barely past 2:00 p.m. and the case I've been assigned is solved. But there's much more going on than my assignment. I can't assume anything here is as it seems. Was I supposed to find the evidence that Per was in Thebes when I scoured his files, or was that an unanticipated outcome of my research? If it was all planted there for me, then by whom? Per or Melanie? If Per had a secret dinner with my uncle on Friday, is it a secret from Melanie or from me?

The man I'm about to confront has information, conveyed to him yesterday by fellow King Family Construction employees who were discussing my client at the Parthenon Diner.

Bashiir Abdi's moral standards may be too high to allow room for any quid pro quo. I know, firsthand, that James Hollings's are not.

———

The lobby of Roberts and Hollings has that office-on-a-Sunday kind of feel: dim, cool, the faint lingering odor of industrial cleaning products from Friday's janitorial service still undisturbed due to forty-eight hours without human stain. The blinds are drawn, adding to the hermetically sealed atmosphere. I perch on a burgundy leather armchair, staring up at the reception desk ordinarily staffed by the one and only Barbie Mitchell. Wouldn't she have a lot to say at her next mommy-and-me gym class or whatever she and her other former cheerleading squad members do with their free time and their babies if she knew I was sitting here right now?

I yank the hem of Izzy's skirt down toward my knees. I want my second first impression to be one of icy control. I'm the one who decides what to offer and when to offer it. He's gaming me right now—he buzzed me into the lobby a full five minutes ago but has yet to emerge from the inner sanctum to escort me in.

Anodyne art hangs on the lobby walls: mauve, blue, and pale green abstract floral prints in plain silver frames. The only personal touches on display are matching headshots of the two partners, one on either side of the long reception desk. Roberts's photo is the same one from years ago; he's in full military regalia with his Korean War service medals pinned to his uniform. Hollings's is more recent, but he has the same empty non-smile smile I remember from his Minnesota state legislature headshot back in the day. He can turn it off as effectively as he turns it on. Is the fire-free James Hollings the one who shows up in the bedroom with his lady's slipper? I shift my position on the chair again. Even though I know his stall tactic is designed to make me antsy, it's making me antsy. Also, the more I think about James in bed the less in control I feel. I close my eyes, breathe myself back to the task at hand. *Information, Toni.* That's the goal. The means to that end is yet to be determined.

"Catching up on lost sleep?"

I open my eyes to see him in the doorway. He's changed his clothes since this morning too. In Christopher's office he wore a suit. Now he's casual, in a T-shirt and jeans. His hair is slightly wet, like he recently showered. Oh, my. He recently showered. I stand up and see him take in my change of clothes as well. I'm the formal one this time. I let him look.

"I have been up since four thirty this morning, when your client so kindly called to summon me here," I say. "I'll admit I'm a little tired."

"Well, we'll have to find you something relaxing to do," he says. "After you finish signing those papers, of course."

Flirtation or invitation? Either way, I find it off-putting. A little too obvious a little too quickly.

I smooth the front of my skirt and pick up my bag.

"We have lots to discuss. And perhaps lots to catch up on. Shall we get started?"

He blinks at my response. I've slowed the pace and he didn't expect it. Did he think I would try to jump him in the lobby and throw us both on top of the reception desk? Okay, based on our history, he probably did. And based on my own tendencies when it comes to sex, I probably would.

James opens his door wider and moves out of the way to usher me in. I'm not above letting my arm brush against his as I pass by. I'm not above walking in front of him, knowing Izzy's skirt is tight and I look good from the back. I do, however, feel a small, surprising pang of weirdness about it.

Everything inside the office is slick and matching. No more Leo Roberts–led Depression-era unbend your used staples and put them back in the stapler mentality. The mauve and burgundy theme from the reception area continues here. Clean, plush carpeting, no threadbare patches. The doors to the offices are burnished glass now—the illusion of transparency but nothing visible from behind them but a shadowy outline of a desk, a lamp. Only the door to the stockroom remains opaque, although it's been replaced with thick plaster painted the same mauve color as the walls, and a large brass door handle equipped with a visibly well-functioning lock. We used to reinforce the old finicky lock by pushing a footstool up against the inside of the door for extra security back in our lunch-hour days.

James comes up next to me.

"Brings back memories, doesn't it?"

Again, that squeamish feeling.

I've fantasized about our days in the stockroom all these years, invoked images of us together during sex with other men to keep things hot for myself—it's my private reel of personal porn. Even this morning, seeing him for the first time brought the images back in the most searing way imaginable. So now that I'm here, in the very place and with the very man who still inhabits my fantasies, why does it all seem so much . . . less? I glance up at him for a gut check—yes, still handsome. Yes, still my type. But that teenaged girl who flew back inside me with a vengeance this morning at my uncle's house to rage and fume doesn't seem to have made it here. That was the girl who found James Hollings to be the most sophisticated, brilliant, powerful, urbane man she'd ever known. The man who inspired her to become a lawyer so she could surpass him. The man who has been in residency in her brain ever since that summer together.

Now Per Olufsen is the most sophisticated, brilliant, powerful, urbane man I've ever known, and the image of him—slovenly, drunk, with his hand down the shirt of a teenaged girl in my childhood home—casts a different light on everything. On my younger self.

James Hollings hasn't changed. The eyes I see him through have.

I cross my arms and turn away from the stockroom to face him.

"Are you ready?" He's holding the same manila folder that he tried to give me earlier.

"James. I'm not here to sign the document," I say. "And I know this might come as a shock to you, but I'm not here to revisit our past. It's a shock to me, in all honesty." At least he looks disappointed. But I'm not about to change course now.

"I have something I need to show you," I continue. "I'd like your promise that you'll tell me exactly what I'm seeing and why I'm seeing it."

He runs his hand through his hair. He doesn't have a read on me right now and he's not pleased. But he nods.

I pull my phone out of my bag. The still from the video Izzy sent me glows to light. I turn the screen in his direction. And wait.

His jaw tightens just a bit. He's thinking. I watch him take it all in, watch his calculations about what he'll say, what I might want.

How many pictures of pretty girls have altered the trajectory of a person's life? When I saw that photo of Denise Hollings in the local paper nearly a decade ago, I viewed it with the detachment I recognize in James right now. I chose not to see a person, but instead a representation of everything I feared and loathed as a sixteen-year-old girl. She was the epitome of female success in the minuscule realm in which I lived and the symbol of how meaningless and powerless female success, even if you achieved it, would always be. A state flower. I didn't want to see a human being. I just wanted to keep James. And hold on to the tiny bit of power I'd found for the first time in my life.

My heart hurts as I send a silent apology for the girl I was in Denise's direction.

"Let's sit down," James says, gesturing to the small mahogany conference table in the center of the room. "I'll answer any questions you have. It's only fair."

The one thing he's always been to me is fair. No pretense—when we were having sex it was about having sex. Now I can see he's made a decision that I'll get the real thing I've come for today: the truth. At least the truth about this.

Sitting across the table from me in his white T-shirt, James looks younger than he did this morning when he was all suited up and businesslike on behalf of my uncle. I could be talking to a friend, a peer. It's a funny element of time that while the number of years in age between us remains fixed forever, the meaning of that difference shrinks as we all move forward. We really are talking lawyer to lawyer; it's not just a gambit anymore. He looks directly at me, no flirting, no double entendres. My phone with that image sits face up on the table between us.

I begin.

"I assume you know that the man in this picture is a client with my firm."

He nods.

"Okay. So why don't you start by telling me how he ended up at my uncle's house for dinner on Friday. I know you won't insult me by pretending this is a coincidence."

The manila folder rests on the table in front of him. He drums his long fingers atop it, a gesture I recognize from years past. His mind is turning over possible replies before he chooses a direction.

"Everyone knows about Per Olufsen's business interests in Minnesota," he says at last. "There's natural alignment between King Construction and Air Trek."

"Uh-huh."

He drums his fingers again. Once, twice, three times.

"I've been a member of the state assembly for five years. We're only paid for the two months a year we're in session, and not well."

Okay . . . where is he going with this? Now he picks up the fountain pen he brought to the table and twirls it in his left hand, like he did in my uncle's office this morning.

"Roberts and Hollings had no conflict of interest as the firm representing your uncle's public dealings. It would have been negligent of me as this district's representative if I didn't try to bring Air Trek's business to Thebes. Public-private collaboration is the only way to effectively lift the region's economic prospects."

I will not roll my eyes. I will not jump in and yell at him for crafting this image of himself as a selfless, devoted public servant instead of directly answering my questions.

"Olufsen has been on my radar for the past year," he says. "Winning a hub for Air Trek in Minneapolis required some legislative jujitsu to get our approvals in before Chicago or Cleveland or Indianapolis nabbed it. The assembly fast-tracked a few proposals and helped make the match. A couple of weeks ago when his secretary reached out to me here in Thebes, I thought it was probably a pro forma thank-you, making nice with the state government hacks—our session ended in May and we don't reconvene in person till October, so the call was forwarded from St. Paul. When it turned out to be about a business opportunity for my district that Olufsen himself wanted to discuss with me personally, I got pretty excited. Understandably. You know Thebes, Toni. How many international corporations come to us like that?"

None. Ever. Which is why this is suspicious. He knows that. This isn't just James telling me the information I've come for. He's building a case.

"Per began to describe his idea," he continues. "He wanted a centralized manufacturing plant, parts for his planes, the space that our area has to offer. I'm on the phone, taking notes about the environmental regulations he'll need to offset, the real estate I think might be available, crunching some initial numbers. Numbers in the tens of millions. It's insane."

It is insane for a place like Thebes. I can imagine his wildfire thoughts about the future of this place with the infusion of capital that Per might bring.

"When Olufsen paused, I shared some of my thoughts. When I came to the part about what it might take to start a manufacturing business

from the ground up around here, he stopped me. 'I'd like to buy an exist-
ing entity. Work with someone who already knows the ropes, has the per-
mits and licenses and relationships. I hear from a new lawyer on my team
that there's an established company in your jurisdiction—King Family
Construction?'"

Your secrets are safe with me, Per said, as springtime rain pinged
against the windows of the Minneapolis Four Seasons.

"What day was this phone call?" I ask. "Do you remember?"

"Yes, it was Tuesday afternoon, June 10, around four. I remember
specifically because we had a freakish storm that day. It was raining, and
suddenly it turned to hail. Golf balls."

When we met at the hotel, I wasn't his lawyer. My coffee with Per was
part of the finalist interview process; he hadn't yet selected us as his firm.
At least as far as I knew.

"He told you about me?"

"Not in so many words. But who else could it have been?"

Per jumped on the information he got from me to make a play for my
uncle's company. Is that part of why Melanie has me on this nauseating
cover-up?

I lean forward, closer to James. "Why would you think I encouraged
him to buy the company? You of all people know I would never spend my
time putting more money into my uncle's pockets."

He shrugs. "Maybe you knew Olufsen was looking for a takeover
opportunity and saw yourself as part of the deal? Help Olufsen get it
for a song, avenge your childhood anguish. Or I figured you might be
throwing me this opportunity because of our . . . history." He flashes me
a loaded look.

I ignore it. "I didn't know he reached out to you. I've been unaware of
any connection until today."

"I've learned that since," he says. "When he called, I wasn't your uncle's lawyer of record. Leo technically still held that position. Christopher was waiting for you come back to the fold. So, when Olufsen talked about the lawyer on his team—who could only be you—I had to keep the secret that you'd made a professional decision Christopher was still unaware of. Toni, you should have heard him go on about how excited he was that you'd be joining the business. About your Harvard Law degree. He was devastated when you didn't come home."

Christopher was devastated when Paul left. I saw it, felt it. But me? Nothing I did when I was still living at home was enough for my uncle's approval. James is trying to twist my heart back to the King camp.

"Why are you shaming me for staying away? Isn't it in your best interest—on every level—if I do? Stop with the setup. What do you want?"

That glint. He admires me for calling him out now. He nods.

"I want the money that a big deal with Air Trek would bring. Because—and this is still confidential—I want to run for national office in 2016. Congress, Toni. The House of Representatives. Can't you see it?"

His green eyes are alight with ambition, excitement. I can read it to perfection—after all, Washington is my ambition too.

"I envisioned everything coming together for me," he continues. "Income to support my family and access to resources to run a statewide campaign through the backing of a man like Per Olufsen. When I heard you were on his legal team, I joined your uncle's. His personal team, not just his public business. I could get what I wanted through working on the King family side of an Air Trek deal. And keep it separate from my role in the assembly."

It makes sense: Hollings sees Per as his ticket beyond Minnesota.

"I started pitching Christopher on the idea and pitching him hard. He could see the upside—all that money, who wouldn't be interested—but he didn't want to sell to an outsider. I promised him I'd get something inked that would ensure your family could run everything on the ground, employment in perpetuity for your cousin Harrison and everyone working for him in Thebes. But there was one sticking point, one issue he just couldn't get over."

I know before he says it. Christopher's baby, ten years in the planning. His vision for Thebes, for transforming it into a retail center of his own making.

"The Big Dig."

He nods. "The Big Dig. Air Trek Industries won't support the project. It will be outdated in three years, Olufsen's people argued. We can't pour resources into brick-and-mortar stores when we need to build a business of the future. I believe they're right. As your uncle's attorney I'll stand behind his business decisions, but it's a dying model. I keep trying to convince him. He won't listen.

"Olufsen was ready to scrap the whole relationship. He can go anywhere he wants with his money. He doesn't need trouble. But I begged him to give it one last shot. I told him I thought if he and your uncle sat down together, broke bread, made a connection, it would change everything. He agreed, one last shot, given how close we were to a deal. And he likes you, Toni, and liked the idea of building a Minnesota family connection for Air Trek's subsidiaries here. Said it works well for him in European hubs. He's secretive though; he didn't want any media pickup in case the deal fell through, so we agreed to keep the face-to-face off the record. As I'm sure you've learned, he likes his public image to be fully under his control. So I arranged for a car to pick him up and bring him to Thebes off the record. And your uncle was too proud to invite Olufsen himself—I had to surprise him and let the man's charm and savvy work its own magic. I bought a spectacular bottle of scotch to help the surprise go down more smoothly."

"I take it the dinner didn't go so well."

"It went incredibly well. They hit it off just as I suspected they would.

The scotch didn't hurt. Neither did the case of Burgundy that Olufsen brought as a gift. Toni, we were minutes from a compromise—the room stank of the money we were all about to make. Everyone was drunk and delighted with each other and your uncle was almost ready to shake on a deal to postpone the Big Dig for eighteen months. It would have satisfied everyone, and I know by then he'd be willing to give it up—when your brother burst into the room."

Paul! Not what I expected to hear. My heart starts beating at twice its usual rate. But I keep steady.

"His eyes were red, he was agitated. Really upset," James continues. "He walked right up to your uncle. Got in his face and screamed 'you're a monster.'"

"That doesn't sound like my brother," I say. Paul is the philosopher between the two of us. I'm the hothead, the yeller. His activism is in the Gandhian vein, all pacifist and impoverished. He always refuses to get angry—in fact, he gets calmer and calmer the more I thrash around.

"He was out of control. Your uncle stood up and said, 'If this is about you and those renters in town again, I'm done hearing about it. Get off my property.' Your brother said, 'You know what this is about. You know what you did.' Then Christopher hit a buzzer under the table and told us he'd called his security team to have your brother removed. I got Per out of there before I could find out what happened next."

My brother. My client. I believed they were separate. Instead, they've smashed into each other with the force of a storm front.

Don't show your feelings. Don't let him stop talking. Silence is a good lawyer's greatest weapon.

I remain still.

"At this point I was desperate to save the deal," James continues. "We were both three sheets to the wind. I suggested we call it a night, no one saw him come and no one would see him go if his car service pulled up to the back of the house. That's the place where your uncle hasn't installed cameras."

"Yes, I know." I'll leave it at that.

"I called Per's car with instructions, pointed him to the back door, and left out the front so everything would be consistent when security came, and I'd be the one on camera if they needed any information. I thought I still had a shot at bringing the deal home."

I imagine the scene: Hollings leaves Per alone to wander on the back patio until his car came. Drunk, most likely annoyed at having wasted his time. And there right in front of him is a beautiful girl, glowing under the staged lighting Izzy rigged.

But Michelle was glowing for herself, not for him. She wanted to star in a GIF that would go viral and set the internet, and her life, on fire. Did he see that? No, he saw some object. A ripe piece of fruit ready to pick. We all treat Per like a god, dazzled by his money, his power. No wonder he acts like he can have anything he wants. James and I dance around him with brooms and dustpans, ready to sweep up his garbage in case we find a few gold coins amid the trash. And we both learned our dirty tricks by dancing around my uncle, the small-town Per, hurling his own lightning bolts hither and yon. I ran away from him; Hollings ran to him. Either way, it was all, always, about Christopher King.

I swallow. Force myself back to the moment.

"James, is there anything else you remember about the evening. Anything at all? About Per or about my brother?"

He pauses, thinking.

"Actually, yes. I recall Paul yelling something else. He said to your uncle: 'You've been lying to us the whole time.' I didn't understand what he meant. I wanted to get Per out of the house, so I didn't stick around to find out."

Us. Paul said *us*.

There is only one *us* in the context of Uncle Christopher's *you* when it comes to Paul—and there's no way that James Hollings would know what it meant.

My brother was talking about me and him.

Lying to us about what? What did Paul learn that forced him to confront Christopher with such venom and fury?

I grab James by the hand from across the table. I sense that my own hands have gone ice cold. He feels it too and his eyes widen.

"Where is my brother?" I can't keep the fear from my voice now. "What is my uncle trying to get me to sign, for real? Tell me the truth!"

I've surprised him. But he doesn't let go of my hand.

"Toni, I told you these papers merely state that Paul is acting on his own, that the rest of the King family supports the Big Dig. Signing them ensures that none of you will make statements to the media."

I feel from his grip, see in his eyes, that he doesn't know. Christopher is keeping whatever Paul learned a secret from Hollings.

This scares me even more.

My uncle is domineering, yes. Overbearing, for sure. But Paul had separated himself from all of that, and what it meant for our childhood, years ago. So if Christopher hadn't pulled any dirty tricks about the Somali neighborhood, what lie could make my brother furious enough to confront him like that?

"Something's wrong," I say, as much to myself as to James.

"What are you talking about?"

What is my uncle hiding? And what does it have to do with me and Paul? I'm frozen in place, a mass of half memories, half nightmares. What's real? What's a myth?

You were Andela, my brother whispered. *And I was Mujo.*

My phone lights up with an incoming call.

Melanie Dwyer.

I pull my hand away from James.

"It's my boss. I need to take this." James steps into another office to give me privacy.

I pick up the phone. Autopilot.

"Melanie." My voice makes the right kind of sound, the sound of a confident first-year associate who just delivered the goods for her supervisor. "I'm wrapping up a couple of things for family and I'm heading back soon. Anything else you need today?"

"We have a problem. A serious problem."

"What can I do?"

"Toni. The problem is you."

Wait. This must be a mistake.

"I got a call from IT. A security alert came to them earlier today—an external server appears to have obtained access to highly confidential files belonging to our client, Air Trek Industries, and downloaded copies of these files illegally."

No. Oh, no.

"Even worse, when our people traced the address, they found it belonged to another law firm: a Roberts, Hollings and Associates in a town called Thebes. I assume that the name of this firm is ringing some bells for you."

"Melanie, it's a misunderstanding."

"A level-two security code appears to have been used by this firm to steal our client's files. Guess who tech told me was issued that code, just this very morning?"

"I can explain. There's no Wi-Fi here, it's like the middle of nowhere, and I couldn't get a signal—I was in the car, not even in the building, but I remembered their password! I swear, everything is only on my laptop, nothing is on the firm's computers. They have no idea I even used their internet. I promise you it's harmless."

"Well, that's an interesting interpretation of what happened—and one that I might even be willing to entertain if it wasn't for a parallel set of circumstances. A quick search of Roberts, Hollings reveals that their largest client is one Christopher King, and his company, King Family Construction. Any relation?"

Any relation to Christopher King. The same question that doomed me when James asked it almost a decade ago.

"No. I mean yes—yes he's my uncle, but . . ."

"So now you know that Per was in negotiations with his company. When I upped you to level-two security, I neglected to realize how much information would download from our files. That's my error. I wanted to keep you out of that piece of the business to avoid any conflict of interest. Before Per began talks, he had us research whether you were a named beneficiary of the company. Turns out you are not, so I gave him the go-ahead."

Christopher must have stripped me from the paperwork within minutes of learning I wasn't coming back.

"Melanie, I promise, this isn't what you think."

"What do I think, Toni? You seem to believe that you know better than I do what I'm thinking. So, you must know that right now, I'm thinking about all the violations of confidentiality you've committed. I'm thinking about how much your family must have to benefit by gaining access to Per Olufsen's financial records during a negotiation. What would you have done next if you were me, Toni, since you're so very skilled at knowing what I think?"

My eyes are closed, I'm sitting at the conference table with my head in my hands, pressing the phone into my ear with my shoulder so hard that pain rattles my neck. "I would have alerted the client," I say in a whisper.

"Excellent! You have a well-trained legal mind. Fine instincts. Raw, of course, but you're young. If you listen to your mentors and supervisors and let them guide you, you have a promising career ahead of you."

"I'm sorry. I'm so sorry. I'll do whatever it takes—"

She cuts me off. "I indeed alerted the client. And since you're so good at guessing games, let's play another one. Guess what he said?"

"I—"

"Oh, never mind, this game has grown tiresome. I'll just tell you. He said that in the middle of a business negotiation with your uncle, things got a little tricky. He was thinking about pulling out. But your uncle's lawyer, James Hollings, convinced him to keep going. The very same Hollings who appears to have benefitted from your level-two security access. A Minnesota state representative, no less! Stealing files for his client and enlisting his client's niece to do his dirty work. *Quel scandale*! This could bring a career to its knees."

"James didn't do anything! It was all me, my stupidity. Please don't pin this on him."

"Is this your confession, Toni? Your mea culpa? Are you ready to admit you've been playing me as well as illegally betraying your client? Do you know how many of your law school classmates applied for your job? But I turned them down in favor of you. I'm under a microscope here that you can't even fathom. Your hire is a reflection on me. If a man fails, it's still regarded as a failure of one man. If I fail . . ."

"You're my idol," I say. I'm not even pleading my case anymore. I just want her to know the truth. "I look at you and see who I want to become."

"Well, lucky for you, you still have a chance. You won't be disbarred, and we won't be filing charges against you. Although what you've done could warrant both."

"Thank you," I say, utterly wrecked.

"Don't thank me. I'm ready to throw the book at you. It's Per who insisted we not take it any further. I guess we all know he has a soft spot for an attractive girl."

I'm disgusted, both with myself and by Melanie's dismissal of me as one of Per's "girls," but now is not the moment.

"You won't regret it. I promise I can make it up to you, Melanie. Whatever I need to do—"

"Stop right there. We're not pressing charges but make no mistake: Antonia King—you're fired."

————

James peeks out of his office. "Are you okay?"

My call ended I don't even know how long ago. Minutes? Hours? Either way, I'm still sitting where he left me, staring at the phone in my hand.

"How much did you hear?"

"Enough to assume you no longer have a job." He slowly comes toward me. Gingerly, as if he's afraid I'm about to run, or leap at him, claws bared. He needn't worry. I'm numb, frozen in my chair. When nothing alarming happens, he pulls out the chair opposite me and sits down.

"I'm sorry. And maybe it's too soon to say this, but . . . what if getting fired turns out to be the best thing that's ever happened to you?"

Ugh. The worst cliché imaginable.

"I have a proposal," he says. "Come work for me."

That snaps me out of my fog. Not in a good way.

"For Christopher?"

You've been lying to us the whole time.

"No. Not at Roberts and Hollings. Why don't you join my campaign? Work on behalf of my 2016 run for Congress."

I put down my phone, fold my hands on the table.

He takes my silence as an opportunity to go on.

"Think about it. The timing is perfect. We have two and a half years to build momentum with fundraising and grassroots organizing. I have all the statewide contacts we need. You can set up my campaign office in Athens. You're a millennial and a woman. Two demographics critical for me if I want to win."

"I'm not a Republican."

"Even better. You'll help bring the swing vote." He's excited now, pressing his hands on the table. His green eyes light up. "When I win, I'll hire you as a legislative aide. You'll be in Washington, DC. You can have more influence there than anywhere else in the world."

The chance I've wanted. What Melanie promised she'd help me find down the road.

"I won't agree with all of your policy positions."

"But you'll agree with some of them. Imagine your future. With this kind of experience under your belt, you could run for office yourself in ten years. Or become a lobbyist. Start your own firm anywhere in the country."

I imagine myself overseeing a campaign office, phones ringing like crazy, running to be the first to see the latest poll numbers scroll across the television screen.

"What makes you so sure you'll win?" I ask. "You just said that you need Per Olufsen's backing. After that dinner, how do you know you'll have him?"

"Because we can get him together."

"I've been fired from his legal team. I don't have any influence with Per anymore."

James points to my phone.

"You do."

The video.

"Oh, no," I say. "First of all, I obtained that video while acting as Per's attorney, so you know it's classified even if I'm not his lawyer anymore. I barely just escaped disbarment for—never mind, it's not important—but Per's the one who saved my ass, and if I use this against him, I'll guarantee you he won't save it again. And second of all . . . this is blackmail! Seriously? Not my style. Is it really yours?"

"Not blackmail. Insurance. I hint just enough, he knows it's out there, it never needs to be seen or spoken of again. There's no reason Olufsen needs to know it came from you. I was there Friday night when Isobel staged that party. I could have asked her for it myself as her family's lawyer, just protecting their interests when I saw them serving alcohol, in case there were any minors. And look what I found!"

"Wait a minute. I didn't say Izzy was involved. And you said you didn't know how Per found the party."

He's silent.

"Did you set him up?"

His jaw tightens again like it did when I first showed him the image. "I did not set him up. But I did notice the kids on the patio. The girl taking pictures of herself. The videographer. Isobel on a ladder adjusting the lights."

"And Per was shit-faced, and you did what? Plant a thought in his head about how the evening could be salvaged? Tell him you were sure that hot girl was at least eighteen because she was a friend of Izzy's? What else? Did you stuff a bunch of condoms in his pocket and tell him to have fun and be careful out there?"

"Don't be so melodramatic."

"But you did see an opportunity and decide to put Per Olufsen in the way of said opportunity."

Our hands fold across our chests in mirror image of each other.

"Per's actions are his own," James says. "I didn't force him to touch that girl."

"But you didn't warn him that she was a minor, either. Though you knew."

"Per Olufsen is not my client."

"So your omission wasn't a legal breach. Isn't it an ethical one?"

"He's an adult."

"But Michelle is not! What about her? Did you even for one second think that you were maneuvering an explosive situation that could impact the life of a sixteen-year-old girl?"

"You're not talking about Michelle anymore, are you?"

This stops me.

Those eyes—I still feel it when he looks at me, even in this moment.

"I . . . actually, I don't know," I say. My voice is quiet now.

The air thickens around us, between us.

He clears his throat.

"When you think back, is that what you remember?" he asks, his voice lowering to match mine. "A pure young girl and a lecherous man?"

The empty office expands. I see myself, my intern self: thrashing, lonely, filled with need I couldn't name. And I trained all that insatiability, all that longing on him. Continents of want. Nothing he could satisfy.

"I researched the age of consent before we ever started anything," I say. "And I chose to keep going, even after I learned that you were engaged. That was my decision, James, not yours. It was probably a stupid choice, but I made it. If this video gets out, Michelle won't have the option to make any choices of her own at all."

James is quiet for another moment. He keeps his arms crossed. This time when he speaks, he looks down.

"When I met you, I thought to myself, *Here's my fling before I propose.* It's idiotic, I know. But in my own mind, somehow, I was still single. I just . . . I never thought I would like you so much, Toni. It's no excuse, but I just shut my eyes and kept going, much longer than I should have. I didn't want to stop."

Finally. After all these years of silence, years of avoiding downtown Thebes, and my secret drunk internet stalking, and messing around with meaningless guys. James has finally said the one thing he never said before. I was angry and inexperienced. He was in denial about his impending marriage. But what we had, at least back then, mattered.

Despite the sting of my lost job, I feel a small beam of something emanate from my chest. It's relief.

"It was both of us, James," I say. "I didn't want to stop either."

He nods. Smiles just a bit. "You were too young for me."

He's right. I was.

"But, Toni, does it have to keep us from combining forces now? I
mean it when I say you'd be a brilliant campaign strategist. Nothing
to do with our past other than I know your mind. I know what you're
capable of achieving." Just like that, his eyes reflect his ambition once
more.

This is your uncle's lawyer, I remind myself. *Be careful.* Is he so far on
the inside now that he'll even use his former feelings for me to get what
he wants? Where is the manipulation and where is the truth? I'm looking
and looking, and I still can't tell.

Did he always think like an operative, and at sixteen, I simply couldn't
see it?

He uncrosses his arms and leans forward. "Let me open this door for
you. All you have to do is walk through it and any career you can dream
of having will be on the other side."

I reach for my phone, still sitting on the table between us.

"Not this way," I say, waving the image in his direction.

If I allow James to use even the implied existence of a video of
Michelle to hold over Per, I'll be colluding with him in a risky game I'm
not sure I'm prepared to handle. The same kind of game I was drawn into
at Grogan. Just what my brother warned me to stay away from.

I stand up. But before I can leave, James puts his hand on my arm.

"The offer's still good," he says. "All you've done today is prove to me
what a great team we make. Give it some thought. And, Toni—don't

screw yourself over because of something we'll never have to use. Michelle will stay safe because we'll be the only ones with this video. Don't let abstract principles ruin your shot. Hanging on to that video is nothing but how the sausage is made."

I hesitate. Even Izzy wanted to keep the video as insurance. Am I being too extreme? Is James making a certain kind of sense?

"How do I know if I give you a copy that you won't use it against me one day? Ruin my career by proving that I stole confidential information from a client while I was his attorney? Maybe I'll be running against you in some close election, and you'll see this as the only way to take me down. How can I trust you?"

James takes his phone out of his pocket and taps on it. Then he turns it around.

A photo of his own. A Christmas tree all lit up, so heavy with ornaments that its needles are barely visible. Torn piles of wrapping paper. An old-fashioned sled, a basketball, a giant teddy bear with a red ribbon around its neck. Denise, wearing a ruffled green bathrobe, sits on the floor with a baby in her lap, smiling at a toddler in red pajamas raising two fistfuls of candy canes in the air.

"James Jr. is the older one," he says. "We call him J.J. He's almost four now. He'll start preschool in the fall. And our little guy, Leo, just turned two. This is from Leo's first Christmas."

Leo, after Leo Roberts, his partner and my first boss. Somehow, that detail above all goes right to my heart.

"If I ever turn on you, Toni, you could come back and turn on me. This is what I have at stake: more than a career. My boys will never look up to me again if they learn that while their mother was picking out china patterns, their father was . . ."

I put my hand out to stop him. This feels like torment, not reassurance. "Enough."

He takes the phone back.

"We know each other's secrets, Toni. I'll keep yours because I need you to keep mine."

———

Back outside under the hot midafternoon sun, I pace the sidewalk. On the one hand, James has given me a way out. A change of plans, I can tell everyone. An opportunity I couldn't pass up to work on a congressional campaign took me off the corporate track and onto the political track. On the other hand, I would be drawn back into the underbelly of this place, the very place that sent me screaming. Even in Washington, how far away could I run from Thebes if the congressman I work for must answer to these people at the voting booth? And what would our professional alliance be based upon? A handshake across time and space set into motion by sex. Kept private through fear. The threat of mutually assured destruction.

But wait a minute. I still don't know where my brother is. If I go back inside and say yes, right now, maybe I can convince James to get me access to confidential information from my uncle. I'll find an excuse to get into the Roberts and Hollings account system. After all, I still know the password . . .

I stop.

No.

Every choice I've made since my phone boomed with the sound of Darth Vader's theme song this morning has been disastrous. I left Minneapolis on top of the world. Now that world is gone.

Thebes didn't bring my life to its knees. I did.

I can't work for Hollings.

James and I might each have an image to flash at each other on our phones. But now, given the origins of the video, I would have to make new decisions, different decisions with different values, if I were to go down this path, whereas he stays exactly in the same place, continuing the decisions he's already made, the path he's already paved.

I have to find my brother. But I can't do it through James Hollings.

My phone vibrates with another call. It's Izzy.

"Toni, thank God you picked up. I'm so sorry!"

"What's wrong?"

She's sobbing. "Please forgive me. It's not what I thought would happen. I was just so worried about you when you left. What if you got into trouble with that guy you're seeing when you confronted him about Michelle? What if you needed backup?"

"Slow down. What are you trying to say?"

"I went to Daddy. I thought he could help because he knows your boyfriend. I told him you came to the house, and that I was scared you were going to find him, and you were alone . . . He said he had a way to stop you from doing anything you shouldn't. To stop you from making the same mistake as Paul."

"What mistake?"

Another sob. "He said he was doing it for your safety. For your own best interests."

"Doing what, Izzy? Doing what?"

"Antonia King?"

I whirl around to see a uniformed Thebes police officer standing before me. Older than Hansen, someone I don't recognize. His car, lights flashing, idles on the street behind us.

"Yes?"

"You're under arrest."

This can't be happening. Melanie promised it wouldn't. Could James have already double-crossed me somehow? Called Per and convinced him I was a snake?

"Officer, I think this is a misunderstanding, if you call Melanie Dwyer in Minneapolis . . ."

"You're under arrest for breaking and entering the home of Christopher King. I need both of your hands in full view."

"I'm sorry, Toni, I'm so sorry." Izzy's weeping is the last thing I hear before the policeman takes my phone and my bag and leads me to the back of his car.

PART III

Late Afternoon

BASHIIR STARES FROM HIS COT AS HANSEN ESCORTS ME, in handcuffs, to the area in front of the holding cell. I can't bring myself to meet his gaze.

"If you asked me to bet on the odds of seeing you back here today," Hansen says into my ear, "I'd have said: really high." He's so close I can smell the chemical stink of Fritos on his breath. "You had that rich-girl uppity attitude, like you were above me. Who's above you now, huh?"

I cringe at his disgusting innuendoes. But I'm too weary to reply.

"Now you two criminals have given me a big problem to solve," he sighs. "On top of the rest of my work. I only got one holding cell here and I can't put boys and girls together. Normally we'd ship one of you over to Athens but it's Sunday. Almost five o'clock. That's the end of my shift. Can't start the paperwork now, I won't have time before clocking out."

I feel him let go of my cuffed wrists with one of his meaty hands and hear the jingle of his key ring as he unclips it from his belt.

"What am I gonna do with you?" he mutters. "It's turning into a freakin' crime spree. I should get time and a half."

"Don't be concerned, Officer." Bashiir's voice is low and calm. "I will maintain respect for the rules and for the young woman."

Hansen is still, contemplating his options. From the sound of their interaction, I get the sense that this isn't the first of our jailor's "problems" that Bashiir has handled since they brought him in last night. He has the practiced tone of a parent negotiating bedtime with his toddler.

No surprise, convenience wins the day. Hansen turns the key in my handcuffs, removing the metal rings brusquely so they scrape across my skin. I shake out my wrists, rub each one in turn as he unlocks the door to the holding cell and gestures me to the cot on the wall across from where Bashiir sits. I climb onto the bare mattress, lie down facing the wall, and curl into a fetal position, yanking Izzy's skirt as far over my knees as it can go.

"I'll be watching you over the monitor." Hansen puts on his best man-in-charge voice, despite just taking what amounts to orders from one of his inmates. "Don't try any funny business."

"If you are watching," says Bashiir, "then you can come back and escort Ms. King to a restroom should she indicate that she needs to use the facilities. I'm sure you would agree that we can't risk the impropriety that might result from sharing this commode. If that's viewed by anyone else through the tapes on the monitor, it could give the wrong impression. About how properly you've administered the rules."

Even in my position facing the wall, I feel a wave of admiration for Bashiir. He has quietly and masterfully allowed me one less humiliation in this most humiliating of situations. And reminded me again that he knows how to access footage from these security cameras. No wonder he's willing to wait out his time until the thirty-six-hour rule expires. Any abuse, any civil rights violation, will be on a hard drive somewhere that he knows how to access. Because he wrote the code.

"Rich girl!" Officer Hansen yells at me. I force myself to open my eyes, lift myself up on an elbow.

"Raise your hand and look into that camera if you need to use the . . . you know what." He's Thebesian through and through: he might denigrate and belittle me, but he's too embarrassed to use a scary word like *bathroom* with a woman.

I turn back to the wall. A strip of little bubbles in the painted concrete greets me at eye level. I focus my attention on them, trying to block out the clang of the iron bars and the turn of the key.

I can't. My head reverberates with the raw screeching sound of metal slamming into metal. The green bubbles on the wall bloat, like I'm looking at them through a fishbowl. What's happening? My chest is tight, I can't breathe.

The echo. The sound of bombs exploding in the streets of Sarajevo. The line between then and now has bled away. I blink, try to retrain my eyes on the paint bubbles, but they blur and re-form into the crisscross pattern of rusted bedsprings. The sleeve, the wrist . . . my mother, my majka.

I see it with a clarity like never before, as if it's happening here.

Her dress isn't just brown, it's decorated at the collar with pink and red and blue flowers that I view up close when she holds me in one arm while stirring a pot of cabbage on the stove with the other. The flowers are ripped away from me when the first blast from the street shakes the apartment. She thrusts me into my brother's arms and screams at us to get down, get down on the floor! We are all there together, all three of us, Mujo holding me and our majka covering us both, while dust blasts through the apartment windows and glass rains down around us.

"Mujo, Andela, hajmo pjevati. Let's sing. All together, come now! The old-time song about Mujo and his horse, the one you love, my own Mujo." She starts, loudly, trying to fight against the boom of cracking concrete outside us, all around:

Mujo kuje konja po mjesecu,
Mujo kuje, a majka ga kune

Mujo is shoeing his horse by the moonlight
while his mother scolds him

My brother's high voice joins her. She's singing louder now, and fast.
I hear my own small voice humming, I know a few of the words too. Another blast from outside, closer now. I shriek.

"Keep singing, Andela, let's sing the bad storm away," Majka says.

Sine Mujo, živ ti bio majci,
Ne kuju se konji po mjesecu,
Već po danu i žarkome suncu!

Mujo, have a care for your poor mother,
Don't shoe your horse by moonlight,
but when it's day and in the hot sun!

We sing to each other in a three-person huddle, our mother almost
yelling the lyrics when the *boom-boom* from all around us rises in pitch
and frequency.

Then it's only our voices. The blasting is gone. The glass and dust stop
dancing around us. Majka says "shush," holds up her finger. Her body
softens over ours.

We've done it: we've outsung the wild storm.

Majka moves away. She leans on her side and looks back at the two of
us, hugging each other still. She smiles.

"My good little children," she says. "Dobra moja djeco—"

The loudest blast of all slams right into the room. Everything is flying bits of tile and glass. My brother's arms tighten around me, he rolls
us away under the cot, shoves me with him below the bedsprings, covers
my ears.

"Let's sing again, Andela," he says. "Just like Majka. Come on." His voice this time is muffled by his hands, but clear:

> *Ja ne gledam sunca nit' mjeseca,*
> *Nit' moj đogo mraka nit' oblaka,*
> *Nit' moj đogo Drine vode hladne.*

> I see neither sun nor moon,
> And my horse ignores darkness and clouds,
> And the cold water of the river Drina.

Where is her voice? Why can't I hear her? I push his hands away and call "Majka? Majka!!" The booming noise is gone, the swirling dust settles around us on the floor.

Then a new sound: the rattle of our doorknob. Insistent, hard. A crash as the door slams open into the room, the clomp of heavy, running feet. Mujo covers my mouth. I turn my head. I see the hand. I see the sleeve. A giant boot steps between me and my majka, then another, and another. A blond, bearded man with startling blue eyes looks down at us . . .

"TONI! ARE YOU OKAY?" BASHIIR'S VOICE CALLS FROM across the cell.

My face is wet with tears. I'm sobbing, my chest heaving up and down.

Everything I've tried, everything I thought would work, has failed. Law school. Corporate job. Antonia King, attorney-at-law: this was my assurance that I'd always be the one either putting someone behind bars or freeing them from captivity. I've lost her. I don't even have Toni King, angry and rebellious high school student, to hide behind anymore. Only Andela remains.

"Try to breathe," Bashiir says. "I can't come over, he'll see me on the camera. Here, listen to me, listen to my voice."

The walls are pulsing, coming closer; he sounds like he's a thousand miles away. My sobs become rasps. I'm clawing for oxygen.

"What are you feeling?" his voice is faint in my ears. "Speak to me."

"I . . . I feel like my heart is exploding," I manage to say between gasps.

"You're having a panic attack. My sister used to have them. You have to try to get more air. Put your hand on your chest and breathe into your palm."

I do as he says. Lying on my back, I focus on the feel of my hand pressing against the rapid-fire beating of my out-of-control heart. The ceiling is high, at least—looking up helps quell the sensation that the walls are closing in around me.

"Let's calm you down," he says. "You were humming just now, before you got upset. Was that a memory?"

I nod.

"Can you tell me?"

Tell him what? That the sound of my mother's voice, just before she was blown to bits, has returned to me after twenty years through my brother's favorite childhood song?

I haven't cried in front of anyone but Paul since we landed on U.S. soil.

"Toni, trying to speak will help you breathe," he says. "Just inhale, then say anything, anything at all, on the exhale."

I press my hand harder against my chest. I'm here, it reminds me. I take a ragged breath in. When I breathe out, I say, "What . . . what would . . . what would your sister do?"

"For her panic attacks?" His voice is back in the room again, just as steady and calm as it was when I first arrived. "Sometimes she would sing herself a lullaby called 'Dhammow' from our past that we loved. It means 'Oh, Perfect Child.' That's why I asked what you were humming. But I think that was a mistake."

I turn my head toward him. He's sitting with his back against the wall, hugging his knees. His eyes are filled with concern. For me. I feel the pounding against my rib cage start to ease off.

"Sing it?" I ask.

"'Dhammow'?" He shakes his head. "Toni, I have the world's most terrible voice. You will definitely have another panic attack just from listening to me sing."

He makes me smile, just a little.

"Okay, that's better," he says, smiling back. "My sister has two children now and she sings it to them. They're growing up in Nairobi, and that song helps keep our childhood, the happy parts, in their lives too."

"You miss them."

"Of course. But everyone is alive and safe and healthy. I'll see them again. My nieces are eight and ten. We video-chat a lot." He touches the two braided string bracelets he wears on his left wrist. "They made me these for my birthday this year."

I can sit up now. I lean my back against the wall on my side as Bashiir has on his. I can't pull my knees up like his without Izzy's skirt hitching all the way up my thighs, so I dangle my legs over the edge of the metal cot. My feet graze the floor. I swing my legs back and forth, listening to the sound that the rubber of my flip-flops makes as they scrape the colorless linoleum.

Bashiir's quiet, his ease in our shared presence, begins to fill the room with something warm, a small but growing light. He makes me feel something no one else has since I set foot back in this town: safe. I take a deep breath, relieved to have the ability to do so again. Also thanks to him.

He's rolling his right hand over the third bracelet he wears on his left wrist, the one strung with black stones, worrying the beads between his fingers.

"Is that from your nieces too?"

A dark look crosses his face. He's struggling with something, some emotion I can't read. He looks at the bracelet, then back over at me.

"It's your brother's, Toni. He asked me to wear it to remind me of a promise I made to him."

He hesitates again, his mouth pressed into a straight line. Then he sighs.

"He asked me to promise that if you returned to Thebes after he left, I would make sure to protect you. He asked me not to tell you anything."

"You do know where he is!"

"Not for sure."

"But you know he's left town. Where? Why?"

Bashiir puts his hand out in a warning.

"Don't show anything over the camera. They might be separately recording our conversation in here too, so do nothing with your body language that would make them go through the audio."

I jump up from my cot.

"Toni, did you hear me?"

I begin waving my hands at the video camera, crossing my legs as if I really have to pee. I even hop up and down on one foot, then the other, for good measure.

"Why are you doing this?" Bashiir asks. I point at the wall clock we can see from between the cell bars, just where the security camera hangs. Same clock from the kindergarten days, a big white face with black numbers and a long needle smoothly traveling around to mark the seconds as well as the minutes and hours. The clock that taught me how to tell time as I fixated on it each day, longing for the small hand on 3 and the big hand on 12 so I could leave.

"It's seven minutes past five," I say. "He said his shift ended at five. You think he stayed a minute longer than he needed to? On a Sunday? And when a new guard takes over a shift, protocol requires detainees to be informed."

"Yes, when the overnight guard left, this one came in. How did you know?"

"When I was here earlier trying to convince him to let me in to see you, I read all of the posted regulations. It's a lawyer thing."

I continue my dance routine. As I suspect, nobody shows. Confident that at least for a few minutes no one is watching, I sit down on Bashiir's cot, next to him. He smells riper than this morning, after more hours in a jail cell on a hot summer afternoon, but not repellent. Not at all.

I pull off a flip-flop and start slapping it against the metal edge of the cot.

"Tell me what you know," I whisper close to his ear. "The audio won't be detectable if I do this." I smack my shoe more insistently to prove my point.

He lowers his head toward mine, so close that our foreheads almost touch.

"I promised to keep you out of it. He wanted you safe. He told me to push you away so you would be too angry to dig any further."

Paul wanted me to stay in Minneapolis and live happily ever after. I was wrong about him. He wasn't rejecting me—he thought making me mad would ensure that I'd keep out of whatever mess was happening here. Despite all our arguments about who is right and who is wrong, my brother, in his own way, is still trying to protect me.

What he doesn't know is that all those years when he shut his bedroom door against me, I was pressed up against it, right on the other side. No matter how much he tries to make me hate him, I will always love him more.

"Does Paul's wife know where he is?" I ask.

His eyes widen.

"You know about Celeste?"

Celeste. So this is the name of my sister-in-law.

"She answered Paul's phone. She told me they were married. Why is it a secret?"

Bashiir hesitates again. I thwap my shoe several time against the metal cot to remind him we won't be overheard.

"Okay," he says at last. "But only because you keep figuring out so much on your own. Which, now that I've seen you in action a few times"—he gestures to my ridiculous but effective flip-flop anti-police-tracking device—"comes as no surprise."

While I bang my shoe in percussive accompaniment, Bashiir begins.

————

"I met your brother a couple of years ago in St. Cloud when I was finishing my master's degree. He was sleeping on the dorm room floor of someone he met at a protest against the American war in Afghanistan. We found common ground quickly. I told him about my prior life in Mogadishu, then in the refugee camps in Kenya, before coming to Minnesota. Paul could remember bits and pieces of the camp you and he lived in with your parents for a few months, before your father was taken away.

"I didn't know where I wanted to go after graduation, but I told Paul that a big city wasn't for me. And Paul said that as much as he hated living under your uncle's roof, he liked the rhythm of small-town life in Thebes. He missed the library, and knowing who everyone was, who their parents were, who their grandparents were."

The very place that repulsed me was beckoning to Paul in ways I never dreamed possible.

"The more your brother talked about Thebes, the more I wanted to move here. All of Minnesota was changing—more newcomers beyond the Cities. Why not Thebes? I applied for a computer engineering job with a video surveillance company in Athens. When it came through, Paul and I agreed to rent an apartment together downtown. Paul picked up odd jobs—I don't have to tell you about his ability to fix almost anything—and I convinced more of my friends to relocate to Thebes. Most of them are like me, no blood relatives in the area but they want a Somali community. Some are married with young children. And most, like me, are no longer religious, not traditionally so. Starting a new community appealed to us. My friends and I have respect for the Somali elders, but their ways aren't ours anymore. I envisioned a community center for all comers, religious or not. And in Thebes, your brother had the contacts and skills to help make it real. We took over the lease of an unused warehouse from an older man your brother knew. He told Paul if we could fix up the warehouse as well as he did the truck that he sold him ten years ago, it would be a blessing."

Mr. Hopper. Still supporting my brother's dreams.

"We all spent nights and weekends cleaning up the community center, doing repairs. Then a notice comes from the landlord: ownership was transferred to King Construction Company. A day later, your uncle's company announces that the center will be razed."

"When was this?" I ask, resuming the banging of my rubber shoe on metal. I'm so wrapped up in Bashiir's story that I've forgotten to keep up my flip-flop trick.

"Late May. An article in the *Oracle* came out that same day showing your family, everyone but Paul, standing in front of the very building that he had been restoring for months, cutting a giant ribbon to announce its demolition."

"I saw."

"Your brother was determined not to let it happen. I argued with him, I said we can find another building, maybe the location wouldn't be as convenient, but it wasn't worth fighting his own family to save it. 'Those people are not my family,' he said. 'Only Toni. And she can't get involved, not now when she's about to start her job in Minneapolis.'"

"Now I've destroyed that too."

Bashiir gives me a quizzical look. Right, he doesn't know that I've been fired. He is still tugging absently at the black beads around his wrist. I reach out and touch the bracelet—our fingers brush lightly, accidentally for a second. Heat. I pull my hand back, but the electrical current of his skin against mine travels through my fingertips.

"Where did Paul get this bracelet?"

"He brought it back from one of his trips to the Bosnian Cultural Center in Minneapolis."

"The what?" Paul never mentioned anything of the sort.

"He's spent the last few years meeting other Bosnians. Looking for any information about your past. Chicago, Cleveland—lots of places with resettled communities. He says you were forbidden from connecting with your own heritage growing up because you were expected to assimilate."

Paul's internet research as a teenager had led to real-life research.

"Why didn't he tell me about the people he met?" I ask.

"I think he didn't want to get your hopes up without concrete information. He found survivors of the concentration camp, called Susica, where your father most likely was sent, but no one who knew him. Paul loved meeting other Bosnians though. They would dance and drink and argue about politics all night, there was always food and a bed. The bracelet was a good luck gift from a Bosnian woman he met in Minneapolis."

"Celeste?"

Bashiir appears amused by my guess. "No, I think the woman was a grandmother. Celeste is from Thebes. She was a couple of years ahead of Paul at school, but they didn't connect until he moved back here."

I try to recall anyone named Celeste growing up, but I'm drawing a blank. She must have been too much older than me; we wouldn't have overlapped.

"Why is he keeping their relationship a secret?"

"There's some complicated background with her father. He's worked for your uncle for years. John Joseph?"

Whoa. Not just anyone who worked for my uncle. His main henchman. Former tormentor of Harrison. And from the looks of him earlier today as he surveyed the Somali neighborhood, he'd have none of Paul and his activism, especially not when it came to his daughter.

"When did they get married?"

"Yesterday. The marriage was his promise to her that he'd come home. I was their witness at city hall in Athens, then we all came back here to execute the plan."

"What plan?"

He gestures toward my flip-flop, which I've let go silent again. I resume.

"The vigil. Paul organized everything in just a day. We all went out at dark. We had candles, blankets, musical instruments."

"A vigil? Not a protest?"

"Your brother wanted it to be a protest. He tried to make it happen weeks ago, during the ribbon cutting for the site. But your cousin convinced him to slow down. Harrison promised Paul that if each of them kept the peace from their respective sides, there'd be no need to go to war."

Of course he did. Harrison being Harrison.

"I was glad that our focus was on positive action," Bashiir continues. "Especially after the wedding. I felt happy, preparing. We were draping the backhoes with fabric, sitting on the front of the bulldozers. Those who pray were planning to roll out their mats. Paul drilled it into everyone: when the team comes, be welcoming. Educate them about everything

that happens inside the community center they were about to take down.
Invite them to join us for a meal.

"But then a line of police vehicles from both Thebes and Athens
pulled up. They came out in riot gear. Paul kept telling everyone to stay
calm, this was a scare tactic, and we all had the right to gather peacefully.
It was so dark by then, and the streetlights on the block have been out
for weeks. Then someone yelled: 'Officer down! One of them has a baseball bat!' The sirens started, and the line of police moved forward. 'No
violence! No violence!' Paul was running among us, trying to find out
what happened, but we couldn't see. So I lit my candle. Someone from
the police line saw the flame and pointed at me and called out: 'He's got
a weapon!'

"Everything from there happened so fast. I was in handcuffs. My
head was against a police car. There was crying, screaming, the police
all mixed in with us. Then I was placed in the back seat. They took me
here."

Bashiir stops, swallows hard. When he speaks again after a long moment, his voice is wobbly. "None of that was supposed to happen. And I
don't know where Paul is now. I don't know what Celeste knows either.
I haven't seen my phone in eighteen hours."

Finally, his calm exterior has cracked. I can feel his exhaustion, his
frustration, his worry. His shoulders slump. Hansen be damned, I reach
out and thread my fingers through Bashiir's, hold his hand in mine. Not
for the heat this time. For the warmth. He doesn't let go.

Everything I don't know about Bashiir wells up in the silence between us. All I don't understand about his history, his life in Thebes, the
shit he faces here. And yet his hand . . . holding it feels like the most familiar sensation in the world. All I want to do is sit this way: in the stillness
we create for each other. The only moment of peace I've had in as long as
I can remember.

But the questions press on me.

"If Paul married Celeste as a promise he'd return," I whisper, "he knew he would leave that same night? Why?"

Bashiir drops his chin to his chest for a moment. I wait, let him feel whatever it is he needs to feel. After a bit, he looks at me again.

"I have to tell you what your brother knows. At this point it's wrong if I don't. The old woman who gave Paul this bracelet. She told him that he should be seeking out Serbian contacts to find what happened to your parents, not Bosnian. 'History remembers the perpetrators,' she said. That's when he started looking online for information about the one man whose name he knew. Someone called Vlado."

Vlado. The man we lived with in Sarajevo. Who slept in our mother's bed.

"He found him. Vlado Jovanović. He was a foot soldier for Milošević. He was tried for crimes against humanity after the siege and found guilty. Paul discovered that he was arrested just weeks after you came to the United States."

I shake my head. "No, that doesn't make sense. Vlado was our mother's boyfriend."

He looks me in the eyes again, with that same intense concern he had when I couldn't breathe. Our hands are still intertwined.

Not my mother's boyfriend. Then what?

Her captor?

Her rapist.

Screens and screens of research from Paul's high school days flicker across my mind's eye. Rape as a weapon of genocide. Bosnian women.

My mother. My majka. Was she protecting us by submitting to him? Was her compliance keeping her out of the camps and us alive?

I'm going to vomit. I'm going to combust into a billion pieces. I'm going to scream until my lungs explode.

But I can't move. I can't let go of Bashiir's hand. He's holding mine tighter now; I can feel his pulse beating between his thumb and his forefinger. Reminding me that I'm here.

I feel something slide over my hand. I look down—Bashiir has slipped Paul's black beads on their elastic string from his wrist to mine.

"It belongs to you," he says. "Your brother was wrong about one very important thing. You don't need him, or anyone, to protect you. You're strong, Toni. I saw it the second you walked in here this morning. You are whole. I can see that having this knowledge will not break you."

I find his gaze again.

"How do you know?"

"My father. Sliced open with a machete. I tried to stop it, but I couldn't. I was eight years old."

The long scar on his forearm. Tentatively, I reach over with my other hand and touch its striations, like branches of a winding river. He doesn't brush me away. Instead, he presses his forehead against mine for a long minute, letting his thoughts be my thoughts. Letting me hear his life. Hearing mine. I close my eyes and rest right here. Both broken and whole.

"Toni . . . There's more . . ."

Bashiir's voice is asking if I can handle more. Forehead to forehead, I nod.

"This Vlado . . . Your brother figured that your uncle had to have more information than he'd been sharing all these years. He became obsessed, he had to find out. When Harrison mentioned in passing some dinner meeting on Friday, Paul knew your uncle wouldn't be in the office. He snuck in and went through his paperwork. Apparently, your uncle still doesn't use a computer. Paul found a file, buried deep in some back drawer, filled with documents of wire transfers. Lots of money. And the most recent payment was only a few months ago. The location on the transfers kept changing—Tucson, Sacramento, Houston. But the payments—twice a year for twenty years."

I move back so I can look right in his eyes.

"Payments? My uncle was paying off Vlado?"

Bashiir shakes his head. "Vlado died in a German prison years ago."

"Then where was he sending money?"

He pauses. Slowly, quietly, he says: "To his brother."

Eddie?

Edward King?

The man who was supposed to be our new American father. The phone call I was too frightened to make. The delay that caused his death.

He isn't dead.

This is what Paul found. Why he ran screaming into Christopher's dinner meeting.

He discovered that our uncle has been lying to us, and lying to the entire town of Thebes, Minnesota, for twenty years. About his own brother's death.

"Paul ran away to look for him, didn't he? That's why he can't tell anyone. He's afraid Christopher will do something if he knows. He's gone underground."

"Your brother is my best friend. I had to help, even though it could cost me my job, or worse," he continues, his low voice in my ear. "The day of Christopher's dinner meeting, I disabled all of the video cameras I programmed for his security company so Paul could sneak in and go through his papers without the guards finding out."

Despite my shock about Eddie, despite the dark stories we've just shared, I can't help smiling.

"Bashiir Abdi!" I whisper. "I thought you didn't have an unethical bone in your body."

I feel him smile back. "Are you disappointed?"

"Oh, no. I'm impressed. I guess it takes a master manipulator to know one when you see one."

"Toni . . . about that, saying that to you before. I'm sorry. After today, I would never—"

I stop him. "Don't apologize. You're right about how I acted."

"But how you acted isn't the sum of who you are. Now I know."

A buzzer blares over the intercom. We both jump. I scramble back to my cot on the other side. The thick metal door outside of the cell area scrapes open.

————

"New guard, new guard, coming through," a gravelly female voice announces just as a uniformed officer strides into the room. It's Brandi Schmidt. Of course. Somehow, she manages to look exactly the same as she did ten years ago, half naked and wasted atop a sewing table, despite being fully dressed in police blues.

"Hey, Toni! What's up! I was just talking with my mother about you. She says you're a lawyer now. From Harvard. Wowie zowie! Aren't you impressive!" Oh, this crab apple didn't fall far from the tree. I refuse to meet her eyes because I will not give her the satisfaction of imagining for one hot second that the tears on my cheeks have anything to do with her power over my situation or the same mean-girl goading tone she perfected back in high school and uses professionally today. She will not have access to anything real, about me or about Bashiir. I feel his words: *you are whole.*

"Well, your little visit to our happy place is over. Your family posted bail, you lucky kid! All cash, hand delivered. Time to check out of this Marriott." I look over at Bashiir with surprise. Why would Christopher bail me out less than an hour after he had me dragged in?

"Is my uncle here?" I ask Brandi, careful to modulate my voice so she can't hear anything of the roil of emotions I'm experiencing.

"Oh, it's not your uncle," she says as she opens the bars. "It's your aunt."

Evelyn! Here she is, half obscured behind the doorway, in her pink dress and kitten-heel pumps.

Why is she letting me out when Christopher locked me in? Does he know?

Eddie . . . does she know?

Brandi turns the key in the lock and slides back the metal bolt with a flourish. The vicious clang this time is to let me go, not keep me in. Yet I won't move. I can't.

"Toni King, you're free to go. Get out of here, what's your problem?" Brandi looks at me like I have six heads.

"I'm fine," I say.

Even Bashiir shakes his head. "Toni, don't be foolish."

Brandi waves the receipt from Evelyn for the bail money right in front of me. "This is more than I make in a freaking year. And you're sitting on your ass."

Fifty thousand dollars.

An insane amount. Absolutely bonkers. This is the price Christopher put on my head to keep me from stirring up more trouble. Only he could wield the influence to set such a price for the crime of crawling up the wall of my own childhood house.

"I can't take his money," I say. "I can't."

"It isn't his." Aunt Evelyn's soft voice calls from the doorway. "It's mine."

Brandi moves aside and I can fully see Evelyn, clutching her oversized pink purse with both hands in front of her body like a suit of armor.

"How?" I ask. Aunt Evelyn has no money of her own. Never has.

Uncle Christopher gave her an allowance—left a check in an envelope on the kitchen counter every Friday morning before he went into the office. He required a full accounting from her of the past week's spending by Thursday night. He tracks every penny.

Evelyn's delicate heels click across the linoleum as she walks toward me, all the way past the bars and into the cell. The incongruity of Evelyn King, first lady of Thebes, Minnesota, still dressed for church, rounding out our little band of cellmates is eyebrow-raising, to say the least. She places her bag on the third cot, carefully lining it up along the edge of the metal frame, and sits, folding her hands on her lap.

"I've been stealing money from King Family Construction for thirty years," she says quietly. "I suppose that means I belong behind bars too." Evelyn looks back at Brandi Schmidt, at her desk, out of earshot. "Oh, dear," she continues. "Did I just confess to a crime at the police station?"

Bashiir starts to laugh, then quickly pretends to cough.

"Hello, we haven't been formally introduced," Aunt Evelyn says. "I'm Mrs. King. What is your name?"

"Bashiir Abdi. I'm one of your nephew's roommates. And pardon the circumstances of our introduction. Other than the location, it's very nice to meet you."

"Aunt Evelyn," I say, interrupting what threatens to become the oddest tea party in history, "please tell me what's going on."

She turns toward me. Even with her expert makeup application I can tell that her eyes are puffy beneath her shadow and liner. But they're clear. Sober. Filled with purpose.

"Isobel ran crying into my room once she learned what her father had done," she says. "She's waiting in the car outside. Oh, and your uncle has no idea we are here bailing you out."

"What did Izzy tell you about why he put me here?"

She looks away. Some emotion is trying to fight its way to the surface.

She hesitates. She's about to speak—but stops. She blinks, then looks back at me again with the same sad, resigned look I remember from sophomore year of high school when she buried her longing to talk with me about *My Ántonia* as soon as she saw my pain.

"It doesn't matter," says Evelyn, her voice soft. "No child of mine belongs behind bars."

Child of mine. My heart rises at the sound of her words.

But wait. Has she known about Eddie all these years as well? Was Evelyn lying to me and Paul along with Christopher? Was she even lying to Harrison and Izzy?

At what price am I a child of hers? Fifty thousand dollars. Does that pay for an hour of jail and twenty years of deceit? Okay then—how much more will it take for her to absolve her own guilt?

"Aunt Evelyn," I ask. "Did you spend all your money to bail me out?"

She pats her purse. "Not even close," she says.

She's proud of her thievery. There is more I can do here.

"Bashiir doesn't belong in jail any more than I do," I say. "Paul is his roommate, so that makes him family."

"No, oh, no," Bashiir is frowning. "Please don't even think about it."

I put up my hand to stop him. "I'm not going anywhere unless you get out too. Nonnegotiable."

He looks at me for a long moment.

"Mrs. King, will you excuse us please? I need to speak with your niece in private."

Aunt Evelyn nods, polite as always. "I'll be outside as soon as you're ready, Antonia."

Bashiir keeps staring at me as the sound of Evelyn's heels recedes.

"Toni, do you truly understand why I'm in jail?" he asks. He's direct, serious, but the coldness he expressed to me earlier today is gone. We've come too far for that.

"For no good reason," I reply. "You're innocent."

"Innocence and guilt are immaterial to them. They're trying to make an example of me to my community. Threatening all of us that if we step out of line, out of 'our place,' we'll be punished. The last thing I need, or want, is some white savior coming around to bail me out. Not your aunt. Not you either."

"That's not what I'm trying to do."

"You don't have to try. That's just how it is. Your brother gets it. That's why he took off. He's trying to fix his own mess, not mine."

He's right. I've been calling Paul out for years on what I thought was his big savior complex. But now I see that Paul found a family here. A true family. What he always wanted. Even if he believes he has to push me away to keep it.

"They can't hold me longer than tomorrow at noon," Bashiir continues. "I'm not afraid of staying here. I'm enraged about staying here. But I can stick it out another day if it means representing who I am, and who my people are."

————

Evelyn and I don't embrace. We don't even touch. But between us now, as we stand side by side to complete the paperwork Brandi hands us, is the invisible pulsing of liquid steel. She showed up for me. Even if I can't ever fully give myself over to her, like Izzy or Harrison, I can't fully leave her either. She's part of all that I am.

Her texts this morning, the ones I ignored—they were warnings. My own inability to slow down and listen to her landed me in this cell, every bit as much as Christopher's actions. Harrison was right about me: I dismiss people too readily, lump them all in with my uncle when it suits my story. And Bashiir is right too: I can't stick myself into other people's business and fix them with my fancy law degree or my family's money.

Who is my aunt, really, behind the façade?

When Brandi is out of hearing range again, I ask her, gently: "Why have you been taking money from the company all these years?"

Evelyn looks at me with her full sad eyes, mascara spikes on every lash. Shakes her head.

"I was fourteen when I started dating your uncle. All I knew outside of Thebes was from books I borrowed from the library. Before you know it, you're in so deep, in a marriage. You turn around and . . . what else is there? I had four children to raise."

She turns back to the forms in front of her. Grips the police-issue ballpoint pen so tightly she scratches the paper.

"But sometimes you feel . . . you just . . . wonder. One morning when I was tallying my expenses—a morning your uncle was distracted, very distracted with other business—I just . . . added a zero to the household bill. And he didn't say a word, he simply reimbursed me from the cash stored in his office safe. No questions. Well, it was a rush, I must say. Legally, what's his is mine. I mean, not what belongs to the business, but technically . . ."

"What did you plan to do with all that cash?"

"I don't know. Nothing, I guess. But when I had it, I could dream. Before, what did I have to dream about?"

She can't look at me directly, just keeps doodling in the margin on the page of legalese.

"I kept upping the ante to see how much I could get away with. I invented a personal assistant who helped me out all day when your uncle was working, and you children were at school."

"You made up an entire person?"

In profile, I see Evelyn's mouth twitch into a smile.

"Poor Lucille. She had a terribly sad situation—a dear girl from Athens whose parents were desperately addicted to heroin and would take her salary to fuel their addiction if they knew how much she made. It was a kindness to her for the company to make her checks out to me and for me to deposit them and pay her in cash so she could save as much as she could from them. I've grown quite fond of Lucille over time. I even paid her tuition to Athens Community College. It was the least I could do."

"Where did you hide it all of these years? We roamed every inch of that house."

Her little Lucille smile grows stronger.

"In the upstairs hall bathroom. There's a secret compartment. You children were so distracted by the bottle of vodka I planted there, you never thought to look behind it to see if there was anything else."

Well. At least some of those daily cocktails were self-congratulatory, not just self-immolating. Evelyn might have been drinking away her feelings of sorrow and loneliness. But part of her was waiting for the opportunity to break free. That part of her squired away money for years without knowing why. That part tried to signal me through poetry and books.

Mrs. Schmidt drops the plastic bin with my belongings on the reception desk before us.

I retrieve my bag and immediately check my phone.

No additional messages.

Why would there be? I've not merely burned all my bridges in the past day—I've destroyed them beyond recognition. The only thing my phone flashes is that still from the video. Per, Michelle, the other Mt. O high school kids—they stare at me like an image from ancient history.

And no surprise, nothing from my brother's number either. Celeste knows that Paul has gone in search of Eddie King.

Does my aunt?

"Aunt Evelyn, can I ask you just one more thing before we leave?"

"Of course."

I take a deep breath. "Please tell me." I'm shivering with the effort it takes to ask the question out loud. "Have I been spending the past day trying to dig up information about the wrong brother?"

At first, she just looks at me with her usual controlled and careful mien. But then the color begins to drain from her face.

She knows Eddie is alive. She's always known.

"Toni!"

It's Bashiir. His voice is jubilant.

I turn around to see him, accompanied by Brandi but without cuffs or restraints of any kind.

"You're out!"

"All the charges were dropped. Officer Schmidt just got the call."

"Really? Who? How?"

Brandi shrugs. "Don't look at me, I just work here. In, out—I do what they say."

Evelyn touches me on the elbow. "Isobel is waiting for us in the car." My aunt has reorganized her expression to mask the revelation of a moment ago. But I have what I need. Years ago, she wrote a note telling me I'd never need to depend on a man to make my way in the world. As a heartbroken teen, I thought it was all about me and my situation. Now I know she was sharing something fundamental about herself. Something she could only articulate through the novel that inspired her to name me Antonia. Was she angry at Christopher for the secret he kept? Was she part of his decision to do so?

It could be guilt that compelled her to dig up $50,000 of pilfered cash and fork it over to get me out.

No child of mine . . .

Evelyn sees me as hers.

It might be out of guilt. But it might be out of love, too.

———

While Bashiir gathers his belongings and cleans himself up, Evelyn and I meet Izzy in the parking lot. After much fuss and more tears and apologies and clinging hugs, my cousin settles her mother in the passenger seat of her Jeep. I promise I'll meet up with her back in her room later, that I won't run off without seeing her again.

As they pull out, Bashiir emerges, his backpack slung over one shoulder.

"Celeste left a message," he says as soon as he's near. His eyes are energized by his news about Paul.

I catch a soft whiff of his newly soaped face and hands. Without thinking, I touch the band of beads around my wrist.

"She said that the chaos ended up being to their advantage—they slipped away and hid until the police shut down the neighborhood. Then they walked most of the night till they got to Athens. She's staying there with friends for a while. Paul took an early morning bus to Indianapolis, but that's just a way station. He left her his phone, his ID. He's on the move, under a false name."

"What's his plan? Where is he ultimately going?"

"He's heading to the last known address on those receipts. He refused to tell us where, or what name he'll be traveling under. He knows it's a risk for any of us to have information about him as long as your uncle wants to stop him from finding Eddie. He'll call Celeste from different numbers, just to say he's safe. But more than that, none of us will know for a while."

"Shouldn't we try to help him? What if he doesn't call her? What if . . ."

"Toni, Paul knows how to lay low and move quickly. He wants to do it this way. I have faith in him and I'm not going to interfere." Bashiir stretches his arms overhead, then turns his face up to the sky.

"But . . ." I stop myself.

This is reality, whether you like it or not.

The lines from *My Ántonia* that Evelyn shared the night I learned that James was engaged come back to me, unbidden.

All those frivolities of summer, the light and shadow, the living mask of green that trembled over everything, they were lies, and this is what was underneath.

I watch him allow the warmth and the quiet of late afternoon seep into his skin. He's been in a jail cell for almost a full day. His community, the one he's building with such love, is under attack. I can't pepper him with questions that are, ultimately, about me.

This is the truth.

Bashiir needs to catch his breath. I need to catch mine. I have so much to figure out, so many pieces to put together about my past. He's got to be thinking about his future, and the future of the Community Center. Yet right now, the simple act of standing in the afternoon heat on an empty street next to this man, seeing the way he squints at the sun's brilliance—it's enough. It makes me feel like a person. A regular person.

I didn't know it was possible to crave something so calm.

Dusk

THE ANCIENT GREEKS REALIZED THE EARTH WAS A sphere long before Galileo got all the credit—the summer solstice marked the first day of their new year. A time of beginnings. The day that Helios, the sun god, preened for endless hours, soaking up the adulation and fear of all the citizens and beaming back at them with his blinding hot light. But evening finally fell on Helios's day in Greece—and here in northern Minnesota, it's beginning to fall now.

As the shadows deepen, I retrace my steps through the woods behind my uncle's house. This time, Izzy and Evelyn wait together for me to sneak back in. *We'll be upstairs,* Izzy texted. *Come figure out a plan. We haven't told him you're out.*

The back of the King family house looms dark before me. Izzy's light is on. I stop, gaze up at her room. Sure enough, there she is, illuminated, two floors up, chatting animatedly on the phone to someone, like a moving picture in a frame.

I pull out my phone to let her know I'm here—but I stop texting before I finish. Instead, I backspace out my message and return the phone to my bag.

No more crawling through windows. No more subversive gestures like those that secretly give my aunt and Izzy a little power of their own but don't upset the structure of the universe as Christopher sees it. Pilfering money is the perfect Aunt Evelyn maneuver; sneaking in forbidden lovers and cousins gives Izzy the thrill she needs.

Today has had an effect on both of them, there's no doubt. Probably a major effect. But here's where our relationship has its limits. Their lives are still their lives, this house is their house, the past is their past. For me, and for Paul, although we called this place home for a time, we have so much left to find.

THE OUTER DOOR TO THE WEST WING IS BURNISHED BY the glow of the almost-setting sun. Touching the brass knob is like touching a fireball. It's unlocked, so his business hours aren't over yet. I enter the foyer—and immediately hear the murmur of voices. He's with Harrison. I duck away from the inner window and press my ear to the door.

" . . . too far this time," my cousin says. "We can dial it back if you call and drop the charges against Toni now."

"Antonia's not thinking clearly. It's for her own good. If I didn't take this measure, she was going to make some serious mistakes."

"The town doesn't want to see her locked up. No matter whether she's liked or not around here, throwing her in jail is a bad look."

"You're being dramatic. Everyone knows what that cell is for—it's a drunk tank. Nothing real. If I excuse members of my own family for wrongdoing, how can I keep the respect of the people of Thebes?"

"Yes, the respect of Thebes! Dad, this is my point. I'm hearing sympathy for Toni through Facebook and Twitter. You don't understand social media. Gossip travels fast, and lots of people saw her around town today. Someone posted a picture of her in handcuffs. This doesn't benefit you or King Family Construction."

For a moment, Christopher is silent on the other side of the door. When he does speak, his tone is measured. "Harrison, are you expecting me to take lessons in business management from my son, a boy barely out of school?"

"Dad, I'm trying to support you from a public relations perspective. And as your son, isn't it useful for me to keep you in touch with what others are thinking? This isn't just a family issue now," Harrison continues to brave through. "Jail is public, and most people don't agree with your assessment that Toni broke the law."

"You're on her side. And Paul's."

"No. I'm fighting for you and for this company. That's why I tried to convince Toni to sign the papers. But she was upset. Understandably. However, there's an opportunity here for good PR. You can show everyone that you own the high road by ending this standoff. That's how to win now: drop the charges against Toni."

"The two of them. They probably cooked this up together. Well, she can sit in that hole until she agrees to sign the statement. That will teach her a lesson about loyalty."

"Dad. Let's focus. We can't let this derail the Dig. The sooner we resolve the situation, the sooner we can get back to work."

"She's tricky. Lied to me for three years, pretending she'd come back after law school."

I never lied! I almost give away my hiding place with my instinctual need to correct him. But I stop. Wait.

My uncle is pacing. I can hear his footfall as his voice rises.

"I built this, all of this, for the family. All they had to do was be part of it. Is it so hard to toe that line? Look at what you and Isobel get, just for showing up each day."

"I think I do more than just show up." Do I hear a note of anger in my cousin's voice?

"How can anyone doubt that I'm doing what's right for Thebes?" My uncle isn't even listening to Harrison. "I've created jobs here for twenty years. The money I brought back from the Balkans saved this town." His voice grows even louder. "My brother couldn't do that. My father couldn't even do that. And Paul and Antonia: they became King family members. I rescued them."

"More reason to drop the charges. Bring her back to talk, at least."

"She was disloyal. I've made my decision."

"But your decision was wrong!"

Silence from inside the office. When my uncle speaks again, he's once more standing close to my hiding place. Close to Harrison.

"Be careful, son," says Christopher. His voice is thicker now, full of portent. "Do you intend to start down this road? Put it away."

Put what away?

"You're right about loyalty, Dad," I hear my cousin say. "It is everything. I've been loyal to you every step of the way. I've worked hard every day to promote you and this company as a force for good to the people in this town, people my age, people who have come here to make a future. I've spent hours talking up the jobs that the Dig will create. And it was working. If you had just let me keep doing it, I would have moved everyone to a peaceful agreement. But you turned out to have no loyalty to me."

"Harrison, you don't want to do this."

Has my cousin finally snapped?

"Family loyalty," Harrison continues. "I supported you after Paul broke into your office on Friday and confronted you over dinner, because his actions put us at risk in front of a potential investor. But I never stopped negotiating with him and his friends, right up through last night. Even though I knew what you had planned. Don't you see? I've been brokering the future of this company you built, for everyone. I've been the go-between, the compromiser, the one working behind the scenes to take our family and this company forward. I've given everything you've asked of me, no matter what I've had to sacrifice to keep the peace. But you couldn't keep the faith long enough to let me see it through. You had to fall back on this."

On what?

"I kept apologizing for your actions and trying to convince everyone to compromise. Until now. Until Izzy called me when I was at the television station—finalizing the deal that you asked me to make to ensure that WKNW would literally be part of the family—to tell me you had Toni arrested."

"Stop overreacting. Listen, you know me, and we understand each other. But Toni, sometimes she doesn't. She needed a little protection from her own worst impulses, that's all."

"No, Dad. Toni might be a pain in the ass, and a hothead, but she came back when you called, didn't she? What you've done is a betrayal of us all. I stand with Toni."

Harrison, who grabbed my hand and pulled me across enemy lines with him in our kindergarten game of Red Rover. Who initiated our pact for life, years ago, at Twin River Falls. How could I have doubted him for even a moment?

"Izzy was sobbing, Dad. She thought it was her fault Toni was in jail. And that's when I saw it so clearly."

"Saw what?" Christopher's voice is wavering now. He's nervous. Whatever Harrison is doing in there, combined with what he's saying— it's cracking something open in my uncle. A vulnerability I haven't heard before. I lean closer.

"I saw that I had to take charge of this myself," Harrison continues. In contrast to his father, Harry's voice is strong and clear. "As an officer of this company, I have the power to speak on your behalf when it comes to King Family Construction. I told the police we were dropping the charges you levied against both Paul and his roommate."

Of course! How could I have missed the obvious? My uncle orchestrated Bashiir's arrest, and the warrant for Paul's, as well as mine. I didn't want it to be true, that's how. And up till tonight, Harrison believed all of it was nothing but a show, like the sign-waving xenophobes downtown.

"That was just the start," says Harrison. "My next call was to the television station. To let Matthew and Charlene know the truth about the injured police officer at last night's protest. And that the evidence is here. What I'm holding in my hands right now. That's the new story that they're holding until the ten o'clock broadcast. That's the new deal. And unless you free Toni, that story runs."

"You. Will. NOT!" My uncle's voice rises to a level of distress I've never heard before. Time to move.

"Harry!" I cry. "I'm here!" I push open the door to the inner office.

The shock that registers on both my uncle's and my cousin's faces, I expect to see.

Harrison standing in front of Christopher wielding a wooden baseball bat, I don't.

A baseball bat. The weapon Officer Hansen told me was used last night to club the sergeant at the scene of Paul and Bashiir's peaceful vigil. This is the evidence Harrison holds in his hands.

"Toni! How did you get out?"

I can't reveal Evelyn's secrets in front of my uncle. Either Evelyn or Izzy can tell Harrison if they want to. I look at Harrison, let him see fully the love and gratitude I feel for him. Then, now, always.

"I'm Batman, remember?"

Harrison returns my look with one of his own: one that says all is forgiven between us. "Yes, you are."

I look at Christopher, who stares in dismay at both of us.

"What did he do?" I ask my cousin.

"He had John Joseph hire a guy to sneak into the protest last night after dark and pretend to be part of the crowd defending the Somali neighborhood. Then he hit the officer so things would get violent, and the police could justify arresting Paul and his friends."

"It was just theater!" Christopher says. "I made sure there would be no serious injuries. I had everything under control." He sounds like the opposite of a man in control. Still working to spin things his way.

Harrison turns to me. "I'm trying to fix it," he says quietly.

"I know," I reply.

There's a rustle from the back of the office, by the door to the house. It's Evelyn and Izzy, standing arm in arm. Izzy's eyes widen as she takes in the specter of her brother wielding a baseball bat in front of her father's face.

"Evelyn," Christopher extends his arm. "We need a united front."

My aunt shakes her head.

"Evelyn . . ." A warning? An admission of fear?

"Harrison," she says, "I think Antonia needs a moment alone with your father." Now she looks straight at me. "I believe they have some old business to discuss."

She's giving me the opening. Permission to say whatever I need to say—ask him what I need to know about Eddie King.

"Evelyn!" A threat this time. Tinged with disbelief.

Whatever reasons she's had to keep Christopher's secret about Eddie—whether it was to protect him or to protect herself—it's over. And for a second time today, she's gifting me freedom at her own expense.

Slowly, Harrison lowers the bat and places it on his father's desk. He walks across the office and stands beside them. Christopher, his face gone white, grips the back of his office chair so hard his fingers leave an indentation in the leather.

Before she leaves the room, Izzy gives me one quick look, a question with her eyes: *Are you all right?* I nod. She slides the door shut.

———

The bank of windows behind Christopher's desk, framed by paisley damask curtains, reveals a bruised purple sky and a blazing orange and red sizzle of setting sun. Christopher himself is practically a shadow. Dusk makes his eyes appear to recede in their sockets. Slowly he sits down in his high-backed chair and spreads his large hands out, palms down on the wide polished wooden desk between us.

"Well," he says, his voice heavy. "I've put this family first my entire adult life. And in a single day you've managed to turn every one of them away from me."

The baseball bat lies crossways, at the center of the desk, over a pile of spreadsheets. So many invisible handprints on the neck of this bat, from Christopher to John Joseph to the thug they hired to take a single swipe at a cop that sent Bashiir to a cell and Paul on the run. Despite all that, it's my peacemaking cousin Harrison who turned it into the most effective weapon of all. He's beaten his father without taking a single blow.

I lean forward, press my own palms on the edge of the desk in a mirror image of my uncle.

"It's the worst feeling in the world, isn't it," I say, "being an outsider in your own home." My voice shakes with the truth of what I'm saying.

The lines across Christopher's forehead seem etched more deeply than just this morning, when he was the passionate orator announcing his vision of a story I was expected to support. I've seen him woo a roomful of people to his causes. I've seen him dominate with his silences. And at his happiest, I've seen him glow in his achievements. But I've never seen him look so completely alone.

I remember sitting in the family pew each Sunday, back in the days when all of us still attended church. Pressed between Paul and Izzy, I would steal glances at my uncle's profile where he sat, in the aisle seat, while the minister gave his sermon. Christopher in those moments seemed truly regal to me. Taller than anyone, back straighter, jaw firmer. Everyone wanted him to shake their hand, admire their children. I used to wonder, then, if he could ever love me like a father, despite my failings. If it was my own fatal flaw that I couldn't find the means within to worship him, as Harrison did, or blithely and uncritically accept him, like Izzy. Wasn't I just making my own life more difficult by resisting his dynamic pull?

Then I would shift my gaze to Paul, beside me, let his profile come into focus and my uncle's blur into the background. Here was my un-equivocal connection to the world. No matter how mad I made him, he was the only one who could keep me safe from my nightmares, the way a father could.

Was it too much pressure on my brother, only three years older, to feel it was up to him to protect me from everything, even my own dreams? I don't know. But I do know, now, that I wasn't imagining Uncle Christopher's distance. He was keeping secrets. Moving his brother from institution to institution. I sensed that a chill ran through his heart, but I never could have guessed it was from fear we'd learn that Edward King was still alive.

"Where is Paul?" I ask him. "Where did he go to look for Eddie?"

The slice of sunset behind my uncle is thin as a thread. The office darkens even as I stand across the desk from him, watching him thinking through his next move. I reach over and switch on his desk lamp just as the horizon line disappears. The arc of light spills between us like a white-gold pool, illuminating the desktop.

"Pittsburgh. That's his last address," Christopher says at last. "But

Paul won't find him there. And don't think you'll find any more evidence about his whereabouts here either—your brother stole what little there was. But now it's all useless, so no matter."

I pause, take this in. Slowly I realize what Christopher has done.

"You moved him again."

"It's better for Paul if he never finds him, believe me. Eddie's overdose left him hideously damaged. There's nothing positive that can come of that reunion. Does he think Eddie's the perfect American father you both should have had instead of terrible me?"

"But why did you move him so many times? Once we grew up, we could have . . ."

"I was hiding him, all right?" Christopher's voice cracks. "It was tragic. Terrible. My own brother would never be fully functional again. I had to decide what to do with him. How would you feel if it was Paul?"

I don't have to think. A loss that would cut to the bone.

"Evelyn was raising you now," he continues. "She said: 'Those poor children have been through too much.' We agreed. You and your brother would be better off if you forgot about Eddie. You barely even knew him. I could support him financially, make sure he was comfortable. I made enough money from working in Sarajevo to care for him and to grow the business. Don't you see? Eddie and I had a deal. One of us goes down, the other one takes care of the whole family. Forever. My brother . . . he's been alive in name only the past twenty years. I freed you—what if you and Paul grew up with Eddie to take care of on top of everything? This was the best way."

Seven-year-old Paul, trying with his tiny hands to pump life into Eddie's chest as he slumped on the floor. Me, incapable of even picking up the phone. Paul would have kept vigil with Eddie to this very day. Would I?

"Now you know," my uncle continues, his tone warming as he sees me hesitate. "Your aunt and I were doing the best we could. But your brother leapt to conclusions the other night. He didn't give me the benefit of the explanation I'm giving you now. That's why I had to try to stop him from making this terrible mistake, by any means I could. That warrant was just to keep him here in Thebes. I had to make certain he wouldn't find Eddie. For his own sake. You too. You were about to follow in his path but thank goodness I stopped you before you could make the same error."

My uncle's methods are extreme, no doubt. But the memory of that terrible time with Eddie—has Christopher been trying through the only means he knows, money and power, to care for us after all?

He leans in. "You and I have the same goal. We want everyone to be safe. I guarantee that I'll send no one after your brother on his futile quest if you convince Harrison to keep this petty, vindictive news story of his off the air. He trusts you. Then we can both get what we want."

Quid pro quo. He always has one more, then one more, then just when you think he's done, he twists you around in yet another direction—an endless maze with only one way out: his way. He'll use my fears for Paul as a threat if it gets him what he needs.

He also strikes a chord. We are alike: we both want to protect the people we love.

"But why did you set Paul up for attacking a police officer? If jail was your only option, why not do what you did to me, arrest him for breaking and entering?"

Christopher shakes his head. "I thought about that. At first, I wanted to have him arrested for theft, so I had John pull up video from the security camera in my office. There was no footage. Paul must have rigged something. John said to add it to the list of offenses—but then I realized: given your brother's history as a vagrant, it would be easier for anyone to believe he was running from the police. It would be my word against his. I'm not worried about who would prevail."

Going up against Christopher King is like ramming your head into an invisible wall everywhere you turn. Paul's confrontation with Christopher on Friday killed the business deal that would have postponed razing the Somali Community Center. Bashiir's ability to disable the video cameras led to the warrant for Paul's arrest. I could probably poke at Christopher's infuriating self-assurance by revealing that his loyal henchman's daughter is now married to his sworn enemy, but that would require betraying my brother's secret. Not an option.

"Antonia, a deal is on the table. Tell your cousin he must stand down before they air the ten o'clock news. Let's work together for the benefit of the whole family."

Work together. His eternal siren call—show your loyalty to me by working together, in business or in blackmail. I'll keep your brother safe, but only if you help me bend the truth, yet again.

We might be alike in some ways. But Christopher will lie, and pretend, and throw any amount of money behind that pretense, to maintain the illusion that he is the head of a perfect American family: an illusion that he believes will heal all wounds.

Nothing can fill those gaping holes for me now other than the truth. Nothing else can seal what's been blown apart.

I'm running out of time. But I cannot let the most important piece of my history stay buried. Not when I have this opening. I take a deep breath.

"My mother. You never talked about her. You told me to forget about the past."

"For your own best interests. You can't say I was wrong about that. Harvard, Antonia. Would you have made it there if you were obsessed about the past, about things you couldn't change? Your brother couldn't let it go, and he dropped out of school."

The same story of us, over and over. The myth he chose for us. The one that I see now I'd been perpetuating myself.

"You knew Vlado," I continue. "Paul learned that he was a convicted war criminal."

"I had nothing to do with Milošević or any of Vlado's beliefs. I'm an American!"

I stand across from him, arms folded. I'm not going to back off.

"It was a different time," Christopher says. He's trying to modulate. "The Berlin Wall fell. Then the Prague Spring. We were democracy builders, helping spread a better way of life behind the Iron Curtain. That's what the Barrington Company bosses told us we were signing on for when we agreed to help build that hotel. My town was dying. The money was good. And my brother . . ." His voice breaks on the word *brother*. My heart breaks a little too when I imagine my own.

He clears his throat. "I worshipped him as a kid. When he lost his leg in the Gulf, he lost everything. His visions of the future, his sense of purpose—gone. It was all up to me then. Our mother and Eddie, they were ready to sit in that farmhouse and rot away together. I single-handedly dragged him overseas to be on the crew with me. Johanna was on board. She saw it was the only way to save their relationship. And Evelyn too. I told her I'd be back before Isobel was born. She understood why I had to go."

Did she? I add it to the list of questions I need to ask my aunt. Did she understand, or was that the time, pregnant, with a toddler and her mother-in-law to manage, that she began to think like a thief because she knew if she wanted anything to belong to her and her alone, she'd have to steal it?

"Sarajevo was supposed to snap my brother out of all his self-pity. But his damn funk just kept going. I worked twice as hard on the crew to cover for him while he moped around about the past."

I've heard and dismissed versions of this story forever. But now that I know there's a different ending on the way, one that leads to the reason he's been hiding Eddie's existence from all of us, I'm listening. And some of what I hear sounds more familiar than I want to admit. *Why are you wasting your time in the dregs of Thebes, Paul? Come to Minneapolis and make a new life. I know better than you do.*

I learned to drink away my feelings from my aunt. I guess I learned how to bully my family from my uncle. Now he sits alone on the other side of his enormous desk, as alone as I felt every minute in this house from the time Paul ran away.

"Eddie wasn't the brother I knew anymore. He would just wander off, limping away on that prosthetic leg, in the middle of work. I could only prop him up with the bosses for so long before they fired him. There we were, on the other side of the earth, and I promised everyone we'd come home with enough money to take care of everything. I left my pregnant wife on that promise, Antonia. Do you see? Do you see now the bind I was in?"

I do, actually. Maybe for the first time.

He exhales, a sigh so full that his shoulders rise and drop from the effort.

"The black market was thriving. One meeting with the right person and I could make ten times the money. No questions asked."

The skin prickles up and down the backs of my legs.

This is what he's never told me before. A window that was sealed shut all of my years in Thebes has just cracked open.

"So much depended on me. Only me. I was responsible for Eddie there and everyone else back here. 'Go to Vlado,' the guys on the crew said. They all knew who he was—the key to the Serbian underground. That's how it worked. The way an American could come home rich."

And the pathway to me and Paul.

The dim room is my ally now; I stay in shadow to keep my face a blur while he continues.

"Vlado said, 'Take your truck and your American passport back and forth to Serbia. Other people will load and unload. All you have to do is drive. You never touch the goods.'"

I'm light-headed, hearing this. "By goods you mean arms." My voice is thin, barely familiar.

"The war was not my fault, Antonia." His tone begins to rise again. "I thought it would all be different. Like the Gulf. You know who you are when you wear a uniform. In Sarajevo it was . . . messy. I was a civilian. It wasn't my fight. I was sent to build a hotel, not choose a side. My side was my family and my community. Always. I did what was necessary and I used the proceeds to start this company. To save Thebes and save you and save everyone. Beginning with my own brother. You know how that feels. You know."

He's trying to keep me with him. But he can't anymore. Not even by invoking Paul again. I'm falling away from his story, backward through the darkness he's thrown into the room.

He ran arms for Vlado.

Vlado raped my mother.

I feel the tears on my face, but I don't care anymore what he sees. I lean out of the shadow slicing through the room, into the artificial light thrown across his desk. Let him know me. Let him know he can't bury Andela by calling me a different name.

"My mother," I whisper. It's a question without asking a question.

He shakes his head. "No. Your mother isn't my fault. You're acting just like Eddie! If only he had just kept his mouth shut . . ."

What?

Christopher's eyes widen as he realizes he's tipped into territory he hadn't intended. Then they narrow, quickly.

"Fine, okay, it wasn't a coincidence we came to your apartment. The siege had worsened, construction on the hotel shut down because of the bombings, and Eddie and I were heading back to the States with everyone else from Barrington. But the guns I pulled in on my last run, they were still hidden in Vlado's apartment. One last job, he said. Destroy the stash."

"Eddie was in on it?"

"No. Never. I did what I had to do to protect him and my family. To keep my promise. Eddie was begging me to get us on the next transport to Germany. I had to tell him why we needed to wait, just a few more hours. We fought; he said 'forget about it, don't you have enough money,' but it was more than the money this time. I knew if I didn't take care of business what could happen. The UN was moving in. There had to be no evidence, no link between me and Vlado.

"Eddie followed me out to the apartment, wouldn't let off telling me to quit. That day—there were bombs going off everywhere. The debris from all the shelling blocked our entrance to the building. Vlado gave me the cash and a grenade, then he ran. Eddie said 'don't do it,' but I had to get in to destroy those guns. I knew from my last tour in Baghdad that no one would know how anything happened in the fog of war."

The sound of bombs. My heart is pounding, like it did when I heard the slam of metal lock me into the cell this afternoon. The embroidered flowers. My mother singing. The fragments fly apart.

Breathe.

Bashiir's kind voice.

You are whole.

The beaded bracelet knocks gently against my chest as I breathe into my hand.

Christopher sits up straighter, tents his fingers together in front of him, elbows on the desk. He wants out of this conversation.

"We rescued you and gave you everything. Now this family is a success. Thebes can be successful too. I'm making it happen. I understand how. After two wars, I know how to keep the peace! We close ranks,

Antonia. Newcomers, renters, these people from countries like yours, they come here with the stench of what they left behind. Our obligation is to the living, not the dead."

He never knew Andela and Mujo, only Antonia and Paul.

He will never understand that our dead live on inside us.

"Look at all I've given you, Antonia. Why can't you and your brother just be grateful?"

It's a rhetorical question, the same question he's asked me all of my life. But now I have an answer that I understand in my gut. He let me believe my whole life that the curse befalling Edward King was Paul's and my fault.

"We knew you were keeping secrets from us," I say. "Kids know. I didn't know what, though, until today. We have nothing from our life before you, Uncle Christopher. Nothing but each other and a few of Paul's memories. You hid a piece of our history from us, and demanded we stop trying to be who we were. The secret you kept never belonged to you. I don't know what you promised Eddie down at Twin River. But it can't be this. You should have told us he was alive."

Christopher lowers his gaze. The dark room is soundless but for the hum of central air that cushions us, ensuring the extremes of Minnesota summers won't touch this house, just like multiple backup generators ensure the extremes of the winters won't either. He's built his home into a fortress against all the elements: weather, strangers, children, change. Could my words have finally cracked through the fortress he's built against the truth?

But when he looks up at me again from across the desk, it's with a level of fury I've never seen before.

"I was protecting you," he says, his blue eyes inscrutable. "I have always protected you and your brother. I brought you here to be Americans. To be Kings. But you never understood what I've given you. First Paul abandoned me, then you. And now you've poisoned Harrison against me, forcing him to use the media to take me down. I don't know who you bewitched into paying your way out of that cell, but no doubt you'll thank him for that favor by turning on him too before long. Just like you turned on James Hollings and his family—whoring yourself out to him when you knew he was going to be married."

I gasp.

"Oh, you think I didn't know? You think you managed to keep that under wraps all by yourself? Your aunt might have romanticized your behavior and made excuses. She spends too much time reading poetry to know what's real. But I wasn't about to let you ruin our family's reputation. I'm the one who buried your reprehensible actions so Denise Hollings would never find out. You've always been a taker, Antonia— you've taken my shelter and protection and now you dare to fling it in my face. Go tell Harrison to kill the story. Then get out of my house."

Slowly I begin to back away. I will not let him see that I'm as furious as he is. I'm expanding in the dark, filling the room with my anger. He will not twist my history into vicious, small-minded smears.

I squeeze my hands into fists and the smooth black beads slide up my left wrist. Bashiir's gift—a symbol of his belief in me. Paul's gift to Bashiir—a promise not broken but recast. And a Bosnian grandmother's gift to Paul—solidarity, faith, and a wish for luck in our shared quest to find any part of the ruined worlds we all left behind.

Why would he throw James in my face now, after all this time pretending not to know, protecting me, as he said? Why is he riling me up like this?

He wants me angry, wants me to storm out and slam the door.

There's something more. Something he's still hiding from me. That's why he changed direction. He knows my temper is my weakest point. I get illogical. Stupid.

Not this time.

Think, Toni. Finish the puzzle.

Eddie. Vlado. Paul on a wild goose chase. Christopher brokering my brother's safety to hide . . . what?

There's no way Christopher is putting Paul's best interests first. Just like there's no way he put me in jail to keep me in Thebes for the night because I was safer locked up than running after my brother.

Fifty thousand dollars. He paid a pretty penny to keep me away from something.

Follow the money, Melanie told me. *Always follow the money.*

Christopher has been paying institution after institution to keep Eddie away from Thebes for twenty years. But why would he need to keep him hundreds of miles away from us and his entire family? Eddie was no threat.

You're acting just like Eddie! If only he had just kept his mouth shut . . .

Wait. What if Christopher isn't paying just for Eddie's medical care . . . what if he's afraid that Eddie has something to tell us? What if his brother isn't as damaged as he claims?

Vlado didn't say there were kids . . .

Christopher said he was surprised to see us in the apartment that day. But he didn't even mention my mother. Why didn't he mention finding a dead woman?

What happened to your mother wasn't my fault.

After the bombing stopped that day, she was still singing.

Then there was another blast, a different one, straight through the window.

Christopher threw a grenade.

"You," I whisper.

The world has gone black.

"You killed her. And Eddie knows."

His eyes narrow again.

"Antonia, now you're jumping to conclusions . . ."

"When did he start threatening to talk?" My mind races. "Was it when you came into the apartment and saw my mother dead on the floor? Or was it later, once you were back here? Was it after Vlado was arrested for war crimes that Eddie put two and two together? Did he threaten to reveal your own war crimes, promises about family be damned?"

Christopher's face is completely ashen. He sinks into his chair. But the light inside of me grows stronger, my back straighter. Everything is clicking into place.

My mother, my mother.

"Was Eddie even addicted to Oxy, Uncle Christopher, before you started 'protecting' everyone from what he knew? Or did he need those pills for more than the pain from his leg? Did he need them so he could blind himself to the truth about his own brother?"

"No!" Christopher's hands are flailing in the air. "All I've done is for you and this entire family. Eddie didn't understand what was best. He was grieving when Johanna left him. He made a mistake bringing two orphans back to raise. And she left. That's what happened!"

"Then why can't you let Paul find him?"

"He'll rant. That's what he does, even from his hospital beds. That's what all the nurses say, everywhere he's been! He spews crazy stories from his drug-addled brain about Sarajevo. Lies! Surely you understand how the ravings of a madman could confuse your brother."

I look at him. I'm filled with calm, with purpose. "All day I've been chasing the wrong man, Uncle Christopher. I should have been looking for your brother, not mine."

"Antonia, what did I tell you . . ." his threat sounds hollow now. Negligible in the face of my discoveries.

"Sending me to the town jail, that price on my head," I continue, "that wasn't to keep me safe. It was to keep me from figuring out your real secret until you had time to get Eddie on the move again. No one else knows, do they? Paul? Izzy? Harrison? Your own wife? They have no idea that your hands stink of my mother's blood!"

"I should have left you behind in that scourge of a country twenty years ago," he shouts. "Eddie made us take you both, out of his sick need to keep punishing me for what I did to preserve our family! I rescued you twice! And you repay me by turning everyone against me."

"Well, guess what?" I say from my side of the room. I'm a hundred feet tall now, grown vast with the truth. "I am very much alive. And I have resources Eddie never had. How long do you think it will take me, with my legal training, to find enough evidence to link the beginnings of your family fortune to conspiracy with a convicted war criminal? And throwing a grenade to cover your crimes and killing my mother as a result? That's manslaughter."

"No, that's not what . . ."

"You do know that statutes of limitations have no bearing on crimes against humanity, right? I will go to the state police, the U.S. military tribunal, the CIA, the FBI, and all the way to The Hague myself with what I know. You'd have been far better off had the accusations come from either your brother or mine instead of me. A drug-addled institutionalized coma survivor? A vagrant high-school dropout on the lam? You might have had a fighting chance. But me? Never."

He's shrinking. A withered tangle, engulfed in his massive chair.

"Please." His voice cracks. "Don't. I . . . I did what I had to do. One moment . . . so long ago . . ."

"You killed her," I say again quietly. More for myself than for him.

And that's when he crumbles. It's the quiet that does it—he disintegrates before me. He puts his head down on the desk, and he weeps.

I see us both as if I'm hovering, floating. My uncle's bowed head, centered in the spreading pool of yellow lamplight. Me, standing in darkness, witness and interlocutor. His pain, mine.

Christopher is trapped in that harsh light his desk lamp throws. Drowning in it. Is it up to me now to rescue him?

Rescue. It's more complicated than that. Yes, Christopher King took us from the rubble of our first life. Fed us, clothed us. Protected us from so much harm. Lived up to the word of the pact he made with Eddie at Twin River.

But rescue us?

No.

Paul and I had to rescue ourselves.

Something diamond-sharp and piercing lodges itself in my chest. An understanding. My history isn't a blight I must deny. It's a truth I must live. Paul ripped one secret out of the past and set me on a course to discover the rest. It doesn't belong to my uncle anymore. It belongs to us.

I won't use blackmail, I told James this afternoon. I meant it. I won't use blackmail to protect my career by threatening his marriage. I won't use it to bring Per Olufsen to his knees to gain his political support. But this isn't about personal gain. I have ancestors to defend. Murdered, raped, left unburied, left to rot.

This shrunken man in front of me—I longed for his approval so many years. And now: if I want to, I could make him beg. I could grab that baseball bat and smash this office and the machinations of a generation to smithereens. Who would blame me if I did?

Destruction. Obliteration. It's my history.

He picks up his head to look at me.

"Antonia . . ."

It's my history, but it won't be my life.

"Okay, Uncle Christopher." I'm calm now. Steady. "I will convince

Harrison to pull the story from tonight's news. But in return, I need your guarantee that the Somali Community Center remains untouched. The Big Dig is off."

He nods.

"And I'm not going to tell the authorities, or Aunt Evelyn, what you really did in Sarajevo," I continue. "At least not right now. You can't pretend, though, not anymore, not to me. So, here's what happens next. You'll text me Eddie's new location. And promise me he stays there. And you won't make any effort to track my brother. No eyes on the ground, no attempts to stop him, no claims that he broke into your office and stole papers. He's protected. Indefinitely."

My uncle is only an outline now, but he manages to nod again.

I begin to walk out, then stop. Turn around as if I've just thought of something out of thin air.

"Oh, and one more thing. You will keep your promise to Harrison and announce that he's the next CEO of King Family Construction. But no conditions. No fake marriage. You can't choose which secrets to keep about any of us anymore. Living or dead."

He starts to rise out of his chair, but I stop him with a wave of my hand. "No negotiations. It happens tonight. What's the breaking local news story on WKNW going to be? A new generation of leadership brings fresh energy to the future of Thebes? Or will it be the start of an investigation into twenty years of lies? From that baseball bat to your brother to your black-market arms deals. To my mother. The decision is yours."

This time when I turn to leave, I don't look back. I don't have to.

At last, I know exactly where I stand with Christopher King.

Night

ALMOST MIDNIGHT. THEBES SITS UNDER COMPLETE darkness now—a darkness I've never seen replicated anywhere else. The proliferation of artificial lights in the cities where I've lived the past seven years has comforted me. With lights come people, throngs of people from a thousand different places. People who don't know about my multiple pasts. I could be anyone I wanted when I was among them.

Here, dark as it is, there's nowhere to hide.

In the parking lot outside the Parthenon Diner, I lean back in the seat of my open-roofed car and look up at the sky. It takes a few blinks to bring into focus, but slowly, the enormous blanket of distant stars begins to reveal itself. They're up there, behind the haze of clouds that started rolling in after sunset. Threat of storms tomorrow.

I've spent the last hour in the parking lot, alone on this dark night, googling what I never allowed myself to look at head-on before. Rape camps. The Muslim women of Bosnia rounded up and tortured through rape as a weapon of genocide. I must have had aunts, cousins, neighbors. Generations of women from my family, even if I have no way of learning who they were—there's no chance they all escaped this fate.

How horrible my mother's end days must have been. What she had to do to protect us. She was Vlado's prize, a spoil of war, and we were there to keep her compliant. He let us live so long as she did his bidding. And he was perfectly willing to let all three of us die when there was a chance he'd be exposed. He handed Christopher that grenade and he fled. Outcome be damned.

No matter how hard I try, or how deeply I research, nothing on the internet can bring my mother back to me. But, at last, I know what happened.

That's something. It has to be.

I'm exhausted now. Deeply bone tired. No more planning, no more searches, no more calls. I press the button to shut off my phone—but before it can power down, the still image of Michelle from Izzy's video glows back to light on the screen.

She's beautiful. Not because of the makeup—because she's filled with hope about her future. Denise Juliette Larson was too, in her engagement photo. Like Helen of Troy: faces that could launch a thousand ships. Did any of these girls, with their heads tilted toward the good light, their hair cascading in waves down their backs, smile into the camera and think: *I'm starting a war*? No—like Melanie had said about us, it was their job to look the part. A Greek beauty. An internet sensation. A perfect wife.

My phone asks me:

Do you want to save this picture?

Do I?

I should delete it.

I might delete it.

Another time.

Yes. Save this picture.

Just in case I want an insurance policy.

Or I need it one day to save somebody I love.

The basin of sky dips low, cradles me, alone in my little car, surrounded by darkness. Night stars shine through the cracks like Sarajevo

Roses in the bombed-out crevices of the sidewalks from my past. Is my brother at a rest stop somewhere off the highway right now, stretching his legs and looking up at the same blue-black sky? Paul chose a serpentine route to Pittsburgh to hide his whereabouts. Indianapolis first, Bashiir said, but from there, it's a secret. Without his phone, and by using an assumed name, my brother has made himself incognito—to everyone except me, that is. I'm certain that I know exactly the identity he's chosen.

If I had level-two security clearance into the records at the Greyhound station in St. Paul, I guarantee I'd find that a Mr. Husein Gradaščević purchased a one-way bus ticket to Indianapolis about four hours ago. Husein Gradaščević, who loves freedom most of all. Who never lets the sound of church bells bother the call to prayer of the muezzin.

I won't tell anyone that I believe Paul is traveling as the Dragon of Bosnia. The more people who know, the more danger he might be in, despite Christopher's promise. Who knows what kind of network my uncle has? If he was willing to conspire with criminals once, it would be foolish of me to believe he wouldn't again. But I'll use my research abilities to track Paul once he's off that bus and onto the next.

My uncle has his skills, and I have mine.

Acknowledgments

Thank you to my editor, Harry Kirchner, for embracing *The Dig* and shepherding the manuscript to completion. Much appreciation to Dan Smetanka and the entire Counterpoint team for their enthusiasm and excitement about this novel, and to Margo La Pierre for early editorial feedback. Huge thanks also to my literary agent, Susan Golomb, her assistant, Madeline Ticknor, and the staff at Writers House for all their support.

Thank you to my village of brilliant, trusted readers and writers: Marina Budhos, Stephanie Carlson, Alice Elliott Dark, Susan Davis, Alex Enders, Bonnie Friedman, Gina Hyams, Pamela Redmond, Clara Baker, and S. Kirk Walsh, and to the Ragdale Foundation for the gift of time and space where the earliest version of the story was born. Special thanks to Christina Baker Kline, who has championed this novel every step of the way. Without Christina's incisive insights and tireless partnership, there would be no Antonia King.

Vanja Pantic Oflazoglu generously shared memories of her early childhood in Sarajevo before her family fled the Bosnian genocide for the United States, helping me deepen the picture of Toni's first years. The Post-Conflict Research Center (Centar za postkonfliktna istraživanja), in Sarajevo, Bosnia and Herzegovina, is an incredible resource for survivor narratives and peace education; thanks to Caroline Hopper Jany for introducing me to Vanja and the Post-Conflict Research Center, and thanks to my sister singers in the Yale Slavic Chorus, circa 1987, for the gift of Bosnian folk music that sparked my imagination as a writer decades later. For additional scholarship about the Bosnian genocide, I referenced *Voices from Srebrenica* by Ann Petrila and Hasan Hasanovic, *The Bone Woman* by Clea Koff, and *Bosnia in Limbo* by Borja Lasheras. *Infidel* by Ayaan Hirsi Ali helped inform Bashiir Abdi's journey from Mogadishu to Minnesota, as did hours of reading news stories of Somali refugees building community across the state over the first two decades of the twenty-first century.

The poem that Toni recalls Evelyn quoting on page 39 is "Shape-changers in Winter" by Margaret Atwood.

Thank you to my Becket, Massachusetts family for their cheers and consolations throughout the multiyear process of bringing *The Dig* into the world: Linda Burt, Jess Burt Donohue, Delayna Feuerzeig, Tessa Ury, Mark Rose, Ted Rose, Craig Feuerzeig, Jesse Donohue, Ann Birmingham, Mari Brown, Eli Donohue, Eli Rose, and Beckett Rose. Thanks to my Montclair, New Jersey friends for the same: Felicia Williams, Skye Amory, Jong Sook Nee, Darin Wacs, and members of both the Montclair Writers Group and my book group (twenty-two years and still going strong). My late father, Bo Burt, modeled living a writer's life and inspired me to persevere. And finally, my boundless gratitude to Joshua Cohen, for all that lies ahead.

ANNE BURT is the editor of *My Father Married Your Mother: Dispatches from the Blended Family* and coeditor, with Christina Baker Kline, of *About Face: Women Write About What They See When They Look in the Mirror*. Her essays and fiction have appeared in numerous publications and venues, including *Salon*, NPR, and *The Christian Science Monitor*; she is a past winner of *Meridian*'s Editors' Prize in Fiction. Anne lives in New York City. Find out more at anneburtwriter.com.